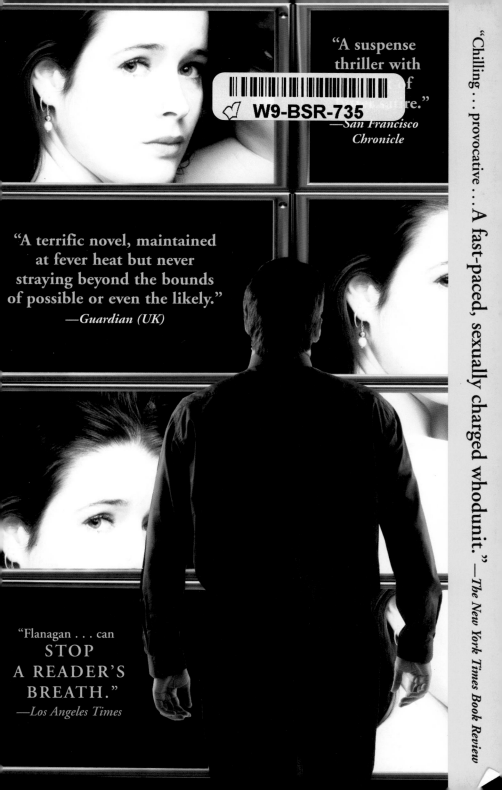

"A suspense thriller with [...] satire."
—San Francisco Chronicle

"A terrific novel, maintained at fever heat but never straying beyond the bounds of possible or even the likely."
—Guardian (UK)

"Flanagan . . . can STOP A READER'S BREATH."
—Los Angeles Times

"Chilling . . . provocative . . . A fast-paced, sexually charged whodunit."
—The New York Times Book Review

W9-BSR-735

Praise for *The Unknown Terrorist*:

"Aims to provoke from the start . . . One is reminded of a fifteenth-century painting of worldly, cackling priests passing out indulgences, the hems of their robes aflame. . . . [Flanagan's] methods name a callousness at loose in the world today, a luridness, and a widespread helplessness before them both. If only they were a product of his imagination."
　　　　　　　　　　　　　　　—*The New York Review of Books*

"Mr. Flanagan's prose is gritty as the outback, naked as a crocodile, and as clear as every postcard photo of Sydney Harbor's iconic Opera House. . . . Thrilling in its helices of luxury and squalor and loyalty and lust; kinetic in its serial events that swell like a tsunami; provocative, in its counterpoint of privacy, security, and politics; inspired in its portrait of Gina, *The Unknown Terrorist* is a cautionary tale well worth reading—if you like your fiction raw."
　　　　　　　　　　　　　　　—*Washington Times*

"A terrific novel, maintained at fever heat but never straying beyond the bounds of possible or even the likely."　　　—*The Guardian* (UK)

"Unflinching . . . Flanagan's tightly crafted narrative is akin to the oppressive power of Kafka's *The Trial*, or Capote's *In Cold Blood*, stark realism revealing underlying sickness. . . . A disturbing gaze at the social and psychological mechanisms of terror."
　　　　　　　　　　　　　　　—*The Washington Post*

"A thriller of genuine importance . . . fired by passionate concern."
　　　　　　　　　　　　　　　—*Daily Telegraph* (UK)

"A deceptively simple potboiler . . . It occupies a niche somewhere between allegory and homage, but Flanagan's hip-hop style sampling is most concerned with the veneer between thoughtful discourse and unsubstantiated accusations.. . . An oddly exhilarating novel. "
　　　　　　　　　　　　　　　—*The Philadelphia Inquirer*

"A searing depiction of how bigotry feasts on rumor and prejudice . . . [Flanagan] twists conventions of character and plot to forge a narrative rich with dark laughter and spiced with political nous . . . To have achieved this feat inside a razor-sharp narrative, and to have done so with humor and a keen eye for the ironies of politics and the muffling blanket of 'the interests of national security' is nothing short of brilliance. Read this novel now, before it's too late for any of us to understand its message." —*Scotland on Sunday* (UK)

"Whips paranoia and a critique of the media into a live-wire thriller." —*Time Out New York*

"A primer on the paranoia that is sweeping the world." —*The Austin Chronicle*

"A funny, filmic, and gripping writer, [Flanagan's] a novelist and philosopher for our time." —*The Daily Mail* (UK)

"A compelling, timely work . . . [Flanagan's] tender characterization renders Gina Davies's tale mightily plausible, and terribly sad." —*Kirkus Reviews*

"Infused with a quiet explosiveness, like a cranial blood vessel bursting while at rest—sudden, violent, and final—a disturbing tale half-whispered and never forgotten. You'll remember The Doll long after reading about her." —Bookreporter.com

Also by Richard Flanagan

Death of a River Guide
The Sound of One Hand Clapping
Gould's Book of Fish

RICHARD
FLANAGAN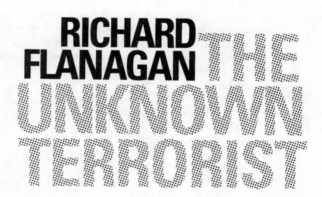

Grove Press
New York

First published by in 2006 in Picador and imprint of
Pan Macmillan Australia Pty Limited
1 Market Street, Sydney

Printed in the United States of America

FIRST PAPERBACK EDITION

ISBN-10: 0-8021-4354-7
ISBN-13: 978-0-8021-4354-9

Grove Press
an imprint of Grove/Atlantic, Inc.
841 Broadway
New York, NY 10003

Distributed by Publishers Group West

www.groveatlantic.com

08 09 10 11 12   10 9 8 7 6 5 4 3 2 1

For David Hicks

THE IDEA THAT LOVE IS NOT ENOUGH is a particularly painful one. In the face of its truth, humanity has for centuries tried to discover in itself evidence that love is the greatest force on earth.

Jesus is an especially sad example of this unequal struggle. The innocent heart of Jesus could never have enough of human love. He demanded it, as Nietzsche observed, with hardness, with madness, and had to invent hell as punishment for those who withheld their love from him. In the end he created a god who was "wholly love" in order to excuse the hopelessness and failure of human love.

Jesus, who wanted love to such an extent, was clearly a madman, and had no choice when confronted with the failure of love but to seek his own death. In his understanding that love was not enough, in his acceptance of the necessity of the sacrifice of his own life to enable the future of those around him, Jesus is history's first, but not last, example of a suicide bomber.

Nietzsche wrote, "I am not a man, I am dynamite". It was the image of a dreamer. Every day now somebody somewhere is dynamite. They are not an image. They are the walking dead, and so are the people who are standing round them. Reality was never made by realists, but by dreamers like Jesus and Nietzsche.

Nietzsche began to fear that what drove the world forward was all that was destructive and evil about it. In his writings he tried to reconcile himself to such a terrible world.

But one day he saw a cart horse being beaten brutally by its driver. He rushed out and put his arms around the horse's neck, and would not let go. Promptly diagnosed as mad, he was locked away in an asylum for the rest of his life.

Nietzsche had even less explanation than Jesus for love and its various manifestations: empathy, kindness, hugging a horse's neck to stop it being beaten. In the end Nietzsche's philosophy could not even explain Nietzsche, a man who sacrificed his life for a horse.

But then, ideas always miss the point. Chopin could offer no explanation of his Nocturnes. Why the Doll was haunted by Chopin's Nocturnes is one strand of this story. In listening to what Chopin could not explain, she heard an explanation of her own life. She could, of course, not know that it also foretold her own death.

SATURDAY

2

THE DOLL WAS A POLE DANCER. She was twenty-six, though routinely claimed, as she had been claiming since she was seventeen, to be twenty-two. A small, dark woman, her fine-featured face and almond eyes were set off by woolly black hair.

"Her body, hey," said Jodie, a fellow pole dancer to whom the body mattered and who, at nineteen, was already a Botox junkie, "it wasn't like, you know, *contemporary*. You know what I mean?" And everyone listening knew exactly what Jodie's lack of expression meant.

The young women who flooded in and out of the pole dancing clubs were of every body type, but their bodies, whatever their differences, shared the toning that only hour after hour of swaying and swinging can bring and a diet of

5

amphetamines and alcohol can hone. They aspired to an ideal they had seen starring in a hundred DVDs and a thousand video clips, splashed across an inestimable number of women's magazine articles and gliding through a million ads. Hard and angular, bones and muscles rippling and bumps and products glistening, it was the ideal of beautiful women as cadaverous children.

But the Doll's body seemed to belong to some different, older idea of what women were. In contrast to the muscled butts and thighs of the other dancers in the club, the Doll's body was more rounded, her arms and thighs and buttocks fuller, and her movements were somehow similarly rounded and full.

She suspected her looks didn't amount to much and did not trust the attention she felt they brought. She did not understand that the attention arose from something else, and that everything that she was—her slow movements, her smile, the way she engaged with people—was what attracted others even more than her looks. But she was twenty-six, pretending to be twenty-two, and looks mattered. She had an open, oval face. It was exactly the wrong face for our age.

3

If the Doll's looks were exotic, her origins were everyday. She was a westie, though from which particular suburb no one knew. She was always going to leave the west, but she was surprised as a young woman how little she felt she had left behind. It wasn't that she had no direction home, but that she had little sense she had ever had a home. The Doll had long ago determined that her early life would mean little to her, and she was of the fixed opinion that origins and explanations were not to be hers.

"I grew up like a cat, my friend," she once told Jodie, who was no friend at all. "My family had no hand in it. You know any cats with an interest in family history?"

Of course, her father came from somewhere, and her mother from somewhere else, and their parents in turn must have had lives of some interest, lived in places and times that might even to our eyes seem exotic, the stuff of mini-series and fat novels discounted at Big W over Christmas; and the further one went back, no doubt the more intriguing it would all become: there might be notorious artists or famous criminals, failed businessmen or successful charlatans, people of variety and interest, of charm and horror. But if this were so, the Doll's parents knew little of it and had interest in none of it. The pattern and passing of lives before and after them meant no more than the ebb and flow of traffic on the freeway.

Their world was one of suburban verities, their world was that of today: the house, the job, the possessions and the cars, the friends and the renovations, the resort holidays and the latest gadgets—digital cameras, home cinemas, a new pool. The past was a garbage bin of outdated appliances: the foot spa; the turbo oven; the doughnut maker and the record player, the SLR and the VCR and the George Foreman grill. The past was an embarrassment of distressing colours and styles about which to laugh: mullet haircuts and padded shoulders, top perms and kettle barbecues. Only this week's catalogue was good and worth getting, no deposit and twenty-four months to pay. Their lives were empty, their lives they regarded as good. The Doll's strongest memories were of television soaps.

She had watched *Neighbours* and *Home and Away*; she had been more upset at the age of eight by Daphne Lawrence dying than when her mother had split from her father the previous year, taking her two younger brothers with her to Hervey Bay to live with a fibreglass swimming pool installer called Ray. Then the Doll hadn't known what was expected of her, or what was meant by such things; but Ramsay Street and Summer Bay made it clear: you cried and you laughed, you went on and on.

She watched music videos with the girls all beautiful and the men all fat and aggressive; the girls outshone the men, the way she saw it, with their looks and their dancing and the way they mostly didn't bother saying anything while the men mouthed off—nothing could have prepared her better for pole dancing.

She claimed that the one enduring memory she had of her mother before she ran off was of a bad trompe l'oeil painting she had done on the Venetian blinds of their suburban lounge room. It was a picture of a window opening onto the sight of Bali's Kuta Beach, where, on holiday, she had first met Ray.

For a time in her teens, she visited her mother in Hervey Bay occasionally. By then Ray had long gone, and her mother talked only of her two sons, two fat boys who dressed like two fat rappers, said *Yo* a lot and greeted each other American style, rubbing fist knuckles; it was as if the Doll were a new and not overly interesting neighbour across the street. Her mother's life was another soap opera but a not particularly good one; a song cycle of drug problems, police visits, prolapses, and new partners. The visits to her mother oppressed the Doll. She went out of duty, and at some point duty seemed not much of a reason and she stopped going.

When, a few years later, she heard her mother had been killed in a pile-up on the Hume Highway she was sad, but not overly. It felt more like the confirmation of a long-standing absence than the beginning of one.

Perhaps the Doll told the story of her mother's painting because the painting was for her about the stupidity of hope and holding on to dreams—or large dreams, in any case. Small dreams, small hopes, small things—all these and only these were what life permitted, and therefore to the Doll were permissible. Anything else, anything larger—as her mother's life so graphically proved—could always be crushed. Which is not to say that the Doll was unhappy; on the contrary. She believed her acceptance of her life was what would guarantee her happiness. She would look straight into the Sydney sun, and never hide from it behind bad pictures of make-believe.

For the Doll was not a dreamer like Jesus or Nietzsche. Rather, she described herself as a realist. Realism is the embrace of disappointment, in order no longer to be disappointed.

4

"So I came to the city, my friend," the Doll then told Jodie, "what of it?"

What of it, indeed? She no more understood her new world than she could explain her loathing and fear of her old, but what did it matter? In Sydney, the five or more millions of the westies detest the stinking snobbery of the north and the arrogance of the east, while the million or so of the rich north and east despise the grasping vulgarity and materialism of the poorer west. Nobody will admit they all think much the same, and that what moves and joins everyone in Sydney is one and the same thing: money; and nobody will admit that the only real difference is that up north and east they more or less have more, while out west they more or less have less.

The Doll wasn't trying to understand any of this, and she would never try. She just wanted to get on, and explanations were simply so much more shit that the mugs talked when all they wanted was to see you with your knickers off.

"I got out of the west," she would say in a nasal twang with its suggestion of Lebanese and Greek–Australian about the edges of its ululating vowels, "and I got the west out of me."

It was untrue, like just about everything she said about herself. At the same time as harbouring a deep desire to one day live northside, she carried a chip on her shoulder about those who already did, and she could, simply because of the suggestion of an upper north shore address, quite gleefully open up on a customer as a snob and a wanker. Nothing could induce her to go further out from the central city than Newtown.

"It's not good for the complexion, my friend," she would say, as she would say about anything that made her sad, as though saying such a thing explained it all.

On the one hand she took an almost perverse pleasure in mocking other girls from the west for their overdone makeup, short skirts, big belts and the amount of product they plastered over their face and hair. On the other, in addition to her prejudices against west Sydney, the Doll had the average run of west Sydney prejudices about the rest of the world. She would on occasion give vent to being pissed off by slopeheads, dirty boongs, cops, and anyone reading the *Sydney Morning Herald*.

"I like to think I'm equally racist about everybody," she would say, "but slimy Lebs I really hate."

5

By the time the Doll got out of bed at ten, the day was already pleasantly hot. The steady traffic outside was the gentlest vibration inside her dark apartment. Her thoughts were too loose to describe. The contrast between the heaviness of her Temazepam-induced sleep and the lightness of the day further lifted the good mood in which she had woken. She gave herself over to what was immediate and likeable: that morning she felt a calm and a joy about the city, and this feeling so infected her she didn't even bother dropping her customary Zoloft.

She caught a taxi to Bondi and as she rode between the tall buildings under a blue and brilliant sky, her eyes filled with tears: for no clear reason she felt happy and small happinesses she allowed herself.

At the beach she went swimming, lay on the sand, let herself fill with sun. She took pleasure in feeling her breasts spreading in the towelling beneath which the sand firmed; in smelling suntan oil and wet sand and air salty from the sea and acrid from the outfall sewage frothing to a latte on distant points.

As she turned her head sideways, one ear on the beach,

one open to the sky, the roar of the waves became louder, the squeals of children a floating accompaniment that began to disappear as she lost her body and mind in the regular swoop and wash of the waves; it was a dream, a dream in which life was worth living after all.

Faraway, she could see a cloud, the only one in the sky. It looked like . . . but it didn't really look like anything, just a slow-moving cloud, beautiful and alone. It kept changing, like the world, and, like the world, it was indescribable.

A nearby radio ran the same news it always seemed to run and its repetition of distant horror and local mundanity was calmly reassuring. More bombings in Baghdad, more water restrictions and more bushfires; another threat to attack Sydney on another al-Qa'ida website and another sportsman in another sex scandal, a late unconfirmed report that three unexploded bombs had been discovered at Sydney's Homebush Olympic stadium and the heatwave was set to go on, continuing to set record highs, while here at the beach, waves rolled in, crashed, and rolled out again, taking all this irrelevant noise with them, as they always had, as they always would.

The radio said: "Live the dream!"

And wasn't that just what she was doing?

There was nothing on earth she wanted at that moment, nothing she felt denied her that she wished to have, no ambition she felt unfulfilled. She desired neither friends nor a man, not money nor clothes nor to be other than who she was. The bad she had known seemed not important. Her body felt neither skinny nor fat, neither weary nor spent, nor excited, nor in need of exercise. She was not beautiful or ugly, but felt her body existed only to receive the gift of this life, and everything at that moment seemed good. It was enough to hear the waves crash and roll, to pour sand from one hand to the other and look at the falling grains.

The radio said: "Congratulations, Australia! We want to thank you with a knockdown sale on our bathroom accessories!"

She dozed, awoke, watched the beautiful surfies in their long boardies and the clubbies in their budgie smugglers, the gays with their tight bods, the girls with their muffin tops poking out proud as can be, the old men with tea bag bellies strutting, and the old women with bodies like weary pavs sagging in the heat, just sitting, watching; breasts and arses and wedding tackle all hanging in such wild disarray and the sun shining like there's no tomorrow and over it all the waves returning the world to some other, better, larger rhythm—who couldn't feel happy as a bird and, as her friend Wilder would say, as free as a fart with all this?

And everything about the beach at that moment blended into something that seemed delightful and comforting, and the name the Doll gave it all was Sydney, and she felt she understood why many had come to love it so.

6

She was dozing when her phone rang. It was Wilder, saying she and Max were at Bondi, that it was a beautiful day, and why didn't the Doll come and join them for a swim?

"It could take me a while," the Doll said, standing, picking up her towel and bag, and scanning the beach, "what with the traffic and all."

She began walking through the throngs of people and spotted the five-year-old Max digging a hole less than a hundred metres away, his mother Wilder lying next to him, majestic and brazen as ever, dark brown and topless.

The Doll rang Wilder back and asked her exactly where she was on the beach. As Wilder began issuing directions, the Doll snuck around behind her and continued talking, until her mouth was right up next to Wilder's mobile phone. Wilder, who was in a splendid mood, turned, looked up with her unforgettable face and shrieked with delight. Max swung around in his hole and, on seeing the Doll, scrambled out and threw himself into her arms.

As the Doll cuddled and tickled Max, the two women chatted. Max soon grew bored and went back to his hole. Wilder told the Doll how she had been invited to be in a Mardi Gras float, Dykes with Dicks, that night. As far as the Doll knew, Wilder wasn't a dyke, but Wilder said someone had taken ill and a friend had rung that very morning and asked her to make up the numbers. Last minute though it might have been, Wilder viewed it as an irresistible proposal, and now it was all arranged, with Max going to his father's.

"Off with the boys tonight," said the Doll, whose view of the hole was obscured by Wilder's body. "Eh, Max?"

There was no answer. The Doll looked up and Wilder twisted around. But Max was no longer in his hole, and was nowhere to be seen. Wilder jumped up, scanned the crowds and then the sea.

"Oh my God," said the Doll. "He's caught in the rip."

And she pointed to a dark snake tongue of water whipping

back through the breakers, on which a small boy on a boogie board was being swiftly carried to the ocean beyond.

They could see Max mouthing screams, helpless and terrified. But with the noise of the waves breaking, people yelling and squealing in the excitement and pleasure of catching waves and having waves crash on them, no one could hear him, and no one, not even the lifesavers, had noticed the small boy's plight. Both women leapt up and began running to the sea.

But before they reached the water or found a lifesaver, they saw a young man strike out into the rip and swim after the now crying boy. The man was a confident swimmer, riding the rip with ease until he reached Max. The two women watched mesmerised, Wilder silently sobbing, as the man took hold of the board and slowly, almost casually, swam it sideways out of the rip. Then he swam Max and the board back to shore, timing their journey inward between the breaking waves. When at last able to stand, he picked Max up and, trailing the board behind them on its wrist leash, walked to where the two women were now making their way through the shore slop toward him, waving and shouting.

He was dark and slender, with short curly hair, and his dark skin was accentuated by the long white Billabong board shorts he wore. Without a word, Max climbed out of his arms into those of his mother.

Wilder stood knee deep in the sea, the larger waves crashing into her waist, crying and smiling, holding her son to her chest, angrily berating him, halting every so often to thank the man before returning to tick Max off, all the while kissing and hugging and burying herself in him, as Max attempted in a half-hearted fashion to shy away from such an embarrassing outburst of maternal affection in front of a stranger.

The young man said little, making light of his rescue, trying not to stare at Wilder's breasts. Then he smiled, said goodbye, shook Max's hand as if they were men who had shared an adventure together, and headed back out into the surf.

"He's a bit of a looker," Wilder said, as he disappeared into a wave.

"Very woggy," said the Doll.

Later, the Doll went for a bodysurf. This feeling she loved above all: diving beneath that wall of white water, feeling its power tumble over her, and popping back up in the confused aftermath of boiling water, the brilliant light slashing her eyes.

The Doll blinked twice because of the brightness and the stinging salt, and then only a few metres away she saw him, similarly blinking and tossing his head, the young man who had so bravely rescued Max.

He smiled. She smiled. He raised an arm out of the water and waved. On impulse, she swam over to where he was treading water, put her arm around his neck and kissed him on the lips. It was a gentle, affectionate kiss, and though neither of their lips opened, her legs washed around his for a moment, and the Doll felt her body tingle.

"Thank you," she said.

And then the water began pulling them apart, a wall of water bearing down and pulling them backwards. They began rising with the wave like sea creatures, and she just had time to give a small smile before she made the split-second decision to catch the wave. She jackknifed and threw herself into the wave's wall the moment before it broke. She felt it lift and hurtle her in its wild aerated force back towards the beach. She seemed to be in the wave for the longest time.

When the wave's power was almost spent and she could feel it bottoming out, agitated sand swirling around her skin, she stood up, gulped a few times, and with smarting eyes searched the glaring sea around and behind her. The slender young man was nowhere to be seen. She half-expected him to surface out of the water and grab her unawares. But he had disappeared. Though the Doll would not admit she was disappointed, she spent some time scanning the waves and wash for his lean body before giving up and going in. She went back up the beach and lay with Wilder and a now sub-dued Max. The sun beat down on them, she slumbered a little, and when she woke, it was time to leave and get to the Chairman's Lounge to start her early shift.

7

How the Chairman's Lounge held on to its reputation as one of the most upmarket pole dancing clubs in Sydney was an achievement not easily explained. Though it had twice won Eros Foundation awards for "Hottest Naughty Nite Spot (NSW)" and once been awarded an impressive five breast rating in *Hustlaz.com Adult Almanac*, such gongs meant noth-ing to anybody other than on the award evening, and, as the Doll herself pointed out, who didn't win prizes these days?

But like much else, the puzzle of its prominence was entwined with the mystery of money. By the straightforward expedient of charging twice the admission price of the other clubs and an even more exorbitant mark-up on drinks, the Chairman's Lounge kept its status bolstered and its punters happy, because they would not throw away such money unless it was one of the best clubs in Sydney and therefore worth every vanishing dollar.

Each day at noon the head bouncer, Billy the Tongan—a large man inevitably clad in an immaculate white tracksuit, gold chains and knock-off Versace sunnies—created the entry to the Chairman's Lounge by rolling a length of grubby red carpet out of the ground storey of an old hotel into the border country that bestrode Kings Cross and Darlinghurst.

Here seemed to be the perfect position for a business that specialised in pompous cock teasing. The city centre was only a short walk distant, while a block away were the brothels and sex shows and streetwalkers of the Cross—an area chiefly known for a dying retail line in old world sleaze, its major feature being a run-down strip mall that parted the hillock on which it sat like a bad mohawk. Here the junkies and the pros, the pervs and the homeless, looked out over their daily shrinking atoll with as much bewilderment and as little hope as the inhabitants of some South Seas micro-nation, knowing whatever the future might hold, it held nothing for them.

Around them, washing up from the gentrified tenements and newly built designer apartments of Darlinghurst and the ceaselessly refurbished mansions of Elizabeth Bay, rushed the incoming tide of property values and inner-city hypocrisy, rising as inexorably and as pitilessly as the nearby globally warmed Pacific Ocean.

Along either side of the carpet that somehow joined all these disparate worlds, Billy the Tongan would set up the brass poles down which he ran an ornate gold-coloured rope. Inside, the true nature of the club began asserting itself. A strip of bare purple neon tubes ran like tracer fire down the half-dozen steps that led into the entry foyer. Here arose the deafening break-beat of doof music and the insistent scratching of the entrance cash register attended by a semi-naked woman charged with undertaking the first fleecing. Beyond this foyer, along a corridor and around a corner, was the main lounge with its scattering of purple felt-lined dancing tables, each replete with a brass pole.

If in the dusty light of morning the club had all the charm and erotic allure of an Eastern European airline's executive lounge, this too was for a purpose. For its dirty, dun-coloured tub chairs and its generic bar and its feature-less tables, its unremarkable nature and meanness of finish pretended to be no other than what it was, more of the bland sameness that was the world of those who came and watched. In its familiarity it relaxed its customers, as in its meanness it reassured them. Its manager, Ferdy Holstein, knew that any attempt to alter this relentless dullness and ordinariness would be an attempt to raise the tone that could only prove an overwhelming commercial error.

Ferdy claimed to come out of rock'n'roll, and frequently dropped names the Doll had never heard of. Ferdy wore Mambo shirts and thought it was fashion, not knowing it was middle age.

The truth was that Ferdy had left his job at a pearl oyster hatchery in Broome a decade earlier with a bootload of

Kimberley dope. He drove two thousand kilometres south, traded the dope and made enough to refill the boot with ecstasy he got through a contact in the Gypsy Jokers. He crossed the interminable length of the Nullarbor and made his way along the Great Ocean Road.

He liked to say he arrived in Melbourne in a '73 Charger and left it a month later in a '96 Beemer, making his way in that same year to Sydney, where he bought a half-share and the job as manager of a run-down bar, and invested what was left of his new wealth on refitting the bar with felt-lined tables and brass poles in the manner of the pole dancing clubs that were then becoming so popular. He would later recall those early years with the tone of feigned humility so many self-made men feel necessary:

"We had our hopes."

Hopes were unnecessary, for the times, as he frequently told his customers, were his. In the Broome oyster hatchery he had spent the first fifteen years of his working life as a technician breeding vats of microscopic algae to be fed to juvenile oysters. All that mattered in that job had been getting several constants right, and thereafter never varying them. Ferdy applied the same principles to his management of the Chairman's Lounge.

For he, a man come out of the red mystery of the Kimberley's pindan dust into the blue certainty of the Kings Cross night, sensed in Sydney that the possibility of human community was a pointless dream, that cities revealed that men shared with algae the most natural destiny: meaninglessness confused by the inexplicable need to live. There were no words for any of it, but a pole dancing club seemed to him a better place than an algal fermentation vat to watch its cracked unravelling. That was what Ferdy felt. What he said, on the other hand, was banal, but not without its own related truth.

"It's all in the show," Ferdy would say.

And indeed it was.

8

Until the moment, a little after 7 pm, that he walked along the red carpet of the Chairman's Lounge, headed down past the purple neon tubes and pulled from his Armani pants' pocket a twenty-dollar note to pay a smiling woman the entry fee, Richard Cody's day had been unhappy. He had slept poorly, woken to yet one more argument with his wife, then been called out by Six's news producers to anchor the live crosses from a terrorist bomb scare at Homebush Olympic stadium.

There was a new makeup girl who had made his hair look ridiculous, then the OB van kept losing contact with the studio on the live crosses, and the whole story in any case quickly grew repetitive, then pointless: three bombs had been found, each in a kid's backpack. The crowd was evacuated, the area sealed off. Nothing else would happen now.

He had continued saying the same thing over and over with his stupid hair and the studio dropping in and out, while a string of so-called experts—mostly consultants wanting a job as an expert in security, terror, politics—commented on each other's remarks, which in turn repeated and elaborated the few brief comments made by the police and government spinners, all pretending that in this vortex of nonsense might be found some sign predicting what might next occur.

Only his Armani summer suit didn't let him down, enduring the heat without crease or crumple. In middle age he had taken refuge in elegance, even when the temperature had not dropped below thirty-eight for five days and the humidity was stuck at ninety-four per cent. As his body thickened and leathered, as his hair thinned, Richard Cody believed his fine clothes helped assert a persuasive idea of himself as charming, sophisticated, clever: in short that his agreeable clothes helped the world concur with his agreeable idea of himself.

After the 1 pm cross, Richard Cody had had enough, and the best of excuses. He had been invited to a lunch at Katie Moretti's home by the boss of Six's news and current affairs division, Jerry Mendes, who had been a not unimportant aspect of Katie Moretti's divorce. Richard Cody was secretly pleased that Jerry Mendes had invited him. It proved, he felt—not least to those to whom he let drop news of the invitation—who was still the senior journalist at Six.

When he finally arrived, Katie Moretti ushered him inside her home—a Double Bay mansion gained in her divorce and refurbished in the contemporary manner of a corporate foyer—and introduced him to her other guests. They came, he learned during the introductions, from advertising and finance and the law. There were also two McKinsey vice presidents—is there anyone, he wondered while shaking hands and smiling, who works for a modern corporation who isn't a vice president?—a Labor Party senator and a graphic designer. You could have greased a hundred barbies with their conversations.

Still, the food had been exquisite, much good wine had

been drunk, and a very fine Armagnac had gone around the table several times. The new furniture and the new paintings and the new crockery and the new caterers all deserved the compliments they received; the view from the dining room over the harbour had rightly been celebrated in several major magazines; and there had even been two wonderful Romanian musicians, a violinist and an accordionist—*my* gypsies, as Katie Moretti called them—earlier in the afternoon. Yet somehow it all seemed tedious, overwrought and as much effort to endure as a day at work.

No one really cared overly about anything; but they still felt the need to repeat what they had read in the *Sydney Morning Herald* which repeated the opinions of people at dinner parties such as the one they were now at, all feeling slightly dizzy with the familiar dullness of everything.

So many ideas to parade, films to have watched, books to have read, exhibitions and plays to have seen, so much to have to have greedily gobbled—and unless you were a glutton and had swallowed the world whole, you were an ignorant fool, unqualified to say anything.

But all these subjects existed only to lard the hard truth of the lunch: the gossip that traded knowledge for money and power; the finessed probings of position and status; the sly seeking of alliances and linking of chains of patronage; the constant aggrandisement of self, as necessary as a bull elephant seal's bark.

Richard Cody would have left even earlier than he did, had it not been for the graphic designer. She was dark, with curly black hair and was wearing a short dark brown dress with a low neckline partly covered with black lace. The lace made the curve and shape of her plump breasts look particularly enticing. Her name was—but what her name was, Richard Cody, for all his interest, was unable to remember.

Still, even without being able to refer to her by name, Richard Cody flirted in a way he believed would not be noticeable, but which he thought would only seem to others like the courtesy someone would show a stranger.

The day dragged on, the graphic designer seemed at first uninterested, and then politely irritated by Richard Cody's attention, and when Jerry Mendes took him aside, ostensibly to admire the view from Katie Moretti's new deck, but rather in order to speak to him in confidence, Richard Cody was both relieved and excited. Perhaps a new program? A promotion? Money? It could only be good, he thought, as he laughed wholeheartedly at some of Jerry Mendes's wretched jokes.

Jerry Mendes was a fat man with a bad complexion. He appeared to have been assembled out of chipped billiard balls. His reputation was as an arse licker, he never seemed to have much to say, and what he said was uttered in an unpleasant voice that was both resonant and high pitched, and always sounded to Richard Cody like one billiard ball hitting another—*clack*—and rebounding onto yet another—*clock*. Still, Richard Cody felt rather important being invited outside for a private chat, and he thought how, in spite of what people said, he was really quite fond of Jerry Mendes.

On the deck the heat was like a weight. The sun was so bright that there was no view, only blinding shards of white light ricocheting off the water like shrapnel filling the sky, slashing at the vision of any who looked. They screwed their faces up to narrow their eyes to slits. Like reptiles waiting to strike, they gazed out on Australia, unable to see anything.

9

"Beautiful, eh?" Jerry Mendes said.

"Exquisite," Richard Cody replied, his head already beginning to ache from the inescapable glare.

"Gotta fag, Richie?"

Richard Cody loathed being called Richie. He wearied of Jerry Mendes always asking this same question and him always giving the same answer: he didn't smoke. He longed for shade.

Jerry Mendes went inside and returned with a lighted cigarette, took one big drag and, as the smoke meandered out of his mouth, flicked the cigarette over the deck and into the blinding white light of Sydney.

Then he turned to Richard Cody and told him that exciting things were afoot at Six, that the board was keen to spend more on current affairs in the chase for ratings. He waited for Richard Cody to say something, and so Richard Cody said something, but it was like telling Jerry Mendes he didn't smoke, for Richard Cody knew whatever he said at this point was irrelevant.

Jerry Mendes then told Richard Cody that he was being transferred from his job as anchor for the network's flagship weekly current affairs program, *This Week Tonight*, to their nightly current affairs show, *Undercurrent*, but not as the anchor, which Richard Cody would have found acceptable, but as "senior network correspondent". He was being replaced at *This Week Tonight* by the young ABC newsreader Zoe LeMay.

Jerry Mendes used all sorts of empty phrases—*reinvention . . . new demographic . . . we are all family . . . synergy*—to dress up what they both knew to be a demotion. All Richard Cody could hear was *clack-clock-clack* and the sound of something sinking. Zoe LeMay! A bimbo even blondes looked down on! It was his face, his age, he knew it. He went to protest, but Jerry Mendes cut him off:

"Well, Richie, if you want it different, you're going to have to get off your arse. Take some responsibility for yourself. Work your way back."

Richard Cody completely forgot how only a few moments earlier he had been rather fond of Jerry Mendes, for now he hated him from the bottom of his heart, hated him completely and utterly, and loathed his grasping mistress, Katie Moretti, and all their awful, dull friends. What made it even worse was that Jerry Mendes, finally weary himself of his own nonsense, had abruptly changed the subject and was now, his repulsive hand on Richard Cody's shoulder, philosophising about journalism as if they were brothers in arms.

"These fuckwits who think it's about the truth, you know where they go wrong?" Jerry Mendes said, neither waiting for nor wanting an answer. "They think the truth has power, that it will carry everything before it. But it's crap. People don't want the truth, you know that, Richie?"

Richard Cody knew he was meant to say nothing. He said nothing.

"People want an exalting illusion, that's what they want. Find that sort of story, ginger it up with a few dashes of fear and nastiness, and you've hit gold. True gold."

This time Richard Cody knew he was meant to say something. He searched for what he hoped was the right note of irony.

"Truth is what we turn into gold, Jerry," he said.

Jerry Mendes laughed so much his laughter turned to wheezing and then a thin, high-pitched choking noise that was only alleviated by an inhaler he wrestled from a trouser pocket. He sucked on it as if it were a giant lollipop.

"Journalism, Richie," said Jerry Mendes when he was once more able to speak, his voice now thin and oddly shrill, "is the art of making a sow's ear out of a silk purse."

10

Walking the length of the Nullarbor Plain did not offer a more dispiriting prospect to Richard Cody than staying one more moment at Katie Moretti's lunch party. And yet, he stayed in order to impress Jerry Mendes that he was a remarkable man who deserved better, so that he would not be thought to be doing what he now desperately wished to do—leaving in a rage. To distract himself he went back to flirting with the graphic designer.

The talk had swung to the mandatory detention of refugees. At first Richard Cody felt compelled—albeit in a qualified manner—to agree that the government's position was less than praiseworthy, but the graphic designer didn't seem to be that interested. Then Richard Cody began putting the other side of the argument, at first tentatively, quoting several sources high up in Foreign Affairs.

And when the graphic designer seemed no more interested than before, Richard Cody began inflating several stories he had heard of "dangerous Islamic types" who had been allowed into the country, playing up a few well-known names with whom he had, if he'd been honest, only the vaguest connection.

And though the graphic designer still appeared no more interested than before, slowly the table began to come round to Richard Cody's views, which seemed like so much common sense from a man who, as a prominent journalist, really had seen something of the world.

"I mean," Richard Cody said, "it's not as if we are Nazi Germany."

"That's what I keep saying, Ray," said the Labor Party senator, who had aioli from the crayfish smeared on his jowl and Richard Cody mixed up with Ray Martin. "We're Australia."

Others murmured their agreement with the senator. There could be no doubt about it; they were Australia and, looking around Katie Moretti's grand dining room and its new furniture and its splendid view, it was readily apparent to them all what Australia was, and all of Australia was as splendid as it was obvious—it was them! It was their success and their prosperity; their mansions and apartments! Their Porsches and Bentleys and Beemers! Their getaways in the tropics! Their yachts and motorcruisers! Their influence, their privileges, their certainties! Who could doubt it? Who would question it? Who would wish to change any of it?

The graphic designer finally seemed engaged; she looked Richard Cody's way, smiled briefly, and leant forward. Richard Cody was relieved. He smiled back.

"Say what you like about the Nazis," the graphic designer said, and Richard Cody noticed that she had an attractive dark mole on her left breast, "but they understood design."

She leant further forward as she spoke, and a heavily ornamented crucifix she wore teetered out from the cleavage that Richard Cody found so appealing, then tumbled out of the pocket between the black lace and her breasts.

"Look at that SS uniform," said the graphic designer. "Now, that's sex in black jodhpurs."

For a moment no one spoke. The crucifix swayed like a talisman in front of them all, beating slow time in that empty space, and the more the crucifix swung, the more Richard Cody looked, and the more he looked the more he imagined her breasts underneath and what her nipples would be like erect, and the more he felt compelled to agree. The swastika was great branding, he said, quickly adding that it wasn't a brand he liked, but that wasn't the point.

Richard Cody was draining another glass of the '97 Moorilla Pinot Noir when the graphic designer got up to leave, and though everyone protested, none more so than Richard Cody, she was going, and going with her was her black lace and her swaying, taunting crucifix and her black-moled breast and her now unknowable nipples. Richard Cody realised that all through that impossibly long lunch she had been bored with them all, not least him.

Richard Cody refilled his glass, determined to make the most of the day, but once the graphic designer was gone so too was whatever small spark had sputtered through the afternoon.

The table talk slowed, then moved on to how terrorism—

when it happened in other countries—had such a positive effect on Australian real estate prices. Richard Cody found himself staring out at the harbour.

"Since nine eleven the Americans love Sydney, because we're beautiful *and* safe," he heard Katie Moretti say. "But whatever will they think of us now with those awful bombs?"

11

Richard Cody turned around. Something about Katie Moretti's inane chatter had captured his attention. With a very real outrage at the graphic designer's complete lack of interest in him, and intent on impressing the table and shaming Jerry Mendes, Richard Cody began talking with passion of the atrocities committed in London, at Beslan, in Madrid and Bali. And as he talked, Richard Cody could feel his anger happily refuelled by the resentment he felt at the people he was sitting with, who thought of terrorism only in terms of their property prices. He felt himself more and more moved by his own unexpected emotion, found himself speaking about the end of innocence and the shocking destruction of the ordinary lives of good people, and somehow the fate of people killed by terrorist bombs and his demotion by Jerry Mendes and his rejection by the graphic designer were all one and the same, and all the wounds of the world were his.

"You won't believe this," Katie Moretti said, "but there's a very sexy Syrian man who comes to our Latin American dancing classes. He's a computer programmer or something. We call him Salsa bin Laden. He's pretty gorgeous, whatever he is."

Richard Cody felt momentarily confused, as if he had

been given a cricket bat to go surfing.

"Well, if you think the death of innocent people doesn't mean anything, say whatever you like," said Richard Cody, who liked saying whatever he liked, and who—if others spoke when he had things to say—experienced a strange sensation that was at once rage and jealousy.

"The era of sentimentality is over," he continued. "Our civilisation is under attack—why, even an afternoon such as this would be illegal under the new barbarians—neither wine, nor women allowed to dress as they wish, nor dancing . . ." and on and on he went, not that anyone had danced or would get the chance while he continued talking.

Richard Cody then argued for the necessity of torture, properly managed. Proper management, sensible policies, agreed procedures—it was possible, after all, to civilise something as barbaric as warfare with the Geneva Convention, and now we needed a Geneva Convention on how we might conduct torture in a civilised fashion.

Sometimes Richard Cody shocked even himself with his opinions and the violence with which he forced them on others. What was even more shocking to him was how other people tended to agree meekly with him, not, he feared, because they thought he was right, but only because he was stronger, louder, more aggressive. People, he felt, merely went where they sensed power.

Still, at first, winning would bring him a feeling of pleasure in victory so acute his face would flush and his nostrils flare. But soon after, Richard Cody would realise he didn't really believe anything he had just so passionately said. Worse, he had only argued because he felt it important that his view, and his view alone, prevail. And then everything he said seemed to him so full of hatred and ignorance, intended only to hurt and to impress, and he despised the way no one would rise to his challenge and call him the fool, the bully, the buffoon that, in his heart, he feared he was.

And because no one ever did, and because he was at once enraged and relieved that they didn't, because they invariably shut up, because no one had the courage to speak the truth or, like the graphic designer, they simply left, Richard Cody would keep on talking and it was hard to know when, if ever, he might stop.

"This is a good world," Richard Cody heard himself saying. "We have prosperity, beautiful homes"—here he held out a hand indicating Katie Moretti's house, recently featured on a magazine home-decorating show on the Six Network—"some more beautiful than others"—here there was laughter—"but there is irrational evil lurking out there."

These were grand words, and Richard Cody felt himself grand speaking them. And then he changed his tone, spoke more quietly, took them into his confidence and told them dark tales of terrible plots foiled, of the mass poisonings and bombings and gassings planned and, through vigilance, averted, offering vivid descriptions of how Australians might otherwise have died en masse in the very heart of Sydney.

Richard Cody could feel the fear take hold. He sensed the pull of a story, the power of its telling, as the table went quiet, their imaginings now hot-wired to his images of conspiracy, fanaticism, horror. He could feel himself cheering up. He was on to something, were it not for the fact there was no new story other than three unexploded homemade bombs at Homebush Olympic stadium.

When the taxi arrived, Richard Cody apologised for leaving early, but lied that he had a shoot at dawn the following morning. That, he said, not looking at Jerry Mendes, was "the truth business".

"A little journalist is a dangerous thing," said Jerry Mendes after he was gone. "Invaluable, really." And once more he laughed until his laughter turned to wheezing, and once more he had to reach for his inhaler.

As the taxi swung out and down the street, Richard Cody leant back into the clammy grey vinyl, took a small bottle out of his coat pocket and sprinkled some fluid onto his hands. It was all a racket, thought Richard Cody as he wiped his hands clean of the germs and bacteria he had picked up at lunch—Six, the media, journalism. He would show them who was the master of such things, he would find the ways and means to restore his standing. He would get a story up that no one would forget. As he reminded himself of his resilience, he wrung his hands, finally clean of Jerry Mendes's slimy touch and the overly moisturised farewell handshake of Katie Moretti, the hand of a mortician, cold and somehow congealed.

His mind returned to the three unexploded bombs and the way he had, for a short time, held the table—prophesying how here in their home town they might yet die wretchedly in some evil cataclysm. But it was hopeless: at a certain point the story petered out. Still his mind raced in circles and the only thing that seemed pleasant to ponder was his memory of the graphic designer's breasts.

Richard Cody leant forward and said to the taxi driver: "We're going to the Cross, mate."

12

On the table the Doll spun, the Doll hugged the brass pole, sat on her arse, spread her legs, worked the floor, walking on her hands and knees over to first this sorry fuck, then that one, then over to a group of suits, dropping her head low so that her hair came close to them, so that they might smell the cheap scent she used solely for work, saying over and over, dragging every word out in a low voice that was almost an orgasmic groan:

"Hi, I'm Krystal."

As though it meant something or everything, so that they would feed her money, the Doll tried to entice them to tip, to persuade them that they needed to see what it was that a woman had beneath her knickers, to pull her knickers away so that they could look, but everything the Doll did, every word she said, every gesture she made, everything she revealed and the many more things she so carefully hid, all of it, she told herself, was about money, to get and to keep money, for all the things that money could buy and for all the things that money made her feel.

And every man, as soon as he entered the Chairman's Lounge, was being measured by every girl only in terms of this—how much money he might have. Every man would be accepted and wanted, flattered and courted, teased and indulged—but in exact proportion to how many dollars the Doll and the other girls thought they would be able to fleece off him.

The long light raking down from far above that high-lighted her body kept everyone else enveloped within the darkness. If any employee had been so foolish as to risk their job and turn the lights up, there would have been revealed an outrageous if rather timid cast of characters assembled beneath the dancing naked woman.

They came from corporate towers, building sites, ware-houses, flats. They were fleeing, if only for an hour or two, the vertiginous suburbs of the west, the tyrannical taste of the inner city; the striving homes of the north, the self-satisfied eastern suburbs. A few came from other places and other countries. But as part of the blackness, they were—no matter how rich or powerful—now nothing. The woman wrapping herself around the brass pole, dropping the see-through top and cupping a breast with her free hand, squeezing her nip-ple—that woman had, for the briefest moment of illusion and truth, become everything.

When she first started, the Doll had expected the clubs to be exotic and erotic, and at first she felt she was simply work-ing in a club with no class. Only over time did she come to realise that all this mundanity was in fact highly honed; that the cheapness and the bad taste was not an error but a pre-condition; that the same music over and over, the absurd platform shoes that seemed to have come out of some seven-ties movie, and the hideous, equally ridiculous gauzy outfits, all served a purpose.

That in the club there was nothing of any note or interest was for a reason: only the women's bodies were to be of note and interest. But to remain noteworthy and interesting, the women's bodies needed to be fed money as regularly as a pokie machine and, like a pokie machine, they offered ongoing small payouts—a tongue appearing, a thigh rubbed, a breast proffered—for each sum dropped into the slot of the hand, the garter, the knicker elastic. If ultimately the grand payout always seemed to be somebody's else's good fortune, at least, as in a pokie joint where the wheels never stopped spinning or the music playing, so too did the bodies here never cease writhing and the music thumping. Because here everything had been reduced and simplified to this: the house spending as little money as possible in order to extract as much money as conceivable from the customer.

And so after a time the absurd outfits, the ludicrous shoes, the ridiculous dance moves no longer seemed absurd and ludicrous and ridiculous to the Doll, but as appropriate and as sensible as scissors to a hairdresser, or an apron to a waitress—simply what was necessary to get the job done and to ensure the customers kept coming. But exactly what they were coming for was less and less obvious to the Doll.

One night a man paid her for two hours of private shows in a row, and she spent the entire time on her knees while he stared up her arse with the solemn intensity of a gynaecologist. Still, as Wilder said, for six hundred and forty bucks you would want to view arses that seriously. Another man paid her over a grand for three and a half hours worth of private shows, in which she sat with him and listened to him talk, until finally, his face swimming in tears, he stood up, and walked out into the night.

Whoever, whatever: they rarely mentioned wives, girlfriends, kids. Except to say they didn't exist or didn't understand or sometimes, when pissed, both. But then, as Ferdy had told the

Doll when she had taken the job, the Chairman's Lounge was a theatre in which everyone had a role.

The girls all had false names and their own act: there was Melissa, whose eyes weren't quite right, and Amber, whose head wasn't.

"You know what I'd really like to be sometimes," Amber said one night. "I'd like to be a man wanking on a woman." And Amber, who rarely smiled, burst into a mysterious smile that no one could fathom. "That must be really something," Amber said, "eh?"

There were some suburban mums and a few students; Jaqui with the breasts, and Maria, who idolised celebrities and who always managed to see celebrity where others failed—whether it was the aspiring actor who had a walk-on in a Cherry Ripe ad on tv five years earlier, or a reserve that never quite made it playing for the Roosters three seasons back—and every time Maria would say:

"Such a lovely guy, and famous too."

There was Rebecca from Adelaide, whom everyone inexplicably called Salls, and who would almost nightly assure the Doll, generally with a sigh, that she was getting out, that she had had enough and was buying a bed and breakfast in Tasmania, or a boutique in Port Douglas. But Salls, who had been there even before the Doll started, never left.

And then there was the Doll herself, who hadn't been there as long as a few, but who had been there longer than most. Like Salls, she had a plan. Unlike Salls, she was close to making it work. She just needed to make a few more hundred dollars.

13

"I knew all her stories," Ferdy would later say to the newspapers, "but not one single thing about her—not even where she lived."

He knew her real name, though, and he knew too why she had been given her nickname, because Ferdy was the bestower of names: hers; the club's; the cocktails—both the old favourites, the Orgasmatron and the Viagra Rocket, and the passing fads such as Schapelle's Sister—along with the girls who worked for him there, Amber and Salls; Jaimee and Maria and Danni and Jodie. To Gina Davies he gave the working name Krystal and, after a few months, the nickname the Russian Doll. For, as he would come to tell the cameras, "whoever you thought you knew, there was always another, different person the next time you met her". But the Russian Doll was too long for a nickname and soon, to the other girls and staff, she was simply *the* Doll.

After, when she only existed as a topic of conversation, people said there was always something different about her—not just who she was, but even how she looked. Her skin could seem almost alabaster, but she only had to walk outside on a hot day and it would turn cinnamon. Her black hair would take on an almost blue lustre under some lights. Sometimes she looked like a child, but on the table she would, in some intangible way, seem far more of a woman than anyone else in the room.

There was something about the promise of her body that made men happy to pay simply to sit in her vicinity, and the Doll was the dancer who almost always pulled the top dollars, no matter how bad the night. But men she mostly cared nothing for. Her sexual life, she said, didn't amount to much:

"Does anybody's?" she would say when the matter was raised. "A few girls, a few more boys. Nothing conclusive," she once told Salls, as if love were a theory that needed proving.

She had an open gaze that met the eyes of others with a certain fearlessness that belied her private nature, and a sleepy, ironic smile that alone was often enough to drive men so crazy they would propose to her. To these Queensland resort developers, Victorian footballers and Sydney management consultants she would always reply:

"Are you completely out of your mind, my friend?"

And when that failed, have Billy the Tongan talk to them as they left the club.

She claimed that it was only about the money, but she had long since learnt that nothing is ever really about money—neither why the women danced, nor why the men watched. She hated the girls who tried to pretend it was some higher calling.

"You talk more shit than floats past Manly," the Doll said to Maria after Maria had claimed it was "for our talent as dancers and our charm as entertainers" that men paid. "Men don't care how an arse or tits wobble," the Doll continued, "just as long as they're wobbling their way, my friend."

The Doll always said "my friend"; it was one of several tricks she employed to make herself appear different from the other girls. There were also her snobberies about clothes, which ran to the more expensive designer labels. She could turn up to work looking as though she were off to a corporate retreat.

Perhaps what the Doll was most successful at doing was keeping up a mystery about herself. She could disappear from the club for months at a time, giving neither notice that she was leaving, nor explanation when she returned, walking in as if it were just another weary day of work like the one before and the one to come.

In the absence of a sense that she had a life of any interest, she rarely spoke of herself. Stories began to cluster, and the Doll, discovering that the surest way of confirming a rumour was by denying it, began taking issue with the wilder tales in order to give them currency.

And so when asked if she had ever made a cast of her vagina and posted it to an ex-boyfriend, she said the tale was just so much crap. That there was no truth whatsoever that she had been Kylie's arse, having her buttocks photographed for promotional shoots, standing in for the pop diva's less appealing backside. She would put off anyone who wanted to search her stories or her heart with a laugh or a threat, mild but sufficient to compel others to leave her alone, but never enough to dispel the myths.

"Get off my arse," she would smile. "It's big, but it's not that big."

What was true? No one much believed the stories of the dead husband which was understood to be a joke that had grown up around one of her private party numbers that Ferdy had dreamt up. For Ferdy milked the exotic appeal of the Doll with various special routines: the Belle of Andalusia; the Harem Dancer; but most successfully for American marines and army groups, as the Black Widow.

There was even a special track for the show: Ferdy, who for a short time fancied himself as a DJ, had sampled "Flight of the Valkyries" off an *Apocalypse Now* DVD and added some explosions, screams, and a thudding rhythm that quickly cranked up to one hundred and sixty beats per minute as the

Doll worked the crowd. She would appear in a long black dress and hijab, then slowly strip to crotchless black knickers and an open cup black bra.

The knickers' split was tied with four black silk ribbons, each with a tiny fake pearl at their end. For fifty dollars, the Black Widow would untie a bow, and when each pearl-heavy ribbon had fallen, the Black Widow would, for a hundred, come up and open her legs wide for the man paying. And as she did so, Ferdy, using a data projector, would cover her flesh with swirling Arabic lettering, which he claimed to the audience was "the Black Widow's most sacred book", the Koran.

"It was a hell of an act," Salls told yet one more tv crew the following Wednesday, recalling what she had seen some four years earlier. "Over the PA, Ferdy'd be hooling the crowd on: 'What ordnance is the Black Widow carrying underneath?' and that sort of stuff. I remember he'd also say something like, 'You might think her fair, you might think her bright, but she's as black as hell and as dark as night.' I thought that was pretty good, and somehow it's stuck in my mind ever since."

14

Girls came and went all the time. The Doll wasn't alone in being selective about her past; many had far better reason than she did to be careful about what they said. A Chinese girl, whom the Doll only knew as Fung, had turned up one night and worked at the Chairman's Lounge for several weeks. There were rumours that she was a snakehead who had escaped from one of the Chinese brothels operating in anonymous CBD tower blocks, the chicken coops where Chinese girls, smuggled into Australia, lived and worked.

Whatever or whoever she was, Fung cultivated Ferdy, who had a thing for Asian women, and she quickly became something of a power within the club. She even rearranged a few of the Doll's shifts, which pissed the Doll off no end. And yet her power was like the wind.

One night a Chinese businessman came to the club. He was middle aged, very polite, and impeccably dressed, with a very large Rolex. Fung had not yet arrived. He caught the Doll's eye and asked her to tell Ferdy that Mr Moon had come to see him. He and Ferdy then sat in a corner, Ferdy ordered a Crownie and Mr Moon Johnnie Walker Blue Label on the rocks, and from a distance they appeared to be having an enjoyable conversation.

The Doll's shift ended and she left. As she walked up Victoria Street she ran into Fung outside an Oporto takeaway. Fung was heading to work, having claimed as her own those profitable few hours around midnight on a Thursday night—pay night.

The Doll was about to tell Fung about Mr Moon, for without knowing she knew that somehow he and Fung were connected, and that the reason for his visit was not to enjoy the pleasure of Ferdy Holstein's company. But she chose to say nothing. What business was it of hers, anyway? Besides, hadn't Fung stolen some of the Doll's lucrative shifts?

"Busy night?" asked Fung, her Chinese accent heavy, the words all sounding to the Doll wrongly tuned.

"Busy as," the Doll replied. "North shore buck's night just walked in as I was heading out."

And for a second time she nearly told Fung about the neat, polite Mr Moon who even at that moment was sitting in the corner of the bar, drinking Johnnie Walker Blue Label, waiting. But why tell a slope who had stolen your best hours anything?

"A mob from a dentists' convention worth getting to know," the Doll continued breezily, all the time the name of Mr Moon so easily said and still unsaid, "and some westie labourers I'd be avoiding."

The two women smiled thinly at each other, then walked on their separate ways. The Doll had reached the lights at an intersection when she turned abruptly and was about to yell out to Fung.

But it was absurd. What on earth would a middle-aged Chinese man have to do with Fung? And anyway, if there was some sort of shit going down, why get mixed up in it?

Having reasoned with herself in this contradictory way, the Doll stifled her cry, swung back around and headed home. She never saw Fung again.

The following night she heard that Fung had left the club with Mr Moon. A week passed and Fung had still not returned to work. A case of Johnnie Walker Blue Label arrived for Ferdy, a gift from Mr Moon. When some months later Fung's body turned up in a cemented wheelie bin in the Hawkesbury River, everyone was both sad and a little terrified, not least the Doll.

But with the Doll, sadness was also a fear that somehow they would find Fung's murderer and through him Mr Moon and through him back to her—to her who had said nothing. And mixed with her fear of the police, of Mr Moon should she ever see him again, was shame and anger. For in her heart the Doll felt she had somehow betrayed Fung and she could not stop thinking that she had cemented Fung in that wheelie bin as surely as whoever had thrown her into the Hawkesbury.

Then she would argue with herself that this was nonsense; that Fung might not have listened anyway. Or that maybe it had nothing to do with Mr Moon. Or that Mr Moon would have caught her come what may. That it was all absurd, for she had done nothing—yet wasn't that exactly her crime?

But no one ever said anything, no police came, no questions were asked and nothing happened. Ferdy shared the Johnnie Walker Blue Label with special guests and a new Asian girl, and every time the Doll saw that bottle being brought out on a tray she felt queasy. For in her heart the same words—*You killed Fung!*—kept playing over and over.

The Doll only saw Mr Moon once more. He was on the tv news at an election fund raiser. He was shaking hands with the prime minister.

15

As she started pushing her buttocks further up and out and opening her legs, the Doll calculated she had made only four hundred dollars so far that evening, and that was including tips. Over her shoulder she caught the eye of a fat suit wearing Bono shades. Maybe he was an anal man, she thought, an idea that was quickly lost in a new calculation.

To make the night worthwhile she still needed another

private show. With some luck she would get the customer to extend it into a second fifteen-minute session and pay the extra, thought the Doll, pressing her knickers in on her anus with a finger. That would give her that extra hundred bucks and, she felt, salvage the night.

"*Ooooh,*" moaned the Doll.

The room smelt like drying ammonia. Her lower back ached and her feet were on fire in the slut shoes all the girls had to wear—hot enough, as Salls used to say, to barbie a T-bone. The Doll turned, going from all fours to kneeling in front of him, trying to keep his wanky Bono shades fixed on her and only her. She slowly squeezed her own breast until her fingers closed on a nipple. She pinched it to make it tauten.

The fat suit extended a trembling hand toward her in which was a folded club tipping dollar. 'Fuck all,' thought the Doll, who was now up very close to him, saying,

"Why, thank you."

She paused, counted three beats like the good professional she was, then in a lower voice said:

"You're different. You're a gentleman. I like dancing for gentlemen."

The Doll spread her legs very slowly and, finally, with a knowing, complicit look that she sealed with a smile, lowered her gaze to her hand that she had begun running between her legs, while all the time thinking of a Louis Vuitton handbag she had seen spectacularly reduced to six hundred dollars. She could buy it tomorrow if the fat suit fell for her. It would make this shitful night worth it.

She let out an almost inaudible moan, a bizarre sound,

really, but it often seemed to do the trick, and then pushed her hand underneath her knickers. She looked up, aiming to start reeling the suit in. But the Bono glasses were no longer fixed on her. Instead, they were focused on the next table, where Jodie was dancing.

The Doll wouldn't give up. There was a Louis Vuitton bag at stake. Though it hurt, because her knees were bruised, she swung back around to being on all fours and once more began swaying her arse, hoping he might return his gaze to her. She swayed, her knees throbbed, her feet burnt, and still she kept on swaying, trying only to see herself striding down a street with her new handbag, imagining how good it would feel, how in control and purposeful she would look.

She would get him interested again, she would. Then when her turn on the table was finished she'd go and sit with him, go to work on him as she had learnt to work for the last five years, all with the aim of getting him to pay her for a fifteen-minute private show. She would give the patter only when it was needed, two ears open and mouth mostly shut, talking only when she had to, as she did with them all: enticing them to tell her their stories, their lives, their dreams; always getting them to talk about themselves, all their shit just pouring out and over her, and her saying,

"Yeah? Wow! Really? Incredible!"

Of late, most said they were mining executives. A few years ago they would have said they were property developers. Before that, dot com entrepreneurs. They were always making money. They always had a major project about to happen. The only constant thing the Doll could ever remember was herself saying, over and over:

"Yeah, wow, really, incredible."

If they ever bothered to ask the Doll about herself, she would tell them that she was just working at the Chairman's Lounge to help with her university fees, that she was a third-year medical student, single, and that she had never found the right man.

Sometimes when she danced up on the table and looked at all the lying going on down below, it seemed to her that the whole world was based on deception. Would any of these men go home tonight and tell their wives and girlfriends where they had been and what they had watched and how they were aroused? And yet everyone accepted that men came here and did such things, and that, after, the men would say nothing about it except to each other.

And so the Doll had come to believe that most of the world ran on such lies and deceptions, pretending to one thing when in truth being secretly desirous of something completely different; and she came to further believe that such deception and lies were perfectly acceptable.

And when Jodie and Amber at their shift's end some-times—if the price was right and they felt like it—went with men to a hotel and turned tricks, they would pretend to the men that they were excited, and the men would pretend that the women weren't pretending, and everyone knew it was all a lie. Deception mounted on deception, people were never who they seemed, told nobody of what they did, felt not what they said, and said nothing of what they felt. And all this was perfectly normal, so normal that when the Doll once raised it in conversation in the change room, Salls looked at her as if she had lost her mind, shook her head, and simply said:

"It's all good."

But when the Doll returned to the security of the brass pole at the centre of the table and turned back around, the fat suit was gone and it was hard to believe anything was good. The Doll held on to the pole, which at moments like this felt the only solid thing in her world, and slowly twirled around, scanning the room for a loaded man.

She spied a lone, middle-aged man coming down from the bar toward the tables. He had a short, keg-like build, wore a flash light-grey summer suit—it had to be Italian—and his face seemed somehow familiar. 'A suit like that,' thought the Doll, 'will either tip with fifties or be tighter than a fish's arse.'

16

Drink in hand, Richard Cody wandered deeper into the enveloping cavern of the club and found a tub chair close to a table on which a topless brunette was dancing. Her rounded arms and real thighs and splendid buttocks seemed a relief after the exposed musculature of the other women. As he took in the spectacle of the woman on the table he thought he recognised something familiar about her. Her name—was it Tiffany? Or was that the one at the Minx Club? Anyway, he thought, what did her name matter? She had a great arse.

He sat down and leant back and felt an odd and deep pleasure—all the sweeter for being familiar—take hold of him. He was thinking of how, for an eternity, people had thought paradise was somewhere else, whereas now it was here; of course, one had to pay, but then whatever pleasure you wanted was yours and you never needed to find out what their names were.

'Ah,' he thought, 'how sweet! How sweet!'

And he leant forward and raised his hand, holding out a twenty-dollar note in his extended fingers. Though a little taken aback when the Doll deftly plucked the note from his hand—for he had not intended to part with it quite so readily—he still felt momentarily enchanted; life no longer seemed so bad, and it was as if the world spun its peculiar way merely in order to ultimately please him.

If Richard Cody had no idea who she was, the Doll, now she could see him clearly, recognised him. He was Mr TV, Richard Cody. In the way of a pine furniture catalogue, Richard Cody was dully reassuring: always the same and telling you what you already knew. He made you feel comfortable. But he seemed a little unreal, even spooky, sitting there in front of her, tipping her, talking to her.

The Doll had heard from Maria that he had become something of a regular in recent months, though normally only on a Tuesday night early in the evening with a few tv executives. The Doll had never been working when he was there, and this was the first time she had seen him in the club. Jodie had turned a trick with him a few weeks before. She said that he had a flat fat cock like a crushed Coke can, and that it was so awful she charged him double, telling him it was her going rate.

"You're a gentleman," said the Doll, smiling as she slid the twenty-dollar note down the side of her knickers. "I like to dance for real gentlemen."

Holding his eyes with her own, the Doll then swung round and fell to her knees, so that her buttocks were very close to Richard Cody's face. She looked over her shoulder at him, and as her arse slowly rocked above his nose, a drink appeared beneath it.

"Compliments of Mr Holstein, the manager," said the top-less waitress indicating, with a slight flick of her head, Ferdy, who was standing over at the bar with a circle of five fat-gutted businessmen. Ferdy raised his glass to Richard Cody.

Unlike the businessmen, Ferdy Holstein was small in both height and girth. He had originally been a budgie of a man who, after years of weight powders, steroids and the dreary round of gymnasiums, had transformed himself into a barrel-chested budgie of a man. Though nearly bald, he had bleached what hair remained a bright blond. For all that was ludicrous about him, he was still able to manifest menace.

A piece of bright icing, Ferdy peeled off from the dough-nut of suits and walked over.

"I'm a great admirer of your work, Mr Cody," he said, "as I've noticed you've become of ours." He reached into an oversized pocket of his baggy jeans, pulled out a business card and handed it to Richard Cody. "If ever I can be of help, let me know." As he spoke, a slight spume of white saliva gathered at the edge of his mouth.

Richard Cody looked at the card. "Ferdy Holstein," he mused, then looked back up. "You've been in the news, Ferdy," he said, pocketing the card.

"Unfortunate event," Ferdy Holstein said.

"That drug rape trial, wasn't it?"

"I was just a witness," Ferdy Holstein said. "As far as I could see, it was consensual sex between my business partner and the girl. But I never said I saw everything."

"Unfortunate," Richard Cody repeated. And then he lit up:

"Terrible thing to be tangled in a trial, Ferdy—you know what the Thais say? 'It is better to eat dog shit than to go to court.'"

"They've got a point," Ferdy Holstein said, taking Richard Cody's hand. "It's good to meet. Like I said, if I can assist you with anything, let me know." He stressed the "anything". "We're a misunderstood industry and we like to help our friends in the media, Mr Cody. Otherwise we all end up eating dog shit."

Yet when Richard Cody flashed Ferdy the briefest of smiles, it was Ferdy who was left feeling both oddly complicit and slightly fearful. Ferdy looked up into the light and, finding the Doll, indicated Richard Cody with a motion of his head.

The music track ended. As the next dancer was announced and the inescapable beat started pushing again, the Doll stepped off the purple felt-lined table and made her way to where Richard Cody once more sat alone.

Later, the Doll would think back on that strange half-hour she spent in one of the private rooms with Richard Cody—two shows in a row, paid for not by him but by Ferdy. At first Richard Cody simply wanting her to fondle her breasts in front of him as he mumbled obscenities. How confident he was—so unlike most men, who, no matter what their bluster, were often like lambs once they were alone with a naked woman: hopeless, lost lambs. But not this man. At one point he even quite cheerfully insulted her, saying:

"Isn't it humiliating?"

"What's humiliating?" said the Doll, picking up her drink, knowing full well what he meant. "Drinking a vodka with tonic rather than straight?"

"Ho ho," said Richard Cody, without smiling. "No." He

opened his hand outwards, extending his little fingers—the tiny fingers of a child, slight, soft and without strength—as though he were a magician who had just conjured a dove out of the air and released it from his palm. The Doll looked down at his hand and felt revolted.

"This," he continued. "Being here. Doing . . . *this*. You are an interesting woman. You could do anything you wanted."

"And your job, my friend," said the Doll, "that's not humiliating?"

Richard Cody made a noise somewhere between a dismissive laugh and a hiss.

"I don't think so," he said. "Now—let's see your arse."

And the Doll smiled the smile that Ferdy had taught them all to use, trying so very hard not to be upset by having to continue dancing naked above this man. And as she danced once more, as he again chanted how he wanted to slide his cock up her arse and then into her mouth and then into her arse, the Doll felt betrayed by her own words.

Why hadn't she shut up, just kept playing the ditz, keeping herself hidden, safe, so that this shit would just pour off her as it normally did? And at that moment, the control, the sass and the front—which at other times seemed so potent and almost second nature—stretched to paper thin, and the Doll felt somehow deceived by life.

At the end, as she was putting her clothes back on, the Doll noticed him pull a small bottle out from his jacket pocket, pour some fluid into his hands and, in a strange ritual, wash them. She felt as if she were filth being flushed down a sink.

17

At the bar Ferdy pulled out a red ledger—no recoverable, traceable hard drives for Ferdy—opened it, ran his finger down a short column of figures, and said:

"Seven hundred and twenty dollars."

He turned the book round, pushed it toward the Doll, and passed her a pen.

"Not bad for an early night, Doll."

While he went to the cash register and from a drawer beneath it pulled out the cash, the Doll checked the figures. When she was sure they were correct, she took out her black Prada Saffiano leather chequebook wallet from the Gucci handbag she now hated, and opened it. The six credit card slots were empty, as was its chequebook compartment. The Doll had neither bank account nor credit rating: the chequebook wallet, she believed, helped convey a different impression. To the eight hundred dollars in its cash compartment, she now added the notes Ferdy handed her, though not before quickly thumb-counting them.

"Good for now, Ferdy. A few years ago we would all have been a little disappointed."

Once outside, the Doll was hit by the pungent, sticky heat of the night. Everywhere there were people, far more people than usual. The Doll walked to the edge of the road and held out a hand.

Inside the Chairman's Lounge, Richard Cody had had enough. Leaving the club, he nodded to Billy the Tongan at the head of the red carpet, then looking up saw the dark dancer, the one with the great arse, now fully clothed, stand-ing by the road trying to flag a taxi. The street was busier than at peak hour, choked with traffic, and the pavements were thick with people, all sorts of people: tourists, families, gays dressed wildly. Richard Cody was thinking how, when he got home, his wife wouldn't be in any mood for sex, and here he was, feeling fit to burst.

Whistles were sounding and a thousand different songs seemed to be erupting from streets not far away. It was, Richard Cody suddenly realised, the night of the Mardi Gras parade. Everyone, he thought, gets sex on Mardi Gras night, and he didn't see why he should miss out.

He casually strode the way of the dancer, and came up behind her.

"Well," Richard Cody said, "if it isn't Tiffany."

"Hello," the Doll said, but avoided his gaze, keeping her eyes firmly fixed on the traffic, holding her hand out more forcefully now, to make her intention clear.

He smiled, his best, most charming smile, turning slightly so she would see him in profile from his left side. As a joke a cameraman had once told him it was a far more handsome profile than his right.

"Tiffany," Richard Cody said, reasonably sure it was her name, and reasonably sure that if it weren't it wouldn't matter: "I pay well for a good blow job."

The Doll turned to him. She noticed his head was twisted in a strange way.

"You've got the wrong idea, my friend," she said, and then walked quickly past him and up to where a cab was pulling in, adding an aside over her shoulder: "Arsehole."

18

A minute later, riding through the crowded, sweating city, the Doll had forgotten about the creepy tv man. Around her the streets surged with colour and sound as Mardi Gras got into full swing. The chaos was exacerbated by the presence of security everywhere—cop cars, uniformed cops, dogs, cordons and spot searches of bags. Pedestrians outnumbered cars and cars were moving slower than people as the taxi shoved through the crowds, crawling the short distance to the Doll's flat in Darlinghurst. The Doll enjoyed the vibrant anonymity of it all. A great city is a great solitude, and the Doll, above all else, liked being alone.

When they became ensnared in a traffic jam, she left the taxi and walked the last block to her flat, past the side lane where an abandoned blue Toyota Corolla continued to accumulate parking tickets as it had done for the past several days—so many that it now looked to be covered by a leaf storm. She turned into the entrance of a dirty and undistinguished brick apartment block.

By the exorbitant standards of the inner city the Doll's third-floor flat was cheap, but for the same reason that its rent was low—its small rooms, its dilapidated kitchen and squalid bathroom—she rarely let anyone come back there. One day she would have an apartment, a real home that she would bring people back to, and everything would be designer—the Alessi sugar bowl, the La Pavoni espresso machine, the Philippe Starck toilet. Until then, she bought the designer products that mattered—the ones other people saw—and that was clothes.

The Doll put both radio and tv on—she hated the flat silent and found any noise preferable to none—undressed, showered in the crappy shower that dribbled like an old drunk, and then naked, preferring not to towel herself but to stay wet in the heat, the Doll went to her bedroom.

With one foot on her bed between the two Garfields with whom she slept, the other balancing on a precarious pile of *Renovating Today* magazines that sat on a bedside table, the Doll stretched her arms up to the low ceiling. She peeled a Beyoncé poster off its Blu-tack, revealing a hand-sized hole in the ceiling, from which, not without difficulty, she pulled out a bulging silk bag decorated with batik patterns.

The Doll lay on her bed, undid the bag's drawstring and took out a fat roll of banknotes bound with a brown rubber band. The Chairman's Lounge paid well, but they paid cash, and she didn't want to get caught by the tax office. And so none of her money went where it could be traced, and all of it went into the batik silk bag.

She had learnt to survive by making the most of the small things of life. The Doll wanted what she could hold on to and that was this fat roll of cash—what she knew without counting to be four hundred and ninety-two one-hundred-dollar notes. To that roll she now added five hundred-dollar notes from her Prada Saffiano leather wallet, for it was her way to always keep a grand in her wallet in case she saw something she wanted.

If pressed, if drunk, if unguarded, she might have confessed to longing for dreams, feelings, sensations that never appeared in a catalogue or a magazine and which no one had ever paid cash for. But as to what these things were, she had neither words nor even images; they were as mysterious as the cloud that had entranced her at the beach that morning, about which she could later not recall one detail. No one remembers a cloud. But $49,700—who could forget that?

The Doll was saving for a deposit on an apartment. Her mind was full of dreams as to what it would be like. She imagined she would find something run-down, some overlooked bargain which, through her hard work and imagination, would be transformed as such places were transformed by magic and seemingly within seven minutes on television DIY programs.

And changed as miraculously with it would be the Doll's life. She would start that uni course; she would ease out of dancing, only doing the minimum to keep up the repayments. Everything was arranged, everything was ready. Because the Doll had no legitimate income, it would be bought in Wilder's name, and then Wilder would sign it over to the Doll. A few days, a week or two at the most, and the life the Doll had so long dreamt of would begin. Her flat was chaotic testimony to this dream of new order. Scattered everywhere were renovating magazines, furniture and homeware catalogues, real estate guides with circled ads and pinboards ruffling with fabric samples and cut out pictures.

Each night after work she would play out the same ritual: shower, retrieve the silk batik bag from the ceiling, lie on her bed, and begin covering her naked body with her hundred-dollar notes. For though the Doll counted the notes nightly, she had come to regard the real measure of her savings as the extent to which she was able to paper over her flesh with money.

Three years earlier the notes had only covered her belly. Then they crept up and over her breasts and the last winter they began to spread down over her groin and thighs. Now she had to start at her odd labour sitting up, delicately placing the first notes on her ankles.

As if her body were a large jigsaw puzzle, she toiled patiently, carefully overlapping each note like fish scales, imagining herself a mermaid of money. Come the day the notes completely covered her naked body, then, the Doll told herself, she would stop dancing full time. Then she would have enough money for the deposit on an apartment.

The notes felt damp and slightly ticklish. They felt like purpose, justification, the future. They felt like what makes a life possible and bearable. They felt good, like only possessing a lot of money can. These days, the Doll preferred the touch of money on her skin to the touch of a man. It was all good. On Monday, dancing for Moretti, she would earn the final three hundred dollars she needed to make $50,000, the sum she had set herself for a deposit. She would place the final three notes on herself. She would put one over her mouth, one over each of her eyes. And, her body finally covered, her new life would begin.

19

After a time the night seemed hotter than ever. The noise of mozzies cut the thick heat in an unpleasant way. The Doll sat up, the dollar notes falling away from her body and fluttering to the floor. She collected the money, counted and rolled it and stowed it in the silk bag, and hid the bag back in its hole.

The Doll stared at the accordion folds of her tightly packed wardrobe, deciding what she might wear. Before she had begun saving, all of her money that wasn't needed for rent and food and a little fun had gone on clothes. Now the Doll proudly told her friends,

"I'm on a budget."

Being on a budget meant the Doll restricted herself to $2,000 a month for clothes. Another grand went out on rent each month, and she allowed herself two grand for living, most of which disappeared on taxis and restaurants. The rest she tried to put away, aiming to add four thousand dollars worth of notes a month to her body. To achieve that the Doll needed to earn nine grand a month.

Sometimes she worked six or even seven nights a week, spent less on clothes and living, and she was able to make her target. Mostly, though, she didn't. Mostly she blew out somewhere or other, or just couldn't be bothered dancing that much and, instead of four grand, it was at best one or two grand or plain nothing that she saved. And so instead of one year it had taken her three years, but still, over time, the money accumulated, and now the Doll and the blue Corolla were competing to be the first covered in paper.

As for the two grand reserved for clothes this seemed to her miserable enough and economy indeed, for in her early years as a dancer the Doll had developed a taste for the best European designers, and so some months her two thousand dollars, even with the most astute shopping, would only be enough to buy two or three things.

Though some of the other girls teased her about her expensive tastes, it was a simple matter for the Doll: she became someone else. No one would imagine that she had ever been other than beautiful, privileged, one of the elect who belonged not in the mortal world, but came down from the world of the gods—the billboards and women's magazines, the films and ads—to walk among mere mortals. It was a fix, like blow, and like blow it always wore off too quickly and left you wanting that feeling back.

Yet the more clothes the Doll bought, the more the Doll spent, the more the Doll was reminded of who she was, where she lived and how she made her money. And after a short time every Bulgari accessory, each Versace shirt, and all the D&G skirts and jeans and Prada shoes only reminded the Doll of one thing: that she was less.

And then she would have to go shopping again.

She would roam the beautiful shops with their beautiful décor and beautiful shop assistants, their exquisite, thoughtful interiors marred only by their awful customers: the rich Asians she resented, the fat rich Australians she despised, the anorexic rich Australians she pitied, the poor rubbernecking westies she hated. So much beauty in service of so much that she found so ugly, so much that was hideous seeking cover, and in all the shoppers she saw only a different aspect of herself: wounded animals desperate that no one else see and know their fatal hurt.

Finally, the Doll put on matching La Perla knickers and bra, beautiful pale green lace embroidered with small pink flowers picked out in Swarovski crystals—how she loved that sweet feeling of them against her skin, so hidden, so secret. They felt like walking around with $49,700 wrapped around her body. Then she wrestled on her favourite rhinestone-studded Versace jeans, draped a gold chain belt around her waist, and over her top slid a little black singlet brightly emblazoned with what, for the Doll, were the most magic of letters: D&G.

Then she headed back out into the night and the Mardi Gras. The scene was much as ever, the same burning smell of Asia: food, crowds, piss, smog. She passed the Aborigine who always slept naked in a driveway just around the corner; the familiar ice addicts; the old men cruising; the same beggars, one of whom even waved to her; a dead cat's skin rippling with the maggots moving beneath.

Her foot rolled and she nearly fell when she trod on a syringe.

"Eh," a voice said. "I know you."

The Doll steadied herself and looked back up to see a beggar standing in front of her, who, in spite of the heat, was wearing an old brown bomber jacket.

"You and the other girls," the beggar said, his head twitching as he spoke. "I see you coming out of the club. You get the rich boys. You girls understand. Couple of bucks ain't much for you." He stank, his skin was scabby and filthy, but his eyes were the brilliant blue she had seen below frozen water on tv documentaries. "My brother fucked me up the arse," he continued. "Twelve, I was. Fucked me so I'd have AIDS, like him. Some brother, eh? I won't lie, I need a hit. Help me, please."

"Twelve?" the Doll asked.

"Twelve," the beggar replied, somewhat taken aback. "That's right. But even a fiver'd do."

The Doll opened her purse and handed him a hundred-dollar note.

Somewhere, the sun was setting.

20

The hot night sky hung over the wild carnival like a damp, filthy rag dripping sweat on the hundreds of thousands squashed in below. The streets were crawling with cops, but everyone appeared resigned to the need for such security after the bomb scare. For nothing, it seemed, could dampen the spirit of the biggest gay parade in the world.

The sticky stench of desire and poppers and spilt beer rose like an intoxicating incense as float after float of near-naked dancing men and women came rolling down Oxford Street. There were men waxed and honed, muscled men with guts of corro and breasts of rippling beef, delicate men in tight silver Lurex; and punctuating the floats were formations of fairies and marching boys and dancing pharaohs and open-chapped cowboys line dancing. There was the roar of the Dykes on Bikes and cheering for the Scats with Hats, and weaving the whole together was a thumping cacophony of cheap fireworks and trilling whistles and a thousand shreds of music, trance and techno and rap and the ballads of beloved gay divas.

Long before she arrived, the Doll sensed the growing vibration of the large crowds massing along the parade's route, milling between the buildings and the barricades like netted shoals of fish, twisting and writhing but largely failing in their desire to move. Some had come to gawk at freaks, some to sneer, some to marvel and some to perv, and some, like the Doll, for a good time. Everyone strained for a view, save for a short weedy man racing through the mob selling stolen milk crates as viewing platforms for a tenner each.

As the Doll worked her way closer to the street and the

spectacle of the parade, she began glimpsing between jammed bodies the sight of sashaying queens with opera house hair, glomesh bags dangling; strutting grizzlies in leathers and chains with harbour bridge moustaches; men dressed in elaborate plumage like fallen birds of paradise.

And then there was the float she had come to see: Dykes with Dicks. Framed between jostling shoulders she saw Wilder topless, waggling a huge black strap-on penis, her great breasts bouncing up and down as she danced.

The Doll thought how Wilder didn't dance the way they did at the club, and it fascinated her how the less Wilder tried to dance the stupid way that was supposed to be about sex, the more sexy she seemed up there on the float. At the club you danced for money, and you danced because you were Krystal or Jodie or Amber. The one thing you never dared dance was yourself.

The Doll was trying to get closer to the barriers so that she could wave to Wilder, when she accidentally knocked a beer a woman was carrying over the side of a man in front of her. The woman swore. The man turned.

He was dark and good looking—too good looking, thought the Doll, to be anything other than gay.

The woman shook her head, swore again, and disappeared into the crowd. The Doll apologised to the man, then pointed to Wilder with her huge, shiny black cock, as if it were an explanation. When the man looked confused, the Doll said as brightly as she could:

"My friend—on the float—my friend."

Rather than being angry, he laughed:

"So—you're the dyke without a dick."

He had the correct pronunciation of a foreigner, yet he seemed somehow familiar. Perhaps it was for that reason, or simply because she was relieved he wasn't furious with her, that the Doll laughed back.

"No, not a dyke. Just a friend. But no dick."

Only then did she recognise him as the man who had rescued Max.

"Compared to her," he said, plucking his soaked shirt out from his hip, "nor have I."

Flustered, the Doll took a handkerchief out of her handbag. When, with a futile gesture, she went to dry his shirt with it she felt her fingertips touch his.

"I'm sorry," the Doll said. "I think we've—"

A float of Dusty Springfield drag queens glided by, and the music was so loud that she could neither finish her sentence nor hear his reply, but it was clear from his expression that he too now recognised her. He mimed a little boy crying and himself swimming in a comic way. She laughed again, and as some men next to them began dancing to the float's music, he put out his hand, smiled, and the Doll, still laughing, took it, not because she really wanted to, but because she felt bad that she had ruined his night soaking him in beer.

And so they began to dance there on the street. At first, they were cramped in their movement, and did little more than an awkward shuffle. But as they continued, he manoeuvred them away from the barriers and the parade to the rear of the spectators. There it was less crowded and people gave them more space. The Doll realised he knew what he was doing as he began leading her into a merengue. They spun and turned, and he pulled her in and let her go right out before tensing his fingers in her hand just slightly, the merest hint of a resolute power, and then she flew back in to him.

As they danced, the Doll found herself looking up at the street lamps spangling the night sky, and her lips formed the easiest of smiles as they swung first this way and then that. As he spun her outwards, she pursed her lips and blew him the softest, gentlest of kisses, and he laughed, and then he pulled her in, somehow twisted her around, bounced her buttocks off his buttocks and sent her spiralling back out.

At first he held the Doll gently and politely: when their bodies touched, they merely brushed against each other as the move demanded they ought. But then she felt her hand being slightly squeezed by his, and she squeezed back. Outwardly their dance remained the same, but the next time he ran his hands down her side, it felt a caress rather than a move, and when he spun her so that she finished with him standing behind her, bodies together, she could feel pressing into her lower back for the briefest, most electric of moments, the firmness of his cock.

The city was like an oven. Around the Doll were not only the floats, the parade, but the endless procession of men and women caught in the mirage of passion, eyeing off thighs, buttocks, waxed skin, walks, head turns, smiles, all alive with the anticipation of what pleasure the evening might yet bring them. The air was taut with desire so animal, it felt to her like some extraordinary annual natural event where hundreds of thousands gathered for one night of parade and rutting.

Someone clapped and the Doll realised it was not a float they were applauding, but them. No more was she separate from the Mardi Gras, a spectator of others, but now part of the exploding street of colour and noise and music, at one with all that was beautiful and all that was grotesque that evening, the plain and the exquisite, the desperate and the hopeful, the predatory and the innocent. No longer did she dance with care about how she might look, but rather with complete abandon, throwing her head back and laughing, suddenly speeding up moves and then slowing them down, so that the rhythm of the dance grew unexpected and wild. And then it was him following her, and he too had somehow become one with the evening and the Doll could feel the lust of the night and his lust joining, and she glowed with it.

Everything seemed to slow down and grow distant—their dancing, the noise and music, the countless thousands of other people, the floats, the carnival, even Sydney itself—as she caught his eyes, and then so casually looked into the night sky, casting him and whatever feelings she was arousing within him away as if they were nothing to her, only to return a short time later with another look, another way of letting her body rest on his, an arm, her breasts; the way, when her nose came close to his mouth, she made a point of closing her eyes and inhaling. She thought she heard him say his name was Tariq. But later, when she thought about it, she wondered if she hadn't got that wrong too.

21

After the parade ended, the Doll found herself walking through the Cross with Tariq. Heading up Darlinghurst Road, the evening was beautiful, and the Cross seemed uncharacteristically upbeat, as they wandered past the he-males and she-males, the offers of cheap pills, tit jobs and blow jobs and quickies down the lane, the tottering junkies and pissed Abos and passing paddy vans and parading trannies, the schizzos and touts and tourists.

One spruiker broke from his established patter and yelled out to some passing young men in rugby tops:

"Carn, boys! Look, gentlemen—" and here he extended an arm toward a dark doorway "—not a great fuck but a cheap one, and I can't be more honest than that, can I?"

They kicked on for a while at Baron's, a pub in the Cross composed of a series of small, oddly angled rooms whose cave-like feeling was accentuated by the dullest of lighting and walls painted a dun yellow trimmed in ochre.

It was a wild, bizarre crush. The crowd surged back and forth, spilling drinks on each other and the hapless sitting on the red leather Chesterfield lounges. There were weary drag queens, stubbled and sweaty, two fat men in rubber masks drinking blue curaçaos, and a man wearing a string vest and no trousers leaning against the wall with his cock out, smok-ing, looking at the melee, while another man leant in on him and stroked him in a dutiful sort of way.

Tariq said if the Doll liked she could come back to his apartment for a coffee.

"What's the time?" asked the Doll.

Tariq lifted his arm and looked at his watch for some moments. It was hard to know whether he was looking at it for so long just to read it, or so that the Doll might see what a beautiful, expensive watch he had, a Bulgari Ipno.

The Doll looked away and upwards, to where all that

seemed to be preventing the sagging ceiling from collapse was a fan staggering through the smoky babble.

"It's Sunday," she heard Tariq say above the din, "and it's only just beginning."

SUNDAY

22

NICK LOUKAKIS STOOD IN THE DOORWAY of his youngest son's bedroom, listening to the sound of his breathing as he slept. Nick Loukakis had had an affair. Maybe he meant something by it, or maybe he didn't. Standing there, he could smell his son's wild dog-like smell, and it was hard to remember. Maybe he'd wanted a way out of his marriage. Or maybe he just wasn't thinking. Maybe the affair ended the marriage. Or maybe the marriage was over when the affair began. The affair lasted several years. He believed it would fall apart each time he saw her again, fearing that she would no longer want him.

Nick Loukakis fell in love with the woman he had the affair with. Maybe he was in love with her from the beginning. Maybe he was still in love with her. His wife never found out. She always knew, but her knowing grew from a vague awareness easily put away, to a bitter knowledge she could still deny, to an enraged desolation when she one day told him she knew, that she had always known, did he think she was such a fool? And he felt his world collapse into a terrifying white hole into which he fell and in which he was still falling.

They stayed together and watched each other slowly become strangers, watched their love die as you watch a great old gum tree succumb to dieback. The affair was over for him, but it was just beginning for her. She never found out then, but it was as if each day now she lived another day of those years of lies and deceit; and his punishment was to witness her suffering. First just the leaf tips in the distant crown brown a little at the edges, then whole leaves, then a branch here and there. Still the tree lives, and everyone says it will be fine, that it is the weather, or one of those things, or anything but the death of something as natural and as seemingly permanent as a tree. But when his marriage began dying back, Nick Loukakis discovered nothing is fine.

Each day some small thing—a joke, a shared intimacy, a sweet memory—he found to have withered and died. Caresses fell like dead leaves. Conversations cracked and then broke. And in the end there was nothing to quicken the trunk with the rising sap that fed and was fed in return by the branches, by the twigs, by the leaves. And in the end what remained, Nick Loukakis discovered, was nothing; nothing to keep it going, just a large thing still standing erect and proud, only everything about it had withered and died.

Nick Loukakis realised that for a long time there had been

something about his life that he now saw as innocence. He would wait up at night until his family was asleep, then walk up and down the corridor of his small home looking into each of their rooms, glad simply to watch them sleeping, knowing they were warm and safe, knowing they were at peace. Sometimes he would pull their covers up, graze their foreheads with the lightest of kisses, and be grateful. Then he would sleep, and in the morning he would rise before anyone, so that he might be awake, sipping his coffee, when they came one by one into the kitchen, sleepy, dishevelled, and he could simply marvel that this joy had been allowed him.

But then this thing happened—something broke and he came to realise he had broken it and that it could not be put back together, not his family nor his life. He realised he could never again be that man, standing in doorways or sipping coffee in the kitchen, that he had been allowed a kind of paradise on earth in his little fibro cottage in Panania, but it was all over, and he could never again be that man waiting to marvel at his life.

Now whenever he tried to hold or hug his wife, she would say,

"Not like that, I don't like it like that. You know that."

Or she would say nothing, and he would fold and unfold her limbs as if she were an inflatable woman. When he tried to make love she made no response. It felt like rape, and he guessed it amounted to much the same thing. He felt the sadness overwhelming him. It clutched at him like death. It dragged him down into the earth. There seemed no good thing left in this life. He drove to an abandoned road with a garden hose, then drove back home. He felt for his children, and he could not escape the sense that it would have been a crime to do such a thing to children, an act for which there would be no forgiveness.

And yet he knew his wife loved him, and he loved her. But something had happened, something had broken and he knew neither how to fix it nor end it. They had continued living together, losing themselves in the dream that is life, because they didn't know what else they could do. The world was large, their troubles insoluble, and they waited together as strangers might huddle together in a shelter biding their time until a storm has passed. He hoped for a sign, a gesture, a moment.

He discovered things he had not known about himself: that after twenty-five years he now preferred to sleep alone; that after half a lifetime of his wife with a sound of frustration pushing away his foot, thigh, hand, he no longer wanted to be rejected every night. The sex was absurd, pointless; an affirmation only of what they didn't have—the affection, tenderness, hope and dreams that had once been theirs. It was a dismal affair of penetration and her body moving only where it was shoved by his thrusts. But the absence of sex he could adjust to as a price, a penance, perhaps. It was the absence of touch, of warmth, of animal connection. She had not let him kiss her for over ten years. When he held her, embraced her, cuddled her, she pushed him away. And yet he knew she loved him and would always love him.

How was it possible to live with another human being so closely, to eat with them, sleep with them, smell their breath, and yet be so unspeakably alone? She rarely talked. She would say:

"That's just me. Take me or leave me."

And if he drove her to talk, she would grow enraged and anguished. She would tell him to go and live with Wilder, because, she would yell,

"That's what you want!"

Never knowing what he wanted, what he craved, what he had not known for so many years was company, the warmth and stimulation of sharing the everyday, a sight one recalled, an idea, a story, a joke—the comfort of intimacy. He came to realise little, perhaps nothing, about him now gave her pleasure and much about him drove her to a silent contempt.

Her passions were her work as an accounts manager at a medical centre, and their two sons, whom she showed all the warmth that she withheld from him. He envied them and he admired her; they were a picture, a beautiful picture in which he did not exist. Outside he knew there was horror, corpses floating in the harbour, bones mortared into dank flats' walls, flesh raked with gunfire; outside there was violence and evil, people waiting to hurt each other, hurting each other at that very moment. As a policeman he had learnt that. It was inescapable. It was unstoppable. In his working life as a detective sergeant with the Kings Cross drug squad he embraced the evil, the horror. He believed it would make him feel better to meet and deal with people whose problems were worse than his own. It didn't. For the same reason, he read books about Hitler and Stalin, about genocides and totalitarian states. That didn't help either.

Policemen, he came to believe, were just the journalists of evil; they described it with reports, photos, videos, forensic reports; they were to their horror what the historians and biographers were to the Holocaust and Hitler. They could not change anything. He could only keep his family safe, while outside, wolves roamed.

He wandered the small house late of an evening when everyone was sleeping, standing in the doorway of each of the bedrooms, listening to the sound of his wife breathing, of his sons breathing, gently, in and out, praying, hoping; waiting for a sign, a gesture, a moment, listening to the human sound of breathing. He was trying not to think that he was falling, that everything was turning to white; trying not to think that the wolf might already be inside, waiting, hoping, listening.

23

Only after she saw him dead did the Doll realise that she had never asked Tariq who he worked for, or where he worked. He had seemed in some way fundamentally bored by what he said he did: talking about it the way students do a subject the night before an exam. Sitting in his apartment early that morning, it hadn't seemed right to ask the questions that later everyone would presume she had the answers to.

"The thing about raster graphics," Tariq was saying, "is that you can precisely manipulate an image by altering a single dot at a time—like when Elvis morphs into an ostrich, that sort of thing." He halted, as if thinking about something entirely different, then said, "What they'd like to do with real people if they could."

"They?" asked the Doll.

"Oh, I dunno," said Tariq. "Governments, corporations—whoever runs the place, I guess, powerful people."

Sydney seemed hushed and calm from Tariq's apartment. He had promised to make her coffee there, but it was too hot; instead they had some chilled Pellegrino he found. They sat on bar chairs at an elevated table positioned in front of a window, watching Sydney's snakeskin scales shifting and glinting far below, talking, sipping their drinks.

The apartment was in Potts Point, a short distance from Baron's in the Cross but a world apart in every other way. They had walked down a road lined with luxury European cars, and then into a flash apartment block foyer. They had taken a coded-card elevator up several storeys, and when the lift stopped, the doors opened directly onto a recently refurbished apartment, white walled and Euro-applianced.

Tariq dimmed the lights that had sprung on as they entered, so that the main sources of illumination were the lights of Woolloomooloo, over which the apartment looked, and, beyond it, Sydney itself. Far below, trains occasionally rushed silently around like toys, making streams of moving light, while car headlights formed thick, dappling lines. It was so different from the rough, stinking streets the Doll knew— a city transformed; a seductive darkness confettied with spots of glowing yellow and white, here and there given more definite form by the red and blue signage of great corporations.

"It's the way computers store an image as individual dots," Tariq continued. The Doll looked away from the city and at him. He was moving his hands around, as though he were a blind man searching for something. "Each pixel is encoded in the computer's memory as a binary digit—what we call bits."

Despite trying to be interested, the Doll found what he

said boring. It was as if he were compelled to say it, although it held no interest for him either. She looked back out over this strange, subdued Sydney. It all seemed so exquisite. The opera house's school of dorsal fins sat on the breast of the city like a brazen brooch on an old tart; the illuminated iron work of the bridge looked like a filigree choker, and the tower blocks studded with their endless little lights reminded the Doll of the most intricate black lacework. She could have stared at this Sydney all night as Tariq continued on about his job in raster graphics, no longer full of fun, but for as long as he talked about his work a rather dull and serious man.

"Together all the bits make up a bitmap," he went on. "I work on software to make better bitmaps to make better pictures. That's raster graphics."

"Bob Marley graphics," joked the Doll, and he spoke no more about it.

What else did they talk about? Later, when the Doll tried to get a better idea of who Tariq had really been, she was unable to remember anything of interest. They talked about some serious things and some trivial things, some general things, some intimate things. Other than when he was talking about computing, he was easy to be with, that was all.

They decided to swap phone numbers. Tariq went searching for a piece of paper and returned with a takeaway menu, wrote a number on it in green felt pen, and passed it to the Doll. She was about to write hers down when he got up again, this time coming back with a mobile phone. It was an expensive looking unit.

"Cool, eh?" Tariq said, holding out a stainless-steel handset. "Got it in KL. It's a Nokia P99 with an MP-3 player.

It's even got its own specially composed Yun Chung Hee mini-symphony ring tones."

When the Doll made no reply, Tariq seemed lost in thought for a moment, as if unsure what to say next. He slid the Nokia P99 open and shut several times. Then he looked up and smiled at the Doll.

"Fuck Yun Chung Hee mini-symphonies. They sound like shit anyway. I found this great site for downloading music for call tones. You can be anyone." He held the phone out in front of her and hit a button. "So, like, when my boss rings this is what happens." And up came a short video of Gollum from *Lord of the Rings* while Tupac Shakur's "Thugs Get Lonely Too" played as the ring tone.

The Doll laughed, because it was vaguely funny and because anything was better than raster graphics. She told Tariq her number and as he entered it he once more asked who she would like to be. The Doll didn't know.

"You can be, like, rap or techno, you can be whatever."

"Maybe classical," the Doll said.

"Cool, classical," said Tariq, who seemed somehow oddly impressed by such a bizarre call. "Wow."

"Do they do, like, Chopin?"

Tariq asked her to spell it, stared at the phone screen a moment, then said, "There's a heap of Chopin here—do you have a favourite? Otherwise every time you call it will be a Chopin concert."

"A Nocturne," the Doll said. "Find his Nocturne in F Minor."

The phone chirruped as Tariq ran his thumbs over the keypad, then quickly took a photo of the Doll.

"Now watch—when you call, this is what happens."

And on the phone's screen up popped a photo of the Doll laughing and with it a tinny version of Chopin's Nocturne in F Minor.

"You actually *like* that shit?" Tariq asked.

"Sometimes," said the Doll.

Another hour passed pleasantly enough, but the Doll began to wonder what, if anything, was going to happen. It was nice, but that, apparently, was that. Perhaps he really was gay—she had, after all, met him at the Mardi Gras. 'Just my luck,' she thought as she stood up, apologised for having stayed so long and told Tariq she would head off.

She leant in and gave him a hug and a kiss on the cheek to say goodbye. She envisaged the kiss and embrace of friendship. It would be firm, warm, fleeting. It would be final. Only it didn't feel like goodbye.

An ocean wind rose from the harbour, shuddered the apartment's window glass, and then the night was once more still.

24

Tariq rolled over to the side of the large bed on which they both now lay naked and took out a small square plastic bag from his trousers on the floor. Getting up onto his knees, he opened the bag's zip lock, then with one hand pushed his erect cock down so that it was roughly level, and with his other hand ran an unruly line of white powder up its shaft, losing much of the powder in the process. With a finger he shaped the powder into a white windrow as best he could, then passed the Doll a fifty-dollar note.

The Doll rolled the note, put an end in one nostril, and flattened the other. She leant down close to his cock and snorted back. Almost immediately she felt her jaw tighten and her teeth pull together, and then . . . so strong, she felt, so strong and so fresh, and so good.

She fell back onto the bed. Tariq leant over her and ran circles of coke around her nipples. He kissed her, then, after snorting the powdery circles, softly drew each nipple in turn into his mouth and ran his tongue around and around them. He sat back up and handed the small plastic bag to the Doll. There was still a good amount of coke left, more than a normal deal.

"Keep it," Tariq said.

"Sure?" the Doll asked.

"Sure," Tariq said. "Plenty more where that came from."

The Doll thanked him and threw the little bag on top of the pile that was her clothes.

As Tariq then lightly licked the cleft from her anus to her labia, as he gently took her lips into his mouth and then found her clitoris with his tongue tip, the idea that she had a soul, that a soul had innate dignity and needs as fundamental and profound as the body, and that some force compelled souls to find others in order not to perish—that idea would have been for the Doll unbearable. People fucked, that was all.

The Doll's head rose and then fell back onto the pillow. Her legs stiffened. She made a small repetitive moaning noise. She frantically pushed Tariq's head out of her thighs as she began coming for the first time and the swirling of his tongue tip around her clitoris became intolerable.

Then she was on her knees, her head resting in the pillow, pushing her arse up, for now she wanted him inside her. She reached between her legs, grabbed his still slightly powdery cock, and pulled it into her while pushing herself back onto him.

They began to rock back and forth, each to a slightly different yet related rhythm. Like their dance, they were spiralling out and then back in to meet each other in strange, shared sensation: unrepeatable, unsayable, her cunt tingling from the coke remnants on his cock, his thumb deep in her puckering arse as if it were a juicy orange, and the Doll felt her body respond as a beast being ridden in a rodeo. As she bucked beneath him, Tariq ran his other hand up her side. For a moment he snared one of her swaying breasts in a loose hold, and she felt it swooning in his palm, her erect nipple brushing back and forth between his forked fingers. Then his hand found her lips and the Doll kissed his fingers, his rough fingers, his gentle fingers, and she took them into her mouth and imagined they were his cock.

She could feel him coming up so deep inside her, in her and in her mouth. For a moment they formed one strange animal pushing back and forth in wild movement and rhythm neither his nor hers, but theirs. They were sweating so much now their bodies slid back and forth on the wet film that arose between them, riding their own moisture as if it were a wave. For a moment the Doll felt that she was that wave, that she was dissolving into pieces that were floating around that strange apartment, that there were no longer two bodies, but only sensations that belonged to them both. The Doll was no longer sure if it was her cries or his, if what she was feeling was his cunt or her cock as she heard the sound of his panting and her moaning at one with the drone of the Sydney night.

At the last moment Tariq pulled out, climbed up her body, and brought his cock up to her face. The Doll noticed how the veins in it glistened. Way above she glimpsed his face, no longer charmingly boyish, but full of blood, twisted in a violent grimace, and the savagery of his desire momentarily frightened her. His body jolted, tears of come ran down her cheeks, and from Tariq's lips she heard an odd, not entirely pleasant sound like the groan of a dead man.

25

The sun pressed on the Doll's face, at first curious, then insistent, and finally with a hard heat that felt like a burning flame. She got up, trying to stay asleep, and went to the bedroom window. The glass of the Deutsche Bank tower block was reflecting the rising sun as a golden fireball straight into Tariq's bedroom. It was blinding. It was as if the sun had fallen to earth and Sydney was being consumed by a brilliant gold flame.

With screwed-up eyes and groggy hands the Doll groped around until she found a toggled cord and somewhat awkwardly dropped what turned out to be Venetian blinds. She flopped back into bed and rolled onto her stomach. Even through the blinds she could feel the sun's power pressing into the room, only now it was a pleasant sensation, falling onto her back and warming her weary body, and even without Temazepam she quickly fell back asleep.

When the Doll next woke and looked across the bed there was no one there. The room was unpleasantly warm and airless. Perhaps there had been no one there before. It was hard to know. But it was clear now: she was alone in the bedroom.

"Tariq?" the Doll said and then, a little louder, so that he would hear her wherever he was, she called, "Oh God, Tariq. What a night."

There was no reply.

The bedroom was an inferno. The Doll found her watch. It was almost midday. Her mouth felt furry. She could feel the dull, unpleasant sensation of dried sweat on her skin. The sheets smelt. She smelt.

The Doll got up. Naked, she wandered through the large apartment. There was no one anywhere. There was nothing personal anywhere. It was featureless, as if it had only just been moved in to. Or borrowed. It added up to nothing beyond an idea of taste.

Unlike her flat, in Tariq's apartment everything was new, and the appliances were all of the best quality. Everything was white, as white as sugar. The walls were white. The wooden Venetian blinds were white-limed. The furniture, the fittings, the frames of pictures were variations of white: ivory, chalk, bone. On a white dining table there was an artfully placed vase with chocolate-coloured roses, but it was as if this was only there to accentuate the whiteness of everything else.

The apartment seemed made not for life, but for photographs in decorating magazines of the type that cluttered the Doll's flat in teetering piles. The apartment was everything the Doll desired, but it no longer seemed to her desirable at all. It felt, if anything, slightly weird. Still, she told herself, disturbed at how all that she wanted now seemed somehow so offputting, it's a cool place.

"It is, it is, it is," she muttered to herself; but deep within her heart—which had fallen and risen with the dramas of a hundred renovating makeovers and a thousand special magazine features—there arose a new unworded suspicion that taste might just be an evasion of life.

She needed to think of something else and she found it in a note that had been left on a smoked glass table. It read simply:

> *Back soon.*
> *T xxx*

She washed in an ornate white-tiled bathroom beneath an elaborate shower that had not one but multiple heads nippling a long pole, so that water flowed in tender thrusts from several angles over her weary body.

After, she went out on the small balcony. There were several grey navy ships berthed in Woolloomooloo Bay, their PAs occasionally sounding a desultory sentence, rasped and choked, that twanged around the bay like a rubber band. She looked out over Sydney Harbour, and thought how it really was a beautiful city, and she felt lucky to live where she did. But she couldn't rid herself of an odd unease.

She went back inside.

"Tariq?" she called. "Tariq?"

She felt a little jumpy. Below Tariq's note the Doll wrote:

> *Had to fly. Call you soon.*

And following his example she signed herself simply with the capital letter of her name:

Gxxx

Though it was hot she shivered. She found her handbag, stashed the coke away, and to steady herself dropped a Stemetil and a Zoloft. It was all good. Then the Doll dressed and left.

26

Before her macchiato was ready to take away, the police had begun arriving. At first the Doll wasn't really aware of anything loud or dramatic but the opposite: a lessening of noise, of traffic—an eerie, spreading peace. The radio in the café, formerly a burr lost in the noise of the city, seemed to be growing in volume.

The radio said: "Can anyone explain why we let them in? Can you?"

The Doll was humming "Crazy in Love", and her belly gave a little flip when she thought back on Tariq's head between her legs. She closed her eyes: she could smell his musky odour, even feel him sweetly pressing inside her still.

"Short mac!" a waiter cried. Her eyes jolted open to see police swarming around the apartment block where she had spent the night with Tariq, and blocking off the street between the apartment building and the café in which the Doll now waited.

Outside no cars moved. Uniformed police were running

up barricades of fluttering blue and white plastic streamers. Paddy wagons, trucks, a police bus had appeared as if by magic. Men in black uniforms with helmets and bulletproof vests and automatic rifles were running into positions behind parked cars, skips, the corners of buildings. It was like a war. Whoever the enemy was, it was clear they were in the apartment block the Doll had just left.

Inside the coffee shop, people were at first excited, and also a little frightened, particularly after a cop came in and spoke to them. He told them that no one was to leave until they were given the all-clear. He said there was nothing to worry about, but that everyone had to keep away from windows. Well away.

The cop turned on his heel and left. There rose in his wake a low murmur of speculation. A waiter claimed to have heard from friends in the force that a man had taken his family hostage and was threatening to kill them. The Doll overheard a woman say it was well known that a prominent drug dealer used an apartment in the building, and that this was some sort of bust. A few were convinced they had found more bombs and some moved as far back into the bowels of the café as they could in case one went off. An older man turned to the Doll and said it was a terrorist they were after.

"They should shoot the bastards," the Doll said, because it's what you said, and in so far as she thought about such things, it was more or less what she thought. But all she could feel was Tariq's flesh on her flesh, his arms around her body, his smell and his touch and his sound. It was as if his body had imprinted itself so strongly on the Doll's that he was still there with her.

Finally people grew bored. Some began talking once more about the Mardi Gras and what they had got up to. Others went back to reading another of the endless supplements that fell like so many dead foetuses out of the Sunday papers. The Doll found the takeaway menu in her handbag and went to call Tariq to see what he might know, but his number rang out to a voicemail box that had no message, only a bleep. She hung up.

The Doll sat down at a table, drank her coffee, ordered another and drank that too, while flicking through a newspaper that was lying there. She skipped past the front pages linking the bombs at Homebush with an al-Qa'ida website threat to bomb Sydney, ignored a story on a gruesome child murder, a feature about another attempt to bomb the Australian embassy in Jakarta, a found dog, a lost British backpacker, until at last she stopped at a spread about Princess Mary and her son.

The Doll looked up and, though sitting deep in the coffee shop, she could see men in combat black creeping along the top of the tower block with rifles, sights occasionally glinting, flickering in and out of the bright sunlight.

She went back to the paper. According to sources close to the Danish royals, the Doll read, Princess Mary was a wonderful hands-on mother, and the young prince was a favourite with everyone at the palace.

'Lucky bitch,' thought the Doll. She dropped another Zoloft to make up for the one she didn't have the day before and read on.

A quarter of an hour later, the same cop came back into the coffee shop, spoke into a walkie-talkie mounted on his shoulder, then asked everyone in the café for their attention.

"The situation," the cop said, "has been successfully neutralised. We thank you for your help with all matters of national security."

No one was sure what he meant. The cop was back on his walkie-talkie, head cocked to the side. Somebody asked if it meant they could leave.

He turned, annoyed at the question.

"Christ," he said. "Haven't I already told you that?"

27

Now came hours of wandering through shop after shop. Though seemingly purposeless, these were rather hours of being impelled by a necessity no less real and profound than that of a nomad hunter to constantly reacquaint himself with the land and game and seasons. There was a ceaselessly unfolding knowledge to it all, vast and necessary to the Doll's life, needing to be endlessly refreshed. The slightest suggestion of new colours or styles, the sudden collapse of a trend as indicated by the telltale discount, an offhand comment by an assistant—all these matters and moments needed to be assimilated, calibrated, judged in determining what might next be · bought, and what was next bought determined how her life might then be.

The Doll's lodestone in these wanderings that day was the Louis Vuitton bag she had promised herself the day before. With its image firmly in her mind and the city as her destination, the Doll left the coffee shop, made her way past the police cordon and up Macleay Street. Needing to walk, to stretch her body, stiff and weary after the lovemaking of the night, she headed past its gay couples and manicured women walking manicured dogs; past its exclusive food shops where a packet of chermoula spice cost more than the powders being pushed at the next street corner; where a few slices of imported jamon would set a gourmand back as much as a streetwalker's weary mouth would a kerb crawler up on Darlinghurst Road.

The Doll headed across to Victoria Street and down the long set of stone steps into Woolloomooloo. As she strode through the empty bottles and cans and streamers and syringes and broken popper bottles left over from the Mardi Gras revellers, everything seemed to radiate more heat.

She escaped from the sun into the welcome shade of the trees of Hyde Park. There a shabby ibis tottering amidst the litter below an overflowing garbage bin was trying to scrape chewing gum off the tip of its long bill. No, she told herself, she was determined not to live on scraps like the ibis, and her thinking turned to how she would soon have an apartment like Tariq's. She would buy when the market was low, and trade when it was up. She had read about such things; it was all about getting onto the real estate carousel, and once you were on, anything was possible. There were countless stories, one heard such tales every day, and soon her story would be one more of them.

A middle-aged couple wearing boxing gloves shadow-boxed as they jogged past the Doll. They seemed radioactive with health and prosperity. The Doll smiled at such idiocy after they had run past. And yet she secretly envied them, wanted to be like them—so affluent, so confident, so oblivious—and the way to become them, she was convinced, was through buying property.

Perhaps her first apartment would not be up to that much, but she would transform it; she wasn't frightened of work, and she had *flair*. Flair, the magazines said, could do so much. Flair was intangible, immeasurable and utterly important. Flair cost nothing but it made money. Flair was invisible but one either had it and got photographed in magazines and real estate columns, or one didn't have it and didn't get photographed. Given she would own property soon, the Doll knew she must have flair and to demonstrate to all who saw her that this was so, she would soon be swinging a Louis Vuitton bag by her side.

But when she got to the Louis Vuitton shop, the bag was gone. Undeterred, the Doll drifted through other shops, in and out of Versace and Armani and Prada searching for an opportunity of equal or even greater worth than the bag she had for a short time so desired.

She was coming out of a shoe boutique back into the main shopping centre when she noticed a large rear projection screen set up outside an electronics store showing crowds leaving the Homebush Olympic stadium after the previous day's bomb scare. That image gave way to a close-up of a kid's backpack being unzipped to reveal a bomb. But only when it cut to armed police taking up positions around Tariq's apartment block did the Doll give it her undivided attention.

28

No sound came from the television, and all that could be heard was the babble of the shopping centre. Somewhere a child was crying. A reporter came on, a young woman, but what the reporter was saying the Doll didn't know. Then a blurry photograph of a bearded man in Arabic dress was being shown, beneath which ran a banner saying, again and again:

'SUSPECTED TERRORIST ELUDES POLICE DRAGNET.'

A salesman came out from the shop with a remote control, looked at the rear projection screen, saw the Doll staring at it, and apologised. The screen momentarily went black and returned to life with *Toy Story*. Buzz Lightyear ran offscreen and the Doll came to her senses.

So that was it! A terrorist in the same block that she had spent the night in. It would make for a good story to tell Wilder, but it was nothing much really, thought the Doll. Yet some feeling so vague she didn't know what it was unsettled her. Her stomach felt tight. Her mouth seemed suddenly full of saliva. She put it down to the drink and the drugs and the late night.

For the second time she rang Tariq, and for the second time his phone rang out to a messageless voicemail, and for the second time she felt foolish and left no message.

How she wished Tariq had been there when she woke. How she wished he hadn't left, or, having left, that he had managed to make it back before she left. And his disappearance now seemed to her strange rather than unfortunate; and his apartment now seemed creepy and unpleasant rather than cool; and all she could think of was the sun filling and burning its rooms. Last night she had felt so happy in his arms, and now she suddenly felt like crying.

The Doll abruptly turned around to leave. A woman in a black burkah walked straight into her, her elbow hitting the Doll.

The Doll's mind leapt back to the police with their guns and black uniforms looking like death, to the television report the day before about the Homebush bombs, and then the woman appeared to the Doll not as another woman, but as something terrifying and unknown, an evil spectre she had seen so often in films, a short, stubby Darth Vader.

The woman, for her part, seemed to be saying it was the Doll's fault, though exactly what she was saying the Doll couldn't understand because she was talking in a strange language. Maybe it was an accusation or maybe it wasn't. It was impossible to say. Later, the Doll wondered if she hadn't actually been apologising. But that was much later.

Perhaps it was the accumulation of the events of the past few days, or the heat, or not taking her pills as she was supposed to, or just a lack of sleep, but the Doll felt strung out, her nerves jagged: the police that morning, the bombs the day before, the way she had worked hard for a Louis Vuitton bag and how there had then been no Louis Vuitton bag; whatever, she snapped.

"Fuck off!" the Doll yelled. "Just fuck off back to wherever you're from."

A few people halted to watch what might happen next, but nothing did. The woman in the black burkah stopped talking, turned, and hurried away.

"Good on you," a middle-aged man in a canary yellow shirt said in a slightly trembling but loud voice. "They won't integrate, you know," he said even more loudly, perhaps intended for the woman in the burkah to hear, though she had already vanished. A large woman clapped. A kid in a Microsoft baseball cap yelled,

"They flew here. We grew here."

The Doll didn't know whether to be buoyed or depressed by this response. No one else said or did anything and, the confrontation ended, they drifted away as if it had been just one more piece of poor plaza entertainment. As she walked towards the main entrance the Doll found herself shaking. She felt ashamed at having lost her temper and unsure as to why she had erupted in such a rage. And yet she was still angry with the woman in the burkah.

'How stupid in this heat!' thought the Doll. 'Why can't they just be like us?' She decided to pity her, and her pity felt a kind of necessary superiority. And it struck the Doll as a particularly humiliating thing for any woman to have to get about in gear as bad as a burkah. But then the Doll remembered the television creep telling her how humiliating it must be to be a pole dancer, and she felt strangely confused.

29

When the Doll got home, she was relieved to finally get out of her clammy Versace jeans, shower and change into old shorts and a singlet, split the coke Tariq had given her, putting one portion in with her bag of cash, and wrapping the other in some tin foil and putting it in the Gucci handbag that she had hoped to no longer need, ready for whenever she might want it.

She put some music on loud and the tv on low. There was

an ad for the new Toyota Prado. Everything in the ad—men, women, roads, and skies—looked beautiful and at peace. It calmed the Doll.

She went and cleaned her bathroom. When she came back a quiz show was on. A reality show. A sports show. She dozed off. She woke to see the screen filled with armed police taking up position around Tariq's apartment block. The Doll grabbed the remote and turned up the volume.

The newsreader was talking about a failed police stake-out of a notorious Islamic terrorist—at which point the vision changed, as before, to the same bad photograph of a bearded man in Arabic dress. The newsreader read out an Arabic-sounding name, the only part of which she recognised was the word Tariq. Then the picture changed again, this time to grainy, dark images taken from on high.

"To assist with their enquiries in regard to yesterday's attempted bombing of Homebush Olympic stadium, police have tonight released security camera footage," the news-reader said, "showing the terrorist suspect entering an apartment building last night with a female accomplice."

The grainy images showed a couple hugging each other as they entered a building. The footage was slowed down so much that she could see the frames clicking through. In contrast with their dark surroundings, they had used some digital effect to spotlight the couple's faces.

"It is not yet known," continued the newsreader, "who the woman is."

The Doll felt her mouth go dry. The man was Tariq. The woman was her.

30

At first, the Doll regarded what she had just seen on the television as she regarded much that she found disagreeable and stupid in this life: irrelevant, and she simply ignored it as she did everything else that she regarded as irrelevant. After all, it was just like all the other crap the journos and shock jocks and pollies carried on with: maybe it had everything to do with their world, but it had nothing to do with hers. It struck the Doll as an excellent idea to simply regard it all as amusing; it arose out of nothing and it would soon all go back to nothing, and none of it was to be taken seriously. She forced a smile, and made herself laugh. What a joke!

"It's so empowering to keep your skin supple," the television said in a voice softly American. As the ad break continued, the Doll went and poured herself a straight Zubrowka vodka, skolled it, and poured herself a second. It's creepy, though, she thought, knowing you'd slept with a terrorist, even one as cute as Tariq.

She rang Wilder, and told her some, though not all, of her story. Wilder, who sounded weary and neither overly interested nor that concerned, told her not to worry.

"Everything blows over, Gina," said Wilder, who always used the Doll's Christian name, "and life goes on as ever. I mean, just focus on the good in your life, and in a year's time we'll be having a drink and you'll suddenly remember when you met another hottie on the beach and became a terrorist for five minutes, and all it'll be is a funny story."

'Yeah,' thought the Doll, 'and maybe not even a year, maybe just a couple of days, and it will all be over except as a stupid joke.'

"Don't worry," said Wilder before hanging up, "you'll be voted off quick enough. Just remind me to come to the eviction party."

The Doll lay back down on her sofa, and after a time drifted off to sleep. When she woke, she surfed the tv, taking none of it in, until she noticed the same security camera footage of Tariq and her on another station, blown up so that their distorted faces filled the screen.

"Police are fearful," said a voiceover, "that two terrorists who escaped a midday raid at Potts Point may strike somewhere in Sydney any day."

The Doll quickly changed stations, then switched the tv off, put some Cat Empire on up loud, then switched that off and put the tv back on. She tried to focus on Wilder's advice, but wasn't able to do what Wilder said; she couldn't *just focus on the good*, and Wilder's *everything blows over* seemed only a dumb cliché that turns out to be a lie. Rather than calming her, it made her uneasy.

The Doll turned the tv off once more. She fought her growing panic by grasping for words that might help hold her up as flotsam does a drowning man. But there were no words of hope, only a dimly perceived sense that something unknowable had changed, something terrible had taken place, and her life was no longer as it had been.

31

The Doll rang Wilder again.

"Wilder . . ." she said, and then she didn't know what else to say.

"Can I come over?" the Doll asked finally. How could she say she was frightened? It was ridiculous—what was there to be frightened of? No, she wasn't frightened.

"It's nothing, really," continued the Doll. "I just don't feel like being by myself at the moment."

Before leaving, she changed once more. She stared for some time at an old black Prada dress that she had never much liked because it seemed somehow bland and inconspicuous. And then she put it on.

She caught a taxi to a run-down brick tenement in Redfern that Wilder had rented for as long as the Doll had known her. 'It'll pass,' she told herself as she walked up to the front door, open to vent the house, thinking of all the shit she had waded through in her life and how, compared to that, this was nothing, really, nothing at all.

She walked down the narrow hallway to the rear of the cottage where a small extension doubled as a kitchen and family room. There, the Doll found Wilder lying on an old red leather couch, wearing only a black bikini and a denim mini, reading a Freedom Furniture catalogue.

"Oh, thank God it's you, Gina," said Wilder. "I'm dead."

Wilder paused, picked up a can of UDL gin and tonic that sat next to the couch, sipped, and started talking again.

"You'll make Max's day. Did you see us last night? My back's shot. That stupid dildo—my God, it was like carrying a baseball bat around. No wonder men moan all the time."

There was a child's yell from a room up the passage.

"Picked Max up an hour ago from his father and all he wants to do is play. All I want to do is die."

A small boy clad only in a pair of wet Spider-Man jocks peeked his white-haired head shyly out from a doorway. When he saw the Doll, his face lit up and he bolted down the hall into her arms.

"Maxie!" the Doll cried, grabbing him and whirling him around. "You're a big fella now! Two days to your birthday," the Doll cooed. "How old?"

Max held up six fingers.

"Three!" said the Doll in mock surprise.

"Six," said Max, "six years old."

"How could I ever forget," said the Doll, and she pulled him in to her, held him close, rubbed her face in his tiny chest, smelt him musty and doggy; felt him writhe, his limbs longer, his thrusts and clutches stronger, and every movement felt at once incredibly sweet and incredibly bitter to her, as if with his growth something in her receded and shrank, as if with his increasing brightness something further dimmed in her. And yet the Doll loved Max as if he were her own son, and Max loved the pretty dark woman who wrapped around him like a towel after a bath.

"He seems well recovered from his near-death experience," said the Doll.

"Rather," agreed Wilder. "Not every day you're saved by a suicide bomber. A tinnie?"

Wilder fetched a can of gin and tonic for the Doll, Max went and got his new radio-controlled car to show her, and while the car bobbed around like a small buzz saw, the Doll and Wilder chatted. The Doll would occasionally make a grab for Max, who would pretend to want to get away and play with his car, but then would allow her to cuddle and nuzzle him.

Wilder was taller than the Doll; lighter featured, snub nosed, and fuller figured, breasts always presented to advantage, hair blonde where the Doll's was dark. Not conventionally beautiful, Wilder would never have got a job at the Chairman's Lounge: her looks were too much fixed in her laugh and her conversation, in her passions and the way she involved those around her in them. One of her past boyfriends had told the Doll that Wilder had presence, and though the Doll had not heard the term used before, she understood what he meant.

Wilder was a good ten years older than the Doll: when the Doll was nineteen and first met Wilder such a difference felt like a world. Wilder seemed wise to her, and experienced, and to have arrived at some serenity about life. She knew a lot about homeopathy and meditation and spoke with authority about these and other matters, not least of which was how one should behave in this life.

One night early in their friendship Wilder, given to discovering revelation in cliché, told the Doll that power corrupts people, and then paused, as if this were some profound new insight, before saying:

"I believe that, you know, I really do."

But at the Chairman's Lounge, where she had been working for a short time by then, the Doll had already seen how people would do most anything for power and money. The Doll saw it was people who made these things, who thought these things mattered, who made these things important. And so she said:

"I dunno. Maybe it's people who corrupt power."

Wilder laughed so much she spilt her drink. The Doll

realised she had said something both naïve and foolish. She felt very stupid and, not wanting to feel so very stupid ever again, the Doll let Wilder do more and more of the talking as the years rolled on.

But what at first seemed clever came with the passing of time to sound to the Doll almost pompous, even ignorant. In the same way, over the years, what was initially captivating became repetitious, while what seemed insightful and wise began, like cheap paste jewellery that flashes brilliantly when new, to grow dull and even tawdry. And what at the beginning appeared an exotic, exciting private life increasingly came across as simply messy.

Wilder had had a string of relationships with men who often seemed as crazy as she was. The most recent, with a married cop, had ended only three months earlier, because, according to Wilder, he wouldn't leave his wife.

"He just didn't get it," Wilder had said. "I thought our love would see us through everything."

The Doll thought that the certainty of Wilder's opinions came from having in some way never quite grown up, while Wilder thought the Doll's blank incomprehension of many of Wilder's opinions was a consequence of not having gone to university. But Wilder liked the clarity of the Doll's directness, and the Doll liked the enthusiastic profusion of Wilder's contradictory thoughts. They frustrated each other and they could not bear to pass more than a few days without seeing each other.

"We're mates, eh, Gina?" Wilder would frequently say. She would hold out her hand with the neatly rolled joint that was never far from her lips and point it in the Doll's direction as though it were a judge's gavel, "I *know* nothing will ever pull us apart."

And when the Doll didn't bother replying to such declarations—because the Doll wondered how Wilder could know such things, and both hated and envied Wilder her certainty—Wilder would end, as she ended so many of her conversations, by saying:

"I believe that, you know, I really do."

And somehow that always seemed to seal the matter.

Wilder believed in so many things: the Labor Party, trade unions and the *Sydney Morning Herald*; the therapeutic effect of porridge in the morning and gin and tonic in the evening. She believed in politics and that the world could be made better, that Australians were good people, the best of people, kind and generous. She believed in belief. And the Doll found all Wilder's beliefs at once reassuring and annoying, for the Doll felt certain about nothing, and had come to believe in little other than what she made of her own life.

Wilder and the Doll went out and sat in Wilder's small backyard. There was a trellis and a grapevine and a bougainvillea that seemed as weary as the world felt that night. There was a brick side wall along which Wilder had placed rocks and where she kept her bonsai plants in a miniature garden. Most were dead.

"My poor darlings," said Wilder. "This heat was the end for them."

Wilder had believed in her bonsai garden, but, she said, when things are not fated to be, they are not fated to be. The Doll knew Wilder to be as careless with her plants as she could sometimes be with her friendships: the lack of regular watering she suspected had as much to do with their demise as destiny. But she said none of this, and they talked for a time about trivial things, and it suited the Doll to lose herself in such triviality.

"People are good," Wilder said at one point, "and in the end goodness comes through. I believe that, you know, I really do."

32

Wilder was always out to convert the Doll to goodness. Whether it was the merits of organic food or the wrongs of globalism, whether it was refugees or minke whales or trade unionists or some other endangered species, she was always seeking to sign the Doll up to good causes, lending her DVDs, books, magazines, all of which the Doll never looked at until Wilder asked for them back and she had to find them, lost amidst an ocean of decorating and fashion magazines.

"Even Athens," she said, referring to the cop boyfriend of whom she had only spoken of violently since they split up. "Even he was a good man, you know. In his way. He gave me that bonsai there," Wilder said, pointing to some dead twigs sticking out of a dried piece of peat in a blue china dish.

Wilder was drunk now, and Wilder was lost in all that she believed was good, in the power of good, and this left the Doll feeling only more scared. Wilder relit her joint, took another sip from her can of gin and tonic, then, giving up on the weary joint, butted it out in an ever overflowing Bakelite ashtray.

"No Tanqueray, I'm afraid," Wilder continued, "only this shit. Kiwi corn syrup with industrial alcohol and some artificial essence of gin. Where was I . . . ? Yeah, people, like, people think they can't do anything against the world. But you watch: their goodness will out." She fixed the Doll with a smile. "Even Athens, you know, even him."

"He was kinda cute," said the Doll, who wasn't displeased at the conversation going elsewhere, and her mind with it.

"When I met him," said Wilder, rolling another joint, "I thought he was *real* cute. We talked a bit—it was that wanky bar in town, the Art Bar—and first it was good, but then he got going on about justice, how there wasn't any."

" 'All these young cops,' he says, 'I tell 'em, I say, just one bit of advice, just one: Don't ever think it's fair. And then in five years they come back to me about this or that, and they say, it's not fair. What'd I say? I say.' "

She went on about Athens then telling her how in his early days as a cop he had been a sniper in their special operations group. One night, they had to stake out a Vietnam vet holed up in the bush out of Newcastle. There was a long siege that ended with Athens getting told to take the vet out, a double tap, one bullet for his heart and one for his head. He shot the vet dead as ordered.

The Doll had heard some of this before—she had known how Wilder had met Athens, and how Athens had been a sniper, but she didn't know that he had killed someone. Not the least pleasure she took in Wilder's company was the way old stories were at odd moments reinvigorated with such fresh, remarkable details.

"And then," said Wilder, "in the middle of the bloody bar

Athens' eyes just fill up with tears. He's pissed, I mean, he's really pissed.

" 'You know,' he says to me, 'I didn't feel bad. That's the worst of it. I felt really good. Pumped, you know. You'd think it'd be hard and bad, but it wasn't. I never felt so alive.'

" 'That's not right,' I said.

" 'Of course it's not fucking right,' he says. 'Nothing's right. Nothing's fair, that's what I tell all the young cops, I say'—and then he was off again, and it was just the same shit over and over. But you know what? He had me after that."

And her story told, Wilder seemed suddenly deflated, as if it was all that had kept her going. "I was down the street just before, and I was thinking about Athens and turned to look at something in a chemist's doorway and I knocked over a whole stupid sunglasses stand," Wilder said. "Fell everywhere. You know that feeling, Gina, when things just won't stop falling?"

33

Richard Cody was not given to consciously thinking out his desires and ambitions. He would have been offended if anyone had suggested to him that he used people to his advantage, or that he had ever hurt anyone in order to better his own situation. And yet, when confronted with the fact of his humiliating demotion on the one hand, and on the other with his recognition of the shadowy face on the television news as that of the pole dancer who had insulted him the night before, his first instinct was to begin to make contact with a range of people, most of whom he had had nothing to do with for a long time, but for whom he now felt a suddenly renewed fondness.

He opened his wallet, took out the card Ferdy Holstein had given him the night before, and rang him. Richard Cody stressed the confidential nature of their conversation and how, if Ferdy were to keep quiet, it could work well for him.

Ferdy Holstein told Richard Cody what Krystal's real name was, but went on to say that he knew little else about her. If he was curious as to why he was being called, he gave no inkling of it.

"She's a loner," said Ferdy Holstein.

Perhaps he too had seen the footage, thought Richard Cody, and was keen to put some distance between him and the dancer.

"You want to know what she thinks?" said Ferdy Holstein. "You never know what she's thinking."

Over that long Sunday evening, Richard Cody wandered his Vaucluse home with his phone, piecing together not so much the truth of Gina Davies' life as rehearsing the story he would present about it. He remembered with pride how he had held the table at Katie Moretti's with his tales of the three bombs and terrorists and evil. He wanted to do the same again, but this time mesmerising not a dozen people, but millions. And so he saw the story as if he were sitting in a lounge room watching his own plasma screen as the shocking tale slowly unfolded.

Yet, as always with such stories, when he began thinking about it he realised that there were key dramatic elements lacking. By degrees, Richard Cody came to see that what was missing was what was unknown: the life of the pole dancer.

The man was obvious—a Middle Eastern name and a no-doubt predictable past—and, from what the news reports were saying, a known terrorist. But the pole dancer was different: an Aussie turning on their own—an unknown terrorist. Because there was no doubt now in Richard Cody's mind that Gina Davies was a killer. The more he thought about her, the more inescapable and logical his thinking was. Just looking back on the time he had spent with her the previous night he could see now that something hadn't been right about her. Hadn't she been secretive when he asked her about her private life? And when he put to her a more than generous proposal wasn't she unpleasantly aggressive? 'No,' thought Richard Cody, 'something was wrong with her—very wrong.'

And the more he thought about it, the more it all made sense, and what at first seemed ludicrous—a pole dancer an Islamic terrorist!—now seemed insidious and disturbing. What better cover? After all, hadn't Christine Keeler slept with both the Russians and Profumo? And wasn't the Chairman's Lounge popular with the influential and powerful? It was obvious what was going on, and it was up to him, Richard Cody, to expose what was happening. And what a story it would be! What ratings they would get! It had everything—sex, politics, even bombs! 'No doubt about it,' thought Richard Cody, 'it's a killer.' He reached for his phone and dialled another number. There was no time to lose.

RICHARD FLANAGAN

34

It was too hot to cook, so Wilder and the Doll walked a hundred metres down the street and entered a small and undistinguished restaurant that sat on the corner of the crossroads, Max leading the way, still in his Spider-Man jocks.

Johnsons was an unpromisingly named ethnic restaurant of a type that had disappeared almost everywhere else in Sydney. It still had cheap chairs with torn vinyl seats, and its plywood panelled walls were decorated with flyblown black and whites of early television stars, long lost to death or the even more relentless obscurity of supermarket magazines, autographed with the doomed flourish of those condemned to Sydney celebrity. Though its colours had long since disappeared with time, a framed photograph of Lebanon also remained, as enduring in adversity as the nation it depicted. For Johnsons was, as a proudly displayed restaurant review from a 1966 *Sydney Morning Herald* reported, Sydney's first Lebanese restaurant, recommended for the adventurous diner.

It was empty, save for two late middle-aged Lebanese men who, though dressed in waiters' black trousers and white shirts, sat in a corner quietly drinking short Arabic coffees and playing dominoes. On seeing Wilder and Max, their faces lit up.

"Mr Maxie! Mr Maxie!" they cried, and Max walked up to them like a caliph returning from exile, acknowledging their attention with a shy smile. He disappeared into the kitchen in the arms of a large, elderly woman.

The Doll began telling Wilder her story in full after their second red wine, but the more she talked the more her fears seemed far-fetched—so improbable and so impossible—and

108

she worried that she was beginning to sound a bit crazy, as if she was spinning fantasies out of a few newsflashes.

The Doll could sense that Wilder felt she had become a little hysterical and that this was now a somewhat boring story. Worse, to the extent Wilder had any interest, she seemed to be suggesting that the Doll might in some manner have brought this on herself, and in some strange way therefore be guilty.

"So this Tariq," Wilder said, "how do you know he was Tariq? Didn't you ever ask what his full name was?"

And perhaps, thought the Doll, it was a very stupid thing to go to a strange apartment with a man you barely knew and whose name you had no proof of, and not ask for ID, but how else does one go to bed with a man?

"And you were drunk," said Wilder, "and had done some coke . . ."

And perhaps, thought the Doll, it was the height of folly to sleep with a stranger in such a state.

"He had an accent," said Wilder, "and he's dark and he's foreign and you never asked where he came from?"

The Doll had been curious, and had perhaps harboured the secret hope that in the future she would discover more about Tariq. But on the night his droning on about raster graphics had merely confirmed to her that, like everyone else, there was a large part of Tariq's life that, far from being illegal, was simply humdrum dullness, hardly worth knowing about. For one evening two people simply had fun together. Questions had seemed intrusive, unnecessary; questions had been superfluous, because for one night they had found something beyond the answers of home and history—maybe something easily broken, maybe not serious, but perhaps all the better and truer for being only about the moment.

But now that something seemed to her the opposite. It seemed small and trivial and stupid, and it made her feel small and trivial and stupid. And all those questions she never asked and all the answers she never got now appeared to matter so much, all the information that might have saved her from the shit she now felt buried in.

"I mean, Gina—*hello*? You get on the gear with a tea-toweller and give him a blow job? I mean, I dunno, but Christ almighty . . ." Wilder shook her head, waved a hand in dismissal, and didn't even bother finishing what she was saying.

In the middle of the Doll describing to Wilder how the police had staked out the apartment block, Wilder struck up a conversation with one of the waiters on the best way of making baba ghanoush. It was, the Doll felt, as if Wilder thought she was overly obsessed with the problem.

"But why me?" asked the Doll at one point. "Why are they doing this to me?"

And Wilder smiled at her like she was some foolish child who, having done wrong, remains confused as to why they are being punished.

"Look, tomorrow you'll wake up and it'll all be over," Wilder said. "There'll be some new story—another bomb, another water crisis, another country being invaded by the Americans, Shane Warne discovered writing a postcard. It's just a bizarre thing. It'll pass."

The Doll laughed. And it was true that there was nothing to be frightened of, because it was, as Wilder pointed out, simply a ridiculous series of associations, and these mistakes would be cleared up quickly. Terrorism was a serious thing, no doubt about it, Wilder said, and that's why the people dealing with it were experts who weren't about to chase a pole dancer, not when there were real monsters out there.

"Do you seriously think they're going to storm through the door of Johnsons," said Wilder, "the most forgotten restaurant in the world, just to arrest you? I don't think so."

The Doll began to feel better, safer. No one was after her. Here, with Wilder, the Doll finally felt secure. Wilder went off on one of her stories, and it warmed her, the gentle Lebanese food, the soft red wine they drank with it, and Wilder's tales.

"When they find out where you work, they'll be the ones who are going to feel stupid," Wilder said after a while.

"Perhaps I should go and see the police," the Doll said. "In the morning, maybe?"

"Yeah, whatever," said Wilder, as though everything were known and not worth knowing at the same time.

"Yeah, whatever," the Doll wearily repeated, trying to sound convinced.

"It's all a joke," said Wilder, again bored, gazing at the curling photos on the wall.

The matter of Tariq remained a mystery.

"Would a terrorist know how to merengue?" the Doll asked Wilder.

And though she didn't say it, the Doll didn't think his behaviour in bed suggested a devout Muslim, but then her experience of bedding devout Muslims was nonexistent.

"And the picture of the bearded man they keep showing

on the television," said the Doll, "that they say is Tariq but doesn't look like him."

"He could have lied," said Wilder, her eyes returning to the Doll.

The Doll was quiet for a moment.

"Or he could be a mistake," she said finally. "Like me."

35

From what Richard Cody could gather from his phone calls there was no motive. Far from being a Muslim, there was no evidence that Gina Davies knew anything about Islam. As much as anyone knew, she had never received any terrorist training.

None of this predisposed Richard Cody to the notion of her innocence. They were merely problems to overcome. His instinct was to create a story in which he more and more believed, in order to allow him to further create that story. He did not say to himself: "Although there is no evidence of any guilt or wrongdoing, I am going to stitch this woman up with concocted assertions." He did not think any such thing, because he would have despised himself if he had ever thought himself capable of making up such monstrous lies.

Rather, as he talked to others on his phone, as he heard from the ASIO spook Siv Harmsen of the capacity of ter- rorist suicide bombers "to kill many hundreds of people at, say, a major sporting event", he was rightly horrified.

"It is horrifying," Siv Harmsen agreed, "and we need stories that remind people of what horrifying things might just happen."

Richard Cody knew there was no need to remind Siv Harmsen of the last story they had worked on together, when Siv leaked him some documents that brought down a police minister with allegations of corruption—allegations that had in that particular case later been shown to be of no particular import or relevance to the police minister, though not without benefit for Siv Harmsen.

"Can I count on you?" was all he needed to say.

"I think we can count on each other," said Siv Harmsen. "Don't you, Richard?"

He went on to say that whoever the woman was, she didn't necessarily have much to do with any of it, as she had never showed up on their surveillance before.

But the more Richard Cody listened to Siv Harmsen, the more persuaded he became that he was on to something. He didn't tell Siv Harmsen he knew who the woman was. If the spooks still hadn't worked it out by the following evening, that would be his first exclusive story.

Once more he could see the pole dancer naked, the bomb belt wrapping around her waist. His horror at the possibility of such an act was as genuine as his smile of jubilation, for the puzzle was coming together, the pieces mostly there, and all he needed now was to persuade Jerry Mendes to give him a special to take such an amazing story to the country.

It was, he told Jerry Mendes, now a race between Six and Gina Davies as to who got the story out first—her with her bombs or them with a tell-all current affairs special. Richard Cody, looking up at a framed photograph of himself shaking hands with Bill Clinton from when they had done a tv special together, could sense Jerry Mendes's growing interest as he began talking about which night would have most impact on the ratings.

Even before Jerry Mendes had said, "Okay, Richie, half-hour prime time, this Tuesday night," Richard Cody had already pointed his finger revolver-like at the Arkansas charmer. Cocking his thumb and smiling, Richard Cody said to himself, "More than one Comeback Kid, Bill."

"Three conditions," said Jerry Mendes, who liked talking at such times in dot points. "One: the special has to be about them both, the terrorist and the pole dancer. Call it 'Al-Qa'ida's Bonnie and Clyde' or something. Two: I have to clear it with the big boss—he'll want to make sure none of his Canberra mates have a problem." The big boss was the chairman of the nation's largest print and electronic media company, Amalgamated Press, and owner of the Six Network, Terry Frith, generally referred to only as Mr Frith.

There was no Three.

Richard Cody agreed—how could he not and why would he not?—knowing the lack of lead time would only help him bend the show his way, knowing also that his name would work like KY Jelly when Mr Frith talked with the government. After all, he had devoted his life to never offending anyone powerful.

When he went to bed his wife was still sitting up watching tv with headphones. A Harvey Norman ad was playing. He watched her lips mouthing the words of the ad's jingle in eerie breaths. He turned over on his back and was soon asleep.

That night in his dreams, Richard Cody was on the stage accepting his fourth gold Logie as tv personality of the year, and all around him people fawned and flattered as they had before, all seeing in him qualities of the greatest intelligence and exceptional humanity as they always had.

"Above all," said a faceless host, "his work in uncovering a terrorist network in Australia showed Richard Cody to be not only Australia's foremost journalist but its most fearless."

And it was only natural to Richard Cody that everyone loved him, and the question of whether anyone meant what they said was irrelevant, for once more he was the centre of everything that mattered, life was as it was always meant to be and life existed only for him.

36

The Doll, too, was dreaming that stifling night. After lying on a mattress on the hot floor of Wilder's lounge room for over an hour, she remained wide awake. It was too quiet for her, the low ceiling felt ever closer, the room ever smaller, the air ever stuffier.

Then she must have dozed off, for suddenly she was looking down on herself. She was alone and naked, being lowered into the earth and, as the dirt began piling up over her, as she saw the leering half-drunken faces of the drones and the suits, the creeps and the pervs, looking down at her like a photo that had been thrown into a garbage bin, she summoned all her strength to wake, to rise, to stand up and not abandon herself to that terrible fate of being alone and naked.

The Doll crept into Wilder's bedroom. Wilder slept quietly, a sheet pulled up to her waist. The only sound in the room was the slow rattle and rush of an old air con vent above the bed head. As gently as she could, the Doll slowly lifted the sheet and slid into the bed next to her friend.

They both lay on their backs, not touching, Wilder asleep in a suitably Wilderish way, hands under her head. The Doll turned and breathed in slowly and deeply, just so that she might smell Wilder and be reassured. She thought how there is some secret of this life in the smell of those you love.

And the Doll stretched out her hand until she could reach Wilder's arm, just so she might touch it. There is a need, thought the Doll, such need in us all and no one can say what it is, and no one can admit that they are dying over and over every day for that need, that wanting, not being answered.

The Doll felt Wilder's arm come to slow life, and Wilder—awake? asleep?—moved one hand out from under her head and gently took the Doll's hand in hers. And in this manner the two women slept, and for a time the Doll's sense of worry passed and was replaced by another feeling, that the world was beautiful and good, that evil and stupidity were not its dominant, necessary forces, and all this was so if one could just hold on to it the way she now held on to Wilder's hand, just hold on and hold on and never ever let go.

MONDAY

37

THE DOLL AWOKE to a warm, slightly sour smell. It was Wilder.

"Oh God," Wilder said.

Wilder sat up in the bed, and the Doll felt the heat of her body billow up from the wrinkled sheet that lay over them. Wilder was beautiful waking, like a cobra disturbed, her broad head darting up on her long neck.

The ageing air con rattled on above the bed like an old friend that had travelled through the long night with them, and with them somehow making it through the darkness. The Doll felt rested and safe. It was some minutes before the events of the last two days began to trickle into her mind, a slight headache that could be ignored.

"Ten past seven," Wilder said, and with that she was out of the bed and gone from the room.

The Doll dozed for a few minutes, but beneath the air con's asthmatic whir she could feel the vibration of peak hour traffic rising through the room and summoning her. She got up and followed the sound of a radio to the small galley kitchen where Wilder was getting Max ready for school.

"I've been thinking," said Wilder, as she stirred the porridge she insisted on making for Max even in the middle of a heat-wave, "you're right. You should go to the police this morning. I'll come with you. Clear this shit up. It's ridiculous." And then she smiled. "It's funny, though. Gina the terrorist!" And they both laughed, and when Wilder handed her a coffee, the Doll could feel that already the morning and life itself were once more turning out to be good and pleasant.

The Doll's thoughts swung to her day. She had her weekly private with Moretti that morning, and there she would earn the last three hundred dollars she needed for her deposit.

"D-Day," the Doll said. But then the news came on the radio, Max yelled for his mother from the bathroom, and Wilder left the Doll with the task of making Max's lunch.

The radio rumbled on with reports of more deaths from another suicide bombing in Baghdad. There was the crash and squeal of a garbage truck outside, Max was crying in the bathroom that he didn't want to go to school, and the radio newsreader was talking of how police were seeking the com-panion of the suspected Middle Eastern terrorist who was photographed by a security camera entering his apartment two nights earlier, before eluding a police raid.

The Doll stopped buttering the bread.

"A police spokesman said they needed the woman to

assist with their investigations," the radio continued. "He refused to speculate on rumours that the woman was also part of the terrorist cell that planted the three bombs at Homebush Olympic stadium on Saturday."

The Doll looked up from Max's sandwiches and saw Wilder staring at her.

"These terrorists are subhuman filth," a politician was now saying over the radio. "The government needs to be doing more to ensure they are hunted down and eliminated."

"Oh, Gina," said Wilder. That was all.

For as long as the Doll had known her, Wilder had been a landscape gardener. Wilder dealt with palettes of pavers, trucks of concrete, tonnes of loam, acres of grass, irate electricians, crazed dogs, cuts by power tools. She transformed stubborn elements of clay and plant, rock and debris and wood, into forms and shapes and shades and colours and sounds that would bring pleasure and arouse admiration. It wasn't in Wilder's way to be intimidated by life.

But when the Doll, margarine and Vegemite-smeared knife in hand, looked at Wilder that morning, as the radio went on about how unnamed security sources had linked the family of the male terrorist to Islamic fundamentalist groups in the Middle East, Wilder, for the first time that the Doll had ever known, looked frightened.

"What were you saying?" asked Wilder.

"I've got Moretti this morning," said the Doll, who had been saying nothing. Her mouth had gone oddly dry and words rolled around in it like marbles. "I've got to do it. I'll go and see the cops after."

Wilder seemed uncharacteristically confused.

"Okay," she said. "Okay." That was all. No strong opinions or plans or certainties. Just "okay okay".

The Doll went to the bedroom, found her Gucci handbag, downed a Stemetil, her last two Zoloft and a Valium 5 all together. Even so, it was several minutes before the shaking stopped.

When she came back to the kitchen the news was over.

"Why?" the radio asked. "Because you've worked for it. Because you deserve it. Talk to your BMW dealer today."

38

Richard Cody turned the radio off and answered the phone as he swung his Mercedes S600 out of the morning glare and down the ramp into the welcome cool cave of Six's underground carpark.

"Richie," said Jerry Mendes, filling the car cabin with his unmistakeably chipped voice as Richard Cody pulled into his personal parking spot. "I managed to get hold of Mr Frith's PA and I've been told Mr Frith can't see a problem. He'll be lunching today with the secretary of the prime minister's office, so if there are any issues, they'll get back to us. Okay?"

And before Richard Cody could reply, Jerry Mendes had hung up. The only sound that remained in the car was the very low hum of his seat's massage function.

39

Though high above the Doll the sky was emptying of cloud and taking on a pitiless blue intent, in the streets below, the shadows were still long and the breeze still that pleasant cool which foretells a scorching day to come. Yet as she walked to Redfern railway station, the Doll felt inexplicably hot and unable to breathe, as if that cruel sky were bearing down on her chest like a great weight.

She was telling herself to keep going, that it would be all right, reminding herself that today was the best of days, the day she had so long dreamt of, when near the entrance to the railway station she came upon a beggar sitting amidst the commuter traffic. The woman's filthy face—not so much lined as gouged, and in places raw and weeping—stuck out of her dirty clothes like a rotting carrot out of a garbage bag. She held up both hands to the countless people walking past and her wretched face nodded up and down as she mumbled something or other, hoping for help.

Still spacey from all the pills she had taken that morning, the Doll slowed and then stopped, and she began to think how, if she could help the beggar, then someone might help her. In the Doll's mind her fate and the fate of the beggar became one and the same. 'She's desperate, I'm desperate,' thought the Doll as people poured past. 'We're no different.' And perhaps overly influenced by Wilder's vague ramblings about karma, the Doll grew excited and happy, for now it seemed clear that somehow in helping the beggar was the solution to her own problems.

But when she stepped closer to the beggar and was about to lean down to talk with her, she found the woman stank terribly of stale piss. Up close it was as if the skin had been peeled away from her face and dirt smeared in its pus-filled sores. The Doll felt queasy. It was so revolting that instead of stopping and giving her some money, as she had intended, the Doll reeled back, turned, lowered her head and quickly walked away. And because her revulsion had so abruptly overwhelmed her empathy, she found herself thinking how someone else—people in authority, or charities, or government departments—should be helping such people, not her.

As she made her way toward the station entrance, the Doll's feelings continued changing, from being annoyed to being angry. She drew the sweet smell of fumes from the crawling cars and heaving buses deep into her chest to be rid of the sour stench of the beggar. 'What was I thinking?' the Doll admonished herself. 'I've got enough on my plate. Besides, once I've seen the police it'll be all over anyway, so why do anything? My life will soon be back on the up.'

And though in her heart such thoughts seemed to her somehow wrong, even cruel, she concentrated on not thinking about the beggar at all, and to her surprise she found it not so very hard. By the time she got off at the Circular Quay ferry terminal the Doll had succeeded in completely forgetting about that awful face and the weird way it had made her feel.

Sitting on a bench seat on a finger wharf, she waited for the welcome prospect of a cooling ferry trip across the harbour. The PA system was broadcasting a radio talkback show.

"Thanks for letting me on your show, Joe," a caller was saying. "I just want to talk about that poor little girl in the paper today all dressed up in the veil and all that garbage and her family making her go to school looking like an alien, well, what's that all about, Joe? They won't integrate, you know."

And hearing this the Doll remembered how the old man in the shopping centre had said exactly the same thing the previous day when she had sworn at the woman in the burkah.

She tried to block out the talkback and lose herself in looking out from the welcome shade of the ferry terminal to where the sky was now a blue kiln ceiling baking and beating everything back down. The Shangri-La tower reflected the sun like a flaming torch, and to avert its glare the Doll's eyes wandered back inside the ferry terminal.

On one side of the bench on which she sat was a woman wearing hot pants, her right leg black with tattoos. On the other side a man was reading a newspaper. Its front page headline read:

TERRORIST LOVERS
SYDNEY READIES FOR ATTACK

The man shook his head, and muttered:

"They should shoot the bastards."

And the Doll remembered that these were exactly the same words she had used less than twenty-four hours earlier. Hadn't she similarly shaken her head when she happened to read a worrying headline? Only now it was Tariq and her he was condemning! Everything she had tried not to think came rushing back. She stood up to get away from the man with the newspaper and walked a few metres, but then had to grab a pole to steady herself.

"I'm sure she's pretty underneath all that," she heard another radio caller say.

"I'm sure she is," replied the shock jock.

"Well, that's my question, Joe," said the caller. "Why do they do it?"

"Joey-fucking-Cosuk," said the woman with the tattooed leg. "Shitty talkback show and they treat him like he's fucking king of fucking Sydney."

"Well, I'll just say this," said Joe Cosuk. "There are more ways than war to conquer a country. Take a look at the front pages of today's newspapers and I think you'll see what I mean."

A man was yelling at the ferry's drawbridge: "Anyone else for Mosman?" The Doll had to let go of the pole.

40

The Doll walked through the ferry's air conditioned cabin out to the open stern deck where there were fewer people who might look at her, and as the ferry turned in a tumbling churn of dirty water, she sat down, adjusted her sunglasses, and looked out at the harbour. The boat moved gently, and the city sparkled in the intense light, its towers radiant, its great roads beautiful, the harbourside mansions splendid.

And yet everywhere the Doll looked she knew people daily endured humiliation and pettiness; saw hate and greed triumph; saw death and stupidity prevail. Worse, they willingly chose to accept it and live their life as a lie, agreeing to everything that was disagreeable, tolerating all that was intolerable, in the hope that they might just be left alone—only now life would not leave her alone. The Doll knew she would still accept everything because, she reasoned, what else could she do? And wouldn't everything then finally turn out all right? If she just accepted enough, swallowed enough, and continued smiling the smile that was not her smile, perhaps it would all end as abruptly, as illogically, as it had started, and life would go back to normal.

The sun exploded off the chop, a thousand screaming fragments of agonising light. The Doll looked down at the ferry's filth-etched metal floor. Her head throbbed, her stomach was watery. The truth was that even on the water she no longer felt safe.

When the ferry reached the jetty in Mosman cove, the Doll disembarked and made her way out of the searing direct light along a bitumen path that gently wound up sandstone cliffs through a lush, green tunnel of mangroves and palms. A mob of parrots rested in nearby gum trees. Even for them it seemed too hot, and for once the jagged calls with which they normally shredded the sky into colourful tatters were subdued. The birds' resigned fatigue and the pleasant, cool walkway calmed the Doll.

Wilder was right, she told herself. It was all a crazy mistake. And besides, they hadn't even identified her, and perhaps never would. There was only one, very bad, piece of video footage showing a blurry figure that could be any one of a million women in Sydney.

She made her way to a road that bordered the cliffs, and from there through avenues of European cars until she came to a grand refurbished Federation mansion on the top side of a street that commanded views of the harbour and city.

In spite of its ornate front door being ajar, she still knocked and called hello before entering.

No matter how many times she came there, the house never failed to impress the Doll with its light and beauty, with the impeccable taste with which it was decorated. She hung her handbag, as she hung it each week, on a coat stand next to a Miró painting in the entry hall, and waited.

The Doll knew nothing about art, but she knew it was a Miró because she had liked the painting and had asked who had done it. Later she had Googled Miró and been astonished that she knew someone who might have the money to own such a work.

The Miró painting showed a bizarre little man with big bug eyes and a square for a body, no arms or legs to speak of, the torso crosshatched so it looked like both a noughts and crosses board and jail cell bars. Imprisoned in the stomach of the Miró man was a red sun and a blue sky.

The Miró and the house belonged to the man she had come to see, Frank Moretti. He lived alone, and he seemed to have a lot of money. Whatever he needed, he paid for. He paid for gardeners, cooks, cleaners. He paid for amusement and he paid for beauty.

"Beauty I prize above all things," he would tell the Doll. He said such things not once, or even twice, but over and over, and there was little that Frank Moretti now said that the Doll had not heard many times before.

It was as if he believed he belonged to some higher race of beings who understood Beauty and Art, who took holidays in Tuscany, and made an odd noise like the rolling of snot in the back of their throat when pronouncing Italian or French words. Once, after listening to one of the Doll's many tales about Moretti, Wilder said that he sounded like a starving man looking for food in an art gallery, and they had both burst out laughing.

Before she started coming, the Doll had never seen a house like Frank Moretti's. It wasn't its size that made it extraordinary, nor the way everything she looked at was not ordinary but exceptional—the way that the more she gazed at it, a chair or a floor rug became remarkable and unlike any chair or floor rug she had ever seen. Nor was it the unexpected manner in which things slowly revealed themselves as more than she had thought; such as the large rounded block rising up from a knee-high wall that turned out to be a piece of marble carved into the shape of a vulva, so purely of itself that it was not until she had looked at it for some months that she realised what the soft ellipses represented.

No; it was the way every furnishing, every decoration worked toward some greater whole, and the greater whole was an environment unlike any she had ever known: none of it brash, none of it shouting for attention, and the overriding feeling that resulted seemed one of serenity. Only after many visits did the Doll come to understand the feeling was rather that of money.

"Perhaps it is because I am Italian," Frank Moretti would say, "that I am so full of *passion*. But I cannot live without beauty."

He didn't seem Italian to the Doll. He just seemed rich. His family, Frank Moretti said, had made a lot of money out of wine. Perhaps, thought the Doll, the rich belong only to money. For when Frank Moretti spoke, that was all the Doll heard in his voice: money. Perhaps he thought it was ideas, wisdom, beauty, taste. Perhaps he thought it was Italy. But it was just money—money he had, money he wanted, money he would get.

If, as the Doll sometimes wondered, Frank Moretti kept an account book in which his considerable expenditure was tallied up, she would have come under the column headed Beauty, along with the latest purchases of mediaeval furniture, Etruscan mosaics, Aboriginal art and New York oils. The Doll's knowledge of art began and ended with Frank Moretti's home: Constantin Brancusi, Rover Thomas, Sean Scully, Fred Williams, Luc Tuymans and, of course, Miró. The title of the Miró was in French, which meant, when Frank Moretti said it, the title sounded like a ball of vibrating phlegm.

"It means," said Frank Moretti, weary at having to explain such obvious things, "the man who ate the sun."

Much as she liked the painting, over time the man who ate the sun and Frank Moretti became for the Doll increasingly the same person.

She was running her fingers over the large decorative nail heads that studded the ornate door of a wooden cabinet that sat beneath the Miró, when she heard the low whir of an electric motor. She turned to see appearing from round a corner an electric wheelchair, in which sat a podgy little man whose emaciated legs dangled from the lambswool-lined seat. His big eyes were exaggerated by the large red-framed Porsche glasses he wore, and the fact that he had almost no hair, so that he seemed simply a pair of eyes in a constant state of surprise.

"Hello, Krystal," said Frank Moretti.

41

"Exquisite, aren't they?" he said, raising a stubby finger from the wheelchair's armrest to point at the nailheads on which the Doll's hand still rested. "Perhaps they are of no interest to you," he said, the sort of stupid thing he always said, when it was obvious she was interested. She had passed the cabinet so many times, yet, like so much else in Moretti's house, not until that day had she noticed its intricate charm. "I had them handmade in Morocco," Moretti continued. "Iron nails hand-forged as they were in the Renaissance. I like them. But perhaps your eye is for the body, not the things the body makes."

There was so much beauty in Frank Moretti's extraordinary home, and all of it the Doll found with each visit a little more unbearable; as if every Blackman and every Nolan, every Williams and every Rover Thomas, every handmade fitting and award-winning architect-designed fixture and Chopin piano note were conspiring with the man who ate the sun to make her aware of only this: that he was more and she was less.

"To understand beauty is not so easy," continued Moretti. "It means that when you see ugliness, it hurts you, it pains you so deeply. But maybe such things do not worry you. Perhaps you don't feel such pain."

As the Doll looked at the strange little man in the wheelchair, at his big insect eyes blown up in his oversized Porsche glasses, she was struck by a cruel thought: 'If what he says is true, what must he feel each time he goes to the bathroom and sees himself in the mirror?'

"I had it specially made," Frank Moretti said, and the Doll realised he was still talking about the cabinet. "I call it my cabinet of human comedy." He whirred over to where the Doll was running her hands over the fine finish. "Do you want to see inside?"

She didn't, but being there—listening, looking, not think-ing—it somehow seemed a welcome respite, and so she nodded her head. In the past he had shown her other strange collections: wooden Assyrian property titles; mummified Egyptian cats; the eggs of extinct birds. They mostly bored her, but for once she felt grateful for the diversion.

On top of the cabinet sat a small carved wooden elephant. Moretti asked the Doll to pass it down to him. With his little hands, he lifted up the elephant's trunk to reveal a hid-den cavity in its body from which he shook out a key. He passed the elephant and the key back to the Doll and invited her to open the cabinet doors.

Inside were a dozen narrow drawers. Moretti's wheelchair hummed and halted as he wheeled himself over to pull one open.

"Now, even you must find this comic," Moretti said, tak-ing out a yellowed piece of paper with foreign typing on it. "It's an official letter from Stalin's secret police in 1937, informing a wife that her husband has been sentenced to ten years without right of correspondence. That means he has been shot as part of the purges." Moretti chuckled. "They were witty men, the old Chekists," he said.

He reached to another drawer low down and took out a machete he said was from Rwanda, darkly marked along its pitted edge. From another, mid-height, he lifted up a rusty old tin can. On its label was a skull and the words Zyklon-B stencilled in fading red on yellow.

"Looks like Albanian tomato paste," Moretti laughed again.

He was truly happy poking around his small museum of infamy. Every item seemed to amuse him one way or another. He reminded the Doll of a child rediscovering a forgotten box of old toys. There were bizarre souvenirs of massacres and genocides from around the world. From Cambodia. From Guatemala. From China. A pair of worn-out shoes he claimed were from a mass grave of Armenians marched to their death in 1916.

It somehow excited him that the world could be evil as well as beautiful, as though all the beauty he owned needed the shoes and the poison gas and the machete to truly shine. For Moretti, the cabinet was what humans did. Art, on the other hand, was what the gods gave, divine revelations allowed a select few.

After a time, the Doll realised the grand tour of the cabinet of human comedy was drawing to an end that Moretti felt would be fitting.

"That drawer there," he said, indicating the topmost drawer. "I'll show you one last thing. It's the only mechanical thing I have ever collected," Frank Moretti said. "Pick it up."

Inside the drawer, carefully mounted on red velvet, was a modern-looking black pistol.

"It's nothing remarkable, really," Moretti said, "but a wonderful tale. It's standard NATO issue, a nine-millimetre Italian Beretta. It belonged to one of the Dutch NATO troops defending a Bosnian Muslim town called Srebrenica." Moretti gestured at the drawer. "Take it out," he said, "try it."

She cradled the gun in her palm as if it were a flower, not

wanting her fingers to stray anywhere near the trigger. The Doll had never held a gun. It felt like nothing much.

"The Serbs demanded the Dutch give them their weapons and get out. The Dutch agreed, handed over their guns—" he reached up and with his tiny hands took the pistol from her—"this included, and left."

The Doll looked down at Frank Moretti. He was holding the pistol as they do in movies, with both hands, aiming it at Miró's man who ate the sun.

"I don't give a shit, really. Unpronounceable people, ugly places, it's what people do, these things. But I like the story and so I keep the gun."

The Doll looked at him, at the gun, lost with Moretti's strange attitude and stranger story.

"After, the Serbs killed eight thousand civilians left unprotected. And this Beretta," Moretti went on, "meant to protect all those people, never used." He was laughing. "That's something, eh? Three thousand Americans die and it changes history. Eight and a half thousand Muslims die and it's forgotten."

And then, presuming her interested in guns, Moretti began instructing her in its use, his voice growing more excited and high-pitched as he spoke.

"That's the safety lever, ambidextrous, clever. It still has all its fifteen rounds from Srebrenica in its magazine, you know, and I leave them there because I feel that's part of its story too. See, now it's off, now it's on—don't worry! Now it's back off. It's not overly accurate, though, and you'd have to get within a few metres of your target to be confident of hitting them."

With his flabby little arm he once more held the gun out, and this time took aim at his reflection in the mirror. From a fanlight window above the front door the beautiful bright light of Sydney fell onto Moretti's back and created a halo around him as he held the gun. He looked like an outline of one of Max's toys of death: part machine, part freak.

"But then—lethal!" Moretti said. "Except when defending Muslims." He laughed once more, let his gun arm fall to his lap, then moved out of the light and returned the gun to the Doll. She let out a long breath, relieved to put it away, lock the cabinet, and hide the key back in the elephant.

42

In the library, as always, Chopin was playing. The Doll, who knew nothing about classical music, knew it was his Nocturne in F Minor because Frank Moretti frequently told her that too.

"It is," Frank Moretti said, "a high point of western culture. When the terrorists have destroyed everything," he told her, "there will still be Chopin's Nocturne in F Minor, and people will marvel forever. But perhaps you have to be Italian to appreciate it fully."

Frank Moretti said this because he believed the Doll did not like Chopin, and it annoyed him, because each Monday morning at 11 am it was her job to undress for him in his library to Chopin's Nocturne in F Minor.

"Perhaps you are simply someone who is beautiful," he would sometimes say, "but who has no ear nor heart for beauty."

The Doll did not dislike Chopin. But each Monday morning as she stripped for Frank Moretti while it played over and over on repeat, she found it ever sadder.

It was also hopeless music to strip to. Bad as the doof music at the club was, its amphetamine beats matched what was expected of the girls, and within its grind was for the Doll both a distance and an escape. The doof music obliterated thought of everything other than movement. The doof music did not touch her. It was a costume within which she felt safe.

The Doll knew she was not, of course, the first woman Frank Moretti had paid to strip for him. He talked of some of the other women who in the past he had paid to look at in private. He would talk of the shape of a neck, or the flow of a calf, or the relationship between thigh and buttock. Isabella had the most exquisite shoulders. Kayleen's hips were beyond compare. Alexa's breasts were small but perfect, and her belly was, said Moretti, irreproachable. He talked of them as though they were paintings that could be bought and sold, things that demonstrated not their own beauty but his superior taste.

So Moretti talked, and he didn't stop talking until she began stripping, and so there was always an incentive for the Doll to begin. But little by little as she took off her Prada dress, as she so very gradually ran her hands down her arms and up between her legs, as she spun and pushed her arse out ever so slowly, then swayed it back and forth, as she stood up so that Frank Moretti might admire the shape of her shoulders and the nape of her neck as she undid her bra, as she turned back around and brought her hands up under her breasts, Chopin was telling her this was all about nothing, nothing, nothing.

Once she was naked, Moretti would come close and investigate her body like a butterfly collector examining minute markings on his latest catch. He would have the Doll turn and then stare at her from behind for several minutes. There would be occasional short dull whirs, like an electric toy being lazily played with, as he manoeuvred his wheelchair here and there to gain different perspectives on her body. Sometimes it felt to the Doll like an appointment with a gynaecologist, but then she would hear those sad piano notes intercut with his squeaky—

"Yes—yes—yes."

And the Doll would know it was something else.

How sad the world was! Doof music lied: it told the girls and the men that they were still young, that youth was forever, death always tomorrow, energy boundless, and that life was as relentless, as insistent in its promise of momentum for the better as the one hundred and forty beats per minute of the track playing. She could strip to a lie, because it gave her a mask. But Chopin brought her soul rushing back into her body, no matter how she fought to keep it out. With Chopin she knew the terrible, wretched truth: she was naked and alone.

When she had finished her undressing and parading, Moretti would leave and she would not see him again. The Doll would get back into her clothes, walk out through the main lounge room, and into the hallway. There by the wall opposite the Miró painting was a Louis XV side table on which was displayed a framed photograph and a blue ceramic tray.

One day she had picked the photograph up and looked

closely, trying to square it with what little he had told her: a
head-on collision with a tip truck in the early morning. The
black and white was of a young man with a magnificent
body, muscled thighs bulging out of the tight shorts fashion-
able in the 1970s. The beach she recognised as the favourite
of the west, Cronulla, and it always struck her as an odd place
for a child of the rich to be. But it was the body that she
could never reconcile with that of the hideous, mutilated
remains of the car smash that she knew as Frank Moretti. For
the young man was beautiful.

If the photograph intrigued the Doll, it was the three
one-hundred-dollar bills lying in the blue ceramic tray waiting for her in payment as she left that compelled her weekly
attention. Such was their arrangement, such was their strange
ritual, as regular as morning tv and just as pointless, though,
for the Doll, at least more lucrative.

But that day she had not even finished her routine when
Frank Moretti's mobile bleeped with a text message. He
looked down at the phone, grunted and, without a word, disappeared into his office. The Doll waited, and when after
some time he had still not returned, she dressed and went
into the kitchen to get a drink of water.

Next to the fridge, a small LCD screen that slid out from
a cupboard at chest height—Moretti height—was on, with a
television infotainment program running. The Doll poured
herself a glass of water. The tv's burbling transformed into an
advertisement for magnetic mattress covers. The Doll could
sense the drugs wearing off and she was feeling scratchy. She
needed to feel zonked again, she told herself. She was shaking so much that she spilt the water.

"Yes, that's right, Holly," a voice on the television was saying as the Doll mopped up the spill, "we have a national exclusive tonight on *Undercurrent*, here on Six."

The Doll glanced up at the screen to see a man, slightly twisted to the camera in a way that seemed familiar, doing some sort of outdoors broadcast, constantly touching with his index finger a coiled wire running into his ear.

"Tonight," said the man, "we're able to reveal the true identity of 'the unknown terrorist' as she has become . . ."

Then she recognised him: it was that creep, Richard Cody.

43

When the Doll came back to her senses there was some amateur footage of a man—or was it a woman?—swaddled in black, brandishing a machine gun on the tv, followed by other scenes she recalled as being from the massacre of schoolchildren at Beslan. And trailing in the wake of these was a series of images that had almost nothing to do with each other, but which to the Doll felt somehow inescapable—as if there were a logic in their ordering that demanded a yet unknown conclusion; as if they were the opening quick cuts summarising a series' shows prior to its cataclysmic finale. On the screen, child's body after child's body was laid out; and this was followed by some of the things she had already seen—one of the kids' backpacks being unzipped to reveal the bomb inside, the armed police taking up position around Tariq's apartment block; the bad photograph of a bearded man in Arabic-looking dress who may or may not have been Tariq;

the slow-motion grainy, dark images of she and Tariq hugging each other.

Richard Cody was talking again.

"Incredibly," he was saying, and here the camera zoomed out to reveal him standing in Kings Cross, with the Chairman's Lounge behind him, "in what may just be the cover of all covers, it turns out that this possible 'unknown terrorist'—I stress possible—is no other than a lap dancer at this club right here, behind me, who was known as—and wait for this—the Black Widow! Now, as we know, this is the same name given to militant Islamic women prominent in suicide attacks in Russia."

It couldn't be, thought the Doll. It wasn't possible. It was a dream, a terrible dream. The television cut back to the anchor, a woman with improbable cheekbones.

"This sounds incredible, Richard. What it does mean in terms of national security?"

There was a long pause while the woman just continued staring out of the television. The Doll felt something dry and round like a pebble on her tongue that she tried to swallow but could not force down her throat. Richard Cody reappeared, touched an earpiece with his index finger, and started talking again.

"I'm sorry, I just lost you there, Holly. Yes, incredible is the word. The Chairman's Lounge is a very exclusive establishment and the Black Widow would have had access to some of Australia's top political and business leaders there. And we will be revealing all this, *and* the lap dancing terrorist's true identity, here, tonight, on *Undercurrent*."

The Doll turned away and, as she did so, felt a strange

dizziness rise inside, as though she were on the verge both of falling into some terrible void while at the same time being that very emptiness. She leant against the sink to steady herself.

"And here at Six," said the woman anchor, "we'll be keeping you up to date with the latest breaking news on this story as it comes to hand."

'Oh God, oh God!' the Doll panicked, 'there's no way out of this!' Her mind raced through the many things she might do and on reflection not one seemed a good idea. The police, if she turned herself in, were not going to believe her; she worried that the media, if she approached them, would set her up, while killing herself seemed attractive but painful and difficult. And so she hoped that something outside of herself would change and prove her innocent, just as something outside her had changed and seemed to be turning her into an outlaw.

Moretti was still talking on the phone. The Doll knocked on his office door. He looked up and she waved a farewell. Without a word or expression Moretti looked back down and resumed talking.

On her way out, she paused in the entrance hallway in front of the Miró. Her phone began ringing. She was shaking. She looked at the phone but it was no number she recognised. She dropped the phone back in her bag and let it ring out. Everything seemed to be swaying as if there were an earthquake: the Miró, the blue ceramic tray, the table, the room . . . and the Doll momentarily tensed her legs so that she might not fall. But the hallway was moving around her, rising, sloping, dropping and shifting, no matter where she stood or how she held herself.

'Focus on the money,' she said to herself, as she had so often said to herself in the past when some aspect of life had gone against her. 'Three hundred dollars will give me . . . will give me . . . makes . . .' But the world was whirling and once more her phone was ringing. Her mind could not do the simple maths. She did not know what it would make, and not knowing what it would make, it became unclear what the money might actually mean.

The Doll snatched up the three one-hundred–dollar notes from the blue ceramic tray, tried to hold on to them, but they were just pieces of dry paper, they were leaves in a park that children chase in the wind and can never catch, and a hundred-dollar note fell out of her trembling fingers onto the floor. She dropped down, snatched it up, and put the cash in her purse as her phone began ringing yet again. 'Focus on the money,' she told herself, as she fumbled for her phone and turned it off. 'Just the money.'

When she stepped outside, the heat hit her body, held her throat. The Doll walked back down the road, concentrating on moving, not hoping, not fearing, but walking, getting on, trying to think of money. But her mind would not work: she couldn't remember whether it was $49,700 she had saved, or whether it was $47,900; if it was $300 left to save or $2,100, or if it was $21,000 that was her target. She couldn't calculate whether it was another three weeks of the man who ate the sun eating her arse out with his eyes, or one week, or several months before she could stop this, be free of it forever.

It was all a blur, everything was a horrible blur of numbers that no longer had any meaning. So instead the Doll tried to see the hundred-dollar notes covering her body and imagine where she would place these next three notes, but all she could see was the wind blowing the notes everywhere and she could not bring her mind to heel and make the wind stop blowing. She tried so hard to see her body slowly disappearing as if by magic, money papering over it. But her body would not disappear, she was naked, the earth was blowing away in a cyclone, and still she was naked.

44

The Doll got off the ferry at Circular Quay. If she was still bewildered by all that was happening, the boat trip had at least been good in helping her mind settle on one thing: she would—she had to—go to the police. But how and where? She paused for a moment under the cool shadow of the Cahill Expressway, trying to think, to decide on some clear course of action.

But as the traffic's violent rumbling seeped into her from the great iron-clad causeway above, her mind returned to its previous turmoil and all certainty abandoned her. For a moment she again toyed with the idea of not going to the police. But, she then thought, if she didn't go they would hunt her down. With their guns and helicopters they would find her anyway and they would kill her.

No, no, she then reprimanded herself, this was just allowing herself to panic. She had to stay cool, she had to go to the police, for only in this way could the nightmare be ended. But she would not turn herself in to the next cop she saw on a street corner, no, she didn't want to be alone with a cop. Far safer, thought the Doll, to go to a cop shop where there were too many witnesses for anything awful to happen. And somehow she felt a certain security in the idea of going into the cop shop as a free and innocent woman.

But as she began walking into town toward the city police station, she started to remember stories about bent Sydney coppers. She began to fear that she would be framed and locked away forever. And in the heat that built the further she got from the harbour and the deeper she went into the city, she found herself beginning to slow and dawdle. But it was only when she turned into George Street that she took fright.

She had walked straight into a police cordon. There were cops and cars and lights and a sense of slight panic everywhere. For a moment—when a big biker cop in jodhpurs turned and stared at her with his thuggish face—she was convinced she was about to be shot dead. It felt to the Doll that they were waiting for her, that it was an ambush. It took all her self-control not to turn and run.

"Anthrax scare," he said to her in a surprisingly soft voice, but it was too late. As she retreated into the heart of the crowd rather than trying to skirt it, she saw through bobbing heads white-suited emergency workers walking beneath portable showers. Staying in the middle of a throng that broke off from the main crowd, she headed away as quickly as she could.

Still, she pressed on. She had to, she told herself, trying to ignore her body that was somehow quivering as she walked. She skirted the edge of Chinatown, past Chinese girls with bleached hair and Chinese punks in bright nylon trackies in spite of the stinking heat. She turned into a narrow street and headed down a hill toward Darling Harbour. At its intersection with a main road was the city cop shop—a wedge-shaped building, mirror glassed down to its ominously black-tiled bottom storey. It reminded the Doll of a chain-mailed fist. 'What goes on inside?' she wondered. 'Why can't you see in?' Her stomach began churning.

But she stuck to her purpose and walked to the police station's public entrance. Inside was a small waiting room full of people, and, apart from a confectionery and drinks dispenser, devoid of furnishings. A man who seemed off his face on something was gibbering beneath a domestic violence poster, a Chinese girl was quietly sobbing near the drinks dispenser, a few others were chatting, while a lone drunk was swearing and mumbling to himself. Behind the counter a couple of uniformed cops and a receptionist were trying to sort the confusion into some order of official documents and formal statements.

She welcomed the strange crowd, seeing in it a disguise and, in the waiting it imposed on her, a final chance to ready herself, to prepare in her head what she would say. A man stood two in front of her in the queue for the counter. He was middle-aged and burly, dressed in big boots, shorts and a t-shirt, covered in concrete dust. Occasionally he turned around and she could see his eyes, bright red from irritation, like vivid make-up against his grey-dusted face. He looked like the ghost of a tradesman. The Doll caught him saying something about a restraining order his wife had out on him. The woman behind the counter was polite. A little later he began yelling how he just wanted to see his kids. The woman remained calm, even, thought the Doll, gentle, and tried to quieten him down, but he only yelled louder.

"I'm the victim here," he yelled. "Not that bitch." A cop came out of a door and was walking up to him, when the man pulled a knife out of his shorts. "Why can't I see my kids?" he yelled. "I just want to see my kids."

And then there were cops everywhere, spilling into the room, some with drawn batons, shoving the waiting room crowd away from the man, who was now waving the knife back and forth, while one pulled a revolver and was shouting,

"Drop the knife and get down!"

'They'll kill him,' thought the Doll, 'just like they'll kill me.'

"Drop it NOW!"

The Doll's body was shaking all over, people were screaming, the man kept yelling, a second cop had a gun trained on him from behind, and the Doll was pushed by someone against the wall between the soft drink dispenser and a reeking Aboriginal woman.

"Fuck this," said the Aboriginal woman, turning to her. "I'm outta here. You coming?"

There didn't seem any good reason to stay. Besides, she could come back later. And these two thoughts brought the Doll a great sense of relief. The cops were preoccupied with the standoff, and seemed not to care what anyone did as long as they stayed out of the way. Keeping close to the wall, the Doll and the Aboriginal woman shuffled the few metres to the door where, following a woman pushing a twin pram, they walked outside.

The Doll was too fearful to run until she was heading up Liverpool Street through the Spanish Quarter, and then she took off, just wanting to get as far away as possible as quickly as she could. She ran wherever there were green lights, open spaces amidst the crowds. When the chasm of a shopping centre entrance opened up before her, she allowed herself to become quickly lost within it.

She breathed in its thick air conditioned chill, felt the sweat on her body cool and her skin clutch. Music it was impossible to recognise rose several storeys to a great clock. Elevators hummed in a way the Doll found oddly reassuring. People sat in a food court eating kebabs and curries and sushi, all staring at some point further on where there were more people eating sushi and curries and kebabs.

She would go back to the cops later. Now she just needed to get herself back together. She wanted another Valium 5, wanted it bad, but resolved to hold out. She needed to keep straight if she was going to talk to the police and sort out this mess with them. Here was good, she told herself. It's all good, she kept repeating. But she knew she was kidding herself.

Like shoals of fish darting hither and thither around a bright coral reef, people moved through the shopping centre's many storeys, its scores of shops, its thousands of shelves, products, lines, with a seemingly instinctive knowledge. Joining with them always made the Doll feel there was once more some purpose and order to her life, though what that purpose and order was she would no more have been able to say than a single fish would have been able to explain its movements. And so, to gather herself, she rode with the crowds, head bowed, up several flights of escalators, trying to summon the determination to go back to the police.

But still she didn't feel good. Her thoughts wouldn't

gather. She felt too visible. To be calm, to think, she needed to buy something, anything, and buy it quickly. Having established an order of action, and with it a vague possibility of progress, she felt momentarily better. Though she had sunglasses, she bought an oversize Christian Dior pair with dark brown lenses and a light gold frame. Feeling once more camouflaged in the guise of the successful woman, the Doll began riding the escalators back down, intent on putting her fear to one side and talking to the police.

At first she didn't pay any attention to the giant screen looming upwards from the ground floor plaza. It was only when the Doll was halfway between the fifth and the fourth floors that she noticed a vast image—broken into a grid by the frames of the scores of plasma screens that stacked together formed the giant whole—of the Twin Towers burning.

The pictures of that collapsing world dissolved into a huge backpack being unzipped and a dark bomb reared threateningly over the shoppers below, before flickering and transforming into giant armed police surrounding Tariq's apartment block.

As the escalator continued descending, the Doll recognised the footage she had seen at Moretti's, only now it had grown into something that was dwarfing and overwhelming everything around it. The bad photograph of a bearded man in Arabic-looking dress filled the shopping centre's plaza like an inescapable image of the devil; the grainy, dark images of Tariq and the Doll hugging each other seemed like something from a horror movie; then the Doll felt as if she too were in that school in Beslan as body after body was laid out while a figure dressed in black brandished a machine gun, threatening every shopper.

The escalator was now falling down the side of the massive grid of plasma screens; taking her past the journalist, Richard Cody. He too was huge, his face monstrous, he was saying something, she was sliding past his mouth, his lips, his obscene tongue, she felt he might swallow her. She turned her head away, tried not to look, but it was unavoidable, and still the escalator kept falling and the Doll with it, while on screen she had now appeared dressed as the Black Widow, something somebody must have videoed at a private show years ago. The Doll felt she was journeying into hell. She was ripping off her dress and then her veil, she was heavily made up, and the bad quality of the video accentuated the whorish look, the plasma grid throwing a mesh over the image that somehow added a final slutty layer. The Doll felt that they had turned her into a murderous porn star. On the vast grid of stacked plasma screens she wore a giant, sick smile. That was the worst thing, the one thing Ferdy made them all wear—that smile that was never hers.

The Doll felt herself seized by panic; she had to run, to hide, to escape this hell. On reaching the ground floor she hurried toward the exit. 'How can I turn myself in to the police now?' she thought, horrified that only a short time before she had been standing in a police station about to give herself up. Whatever was she thinking? Was she insane? Trust cops in this town?

'It's gone too far, it's all gone too far! They'll fix me up somehow, say I threatened them or had a weapon, something bad. And then they'll have to kill me,' thought the Doll. 'It's obvious, because I'm the only one who can prove how wrong they are. Just like the tradey, they'll pull a gun on me.'

As she hurried past the KL Noodle Bar she noticed a middle-aged woman—a nice, round-looking woman, a woman who could well be an aunt, thought the Doll, a woman she might like to become one day, if she could cope with dressing that badly—get up to go. As she walked away, the Doll noticed she had left her mobile phone sitting on the table.

It was an old person's mobile, a clunky, outdated Nokia 3315. Before she even realised what she was doing, the Doll had circled back around, leant slightly in to the woman's table and, with a movement that surprised her with its deftness, placed a hundred-dollar bill under the stranger's coffee cup and scooped up her mobile phone. And with that she was walking out of the food court and heading to an exit. As she scurried along she was already dialling a number on the stolen phone.

"Hello," said a voice.

"Wilder?"

"Oh Jesus, Gina. Are you crazy? Have you seen the news? Are you ringing on your phone?"

"Wilder," said the Doll, and she could hear that her own voice was trembling, "have you still got your scissors?"

45

The Doll resolved first to head back to her home. If the police had it staked out, she would see them—if they didn't she would go in, get her cash out before it was too late, quickly grab a few clothes and then clear out to Wilder's. The cash!—that was what would get her out of this mess, thought the Doll.

Only two hours before, with Moretti's money added to what was left from the last two days, she had had eleven one hundred-dollar notes plus change. But the sunglasses had set her back five hundred dollars, and then after leaving the hundred for the phone, the Doll had just four hundred dollars and some change left in her wallet. It was nothing.

With her cash back at her flat there was freedom, possibilities, hope. And just thinking about all her money there, imagining the feel of those hundred-dollar notes on her body and her body once more relaxed and comfortable beneath them, made the Doll feel better. She didn't know what she was going to do with the money, but she knew money could buy a lot of things, and the more money, the more you could buy: time, space, people. But without the money she would be lost.

Feeling she needed to walk, the Doll headed through the city, up William Street, feeling safe in the great onrush of traffic, of crowds looking through and beyond her, reassuring her that she was still unknown.

It was a long, hot walk, but she didn't mind. It kept her panic at bay; it made her feel she was doing something, that she was getting somewhere. Her mind clearer, it occurred to the Doll that she still had Tariq's number and a phone that couldn't be traced to her. Maybe Tariq felt as bad and as scared as she did. Maybe Tariq knew whatever it was you needed to know at such a time. Maybe Tariq had an idea, a plan.

Suddenly excited, the Doll searched through her Gucci handbag until she found the crumpled takeaway restaurant menu with the green inked number. 'Yes,' she thought,

'Tariq will know what we should do.' And in the Doll's mind it was now not her alone, but her and Tariq, and when she thought about Tariq, she realised what a remarkable and strong man he was, and how together they might be able to sort something out. If he could, she was sure he would find her and help her, and together they might get themselves out of this awful mess. But when she found cover in the shadows of a narrow side street and called, there was again no answer, only the same stupid American voice welcoming her to voicemail.

She hung up and was making her way along the narrow street, when she heard noises up ahead and came upon a woman squatting in the deep black shadow of a driveway, back against green wheelie bins, knickers around her ankles, a puddle beneath her. Three young boys with skateboards were laughing happily, running in and out of the darkness, yelling at her and giggling.

"You heap of stinking shit!"

"You old scrag! Go and piss somewhere else."

"Lick it up, Mum!"

The Doll looked at her watch: she was meant to be at work in two hours. She hurried past, so caught up in her own problems she scarcely noticed the old woman. It was dawning on her that if she was too scared to go to the cops, it would be far too dangerous for her to go to work. And this thought made her furious. How was she to make the money she needed to live? How was she to get the cash she would need for her mortgage repayments? She told herself that perhaps she would still go to the cops when she felt ready, so why not go to work? But in her heart she knew that this was lying to herself. She would never go to the cops now, and she would not be going back to dance. And these thoughts made her far angrier than anything else.

Once more, her mind returned to Tariq, who by never answering his phone somehow seemed to grow in her mind as the person who could help her out of her ever worsening situation. And the more she kept on ringing him, and the more she heard only his infuriating American voicemail message, the more she realised she needed to speak to him and the more she understood his ongoing silence meant she must turn to him, that she must find him: fate had brought them together, and only together could they alter fate.

And so as the Doll continued making her way to Darlinghurst, she sought small refuges and nooks where she could ring Tariq's phone, and each pick-up by his voicemail only confirmed in her own mind the urgent necessity of finding him. And then the Doll would step back out of the shadows with their dead rats and syringes and leaking black plastic bags and resume walking along the sticky bitumen pavements, past the skips with the ice addicts unravelling their minds in their meticulous search of junk, and the Doll began wondering if she was any less deluded than they in her own hunt.

Still she kept on walking and dialling. After a good half-hour she had almost reached her flat when yet again she took cover to try once more, this time in the alleyway in which the blue Toyota Corolla was still parked, still covered in tickets, its windows now all smashed.

The alleyway was particularly muggy and there was a bad smell, as if a dead animal were rotting in its shadows. As she reached into her handbag and found the phone, the Doll fanned her face in a pointless attempt to be rid of the stench and the heat. Fumbling around for the Nokia 3315, the Doll realised why Tariq wasn't answering. It was because she had been ringing from the stolen phone that he hadn't recognised the number and so ignored her calls. She paused, then grabbed her own phone. If using it was what it took to make contact, she would run the risk. She switched it on, ignoring the missed calls and messages. She dialled, and as she waited for an answer she heard something nearby. It was muffled, at once distant and close, but familiar. Then she recognised the sound. It was Chopin's Nocturne in F Minor.

She looked around. There was nothing save walls, some garbage, and the Toyota Corolla. It was a good omen, though, she thought, her thinking of Tariq and hearing Chopin. It meant something was meant to be. The Chopin stopped playing. In her ear the Doll heard the usual voicemail message. She hung up.

Something that was not a thought nor an idea, but a need without form, an awareness of a desire that had to be fulfilled, came into the Doll's mind. She took a few tentative steps deeper into the alley, then slid into the small, stinking space between a dark brick wall and the blue Corolla.

She flicked sweat off her cheek with a finger. With her back to the wall, she redialled Tariq's number. She didn't bother raising the phone to her ear. Even with the phone at her waist she could hear the dial tone. Again, from somewhere now closer and a little louder, Chopin's Nocturne in F Minor began playing.

As the Doll edged further down the alley, the stench grew

worse, and then the music stopped. Down by her waist the voicemail message began. The air was now so bad that for a moment she thought she might vomit. She concentrated on adjusting her vision to the darkness. Her eyes fixed on the car, she hung up without looking at the phone, counted a few beats, and then hit redial. For the third time there were a few seconds of nothing. She rubbed her damp cheek with the phone. She had just noticed that the Corolla's boot wasn't properly closed when the ringing tone and the Chopin began simultaneously.

The Doll slowly stretched out her arm. With the back of the phone she lifted the boot up. A swarm of blowflies rose with it, accompanied by the Chopin, now clear and loud. She moved closer. Just as she glimpsed inside the boot, the full force of the stench hit her. She jerked backwards as if she had been punched. The boot lid dropped and then bounced slightly back up. But in that fraction of a second the Doll had seen everything, including the stainless-steel tip of his prized Nokia protruding from his trouser pocket.

46

After some time she stepped back, raised the boot lid again and looked inside for a good minute. Tariq's corpse lay curled up in the boot, clad in the same clothes in which she had met him only two nights before.

She tried to wave the blowflies away from his face, but her hand passed through the vibrating black cloud as through water. Tariq's face was harrowed, a husk. His cheeks were hollow and sunken, like an old man's, as though something had been pulled out. There was a big scab of dried blood on his forehead. It had a tail that ran down the side of his face onto the boot floor where it formed a coagulated puddle that in the darkness glistened dully like wet bitumen.

The Doll smiled as she had taught herself to smile when things were unpleasant and she didn't want anyone to know what she was feeling. She forced herself to hold her smile as she looked through the blowflies at his still-open eyes that she wished were not open, at his slightly swollen lips, at the whiteness of his skin that did not seem that of an adult but of a child, a beautiful child sleeping soundly after the longest of days.

The Bulgari Ipno was gone from his left wrist. But it was his right hand lying open and outstretched across his belly that undid her. Those gentle fingers that she could still feel in her and in her mouth were now oddly stiff and frightening.

She fell to her knees, hands on the boot sill, and vomited what little she had in her stomach. She knelt in the filth and the stench and the wet heat of the alleyway, head dangling between her outstretched arms, dribbling strings of green bile, trying to get the sensation of his fingers out of her mouth.

Somewhat unsteadily, she got to her feet, shuffled back between the car and the wall, and walked out of the alley. On the street the full white glare of the day hit her like a spotlight in the club. She felt dazzled. It felt like a punch and she had to take a half-step backwards to get her balance. Her phone rang, she switched it off. It was difficult to breathe the oven-like air. Her mouth still tasted foully of

bile; her eyes were still full of blood, there was blood everywhere; the world seemed to need it, thrive on it; up and
down the street people seemed to have trouble seeing and
breathing, their eyes and throats were so full of it. She
would not go to her flat now. She could get the money
later, sometime soon. But for now, she felt too frightened
and needed to get away. She swallowed another Valium 5.
Not having any water, she sucked on her fingers to force
the tablet down.

After a time, it was all good.

She raised her head slightly, as if she were about to start
another show on the table, gave herself over to the sense of
oblivion that bright light always brought out in her, and
turned away from her apartment block. She caught a train
from the Cross to Redfern. There were cops with guns
everywhere in the train stations; their eyes darted back and
forth, she could smell the apprehension. But the Doll felt
momentarily without fear. She expected them to shoot her
at any moment and part of her hoped they now would and
part of her no longer cared if they did.

47

Wilder said nothing when she opened the door and saw the
Doll. She hustled her in as quickly as possible and then
slammed the door shut.

Inside, Wilder's home was as ever: Max's toys everywhere,
a chalkboard, the mess of a family, telly rumbling on in the
background. Only Wilder was changed. There was no gin,
neither Tanqueray nor UDL. Nor were there any of Wilder's

interminable stories about herself that the Doll listened to as others do talkback radio.

"He's at a mate's," was all Wilder said when the Doll looked around for Max. Neither knew what to say next.

Wilder finally came out with it.

"Look," she said, "I can do something with your hair, but wouldn't it be better to turn yourself in before this shit gets any worse?"

The Doll said nothing.

"I just don't get it," said Wilder. "It's a fuckup, sure, but in the end it'll be clear that you're innocent. Why won't you trust them?"

But the Doll was staring at the tv, where a politician was talking, with a banner running across the bottom of the screen declaring TERRORISTS STILL ON RUN. SYD-NEY ON HIGH ALERT. He was a large man who had slightly narrowed his eyes, as if he were trying to read an eyesight chart but was having trouble with the finer lines.

"As leader of the Opposition," an invisible interviewer was now saying, "what do you say to government claims that your party is soft on terror?"

The politician leant slightly forward, as if trying to focus better on that tantalising, elusive eyesight chart.

"Let me just say this: we are not going soft." He made an emphatic movement with his hand. "Terrorists are not Australians. Australians are decent people. Let me just say also that we welcome calls to change the law to strip any Australian citizen of their citizenship, whether they be native born or naturalised, if they are involved in anti-Australian activities. Either you are with Australia or you are no longer Australian and have lost your right to the rights of other citizens."

"My God," said Wilder, then swung to another station where a current affairs show anchor was talking.

"Does your government have a shoot-to-kill policy?" said the anchor, and the screen cut to the prime minister who, Wilder realised, was being interviewed.

"We have an appropriate policy which—" The prime minister never got to finish, for Wilder had already changed stations again. But on the next channel the same armed police were surrounding Tariq's apartment building.

"This is insane," whispered Wilder, once more pointing the remote at the tv with the intention of switching it off, but the Doll pulled her arm down.

"Let it play," she said. "I have to watch."

And so standing together they watched the same footage run again—the same bomb in the same kid's backpack; the same bad photograph of the same bearded man in Arabic-looking dress; the same slow-motion grainy images of Tariq and the Doll hugging each other. The repetitive images clicking over filled the tv like loose change filling an empty pokie.

The Twin Towers fell again; the same children's bodies were laid out once more in Beslan; the same man or woman dressed in black brandished the same machine gun; the Doll continued dancing naked. And there were new scenes—a murky London tube train moments after it had been bombed; the Sari nightclub burning after the Bali bombing; wounded being taken away from the Madrid train bombing, the montage culminating in a shot that zoomed in on the

Sydney Opera House before blowing out to white, a cheap effect accompanied by an ominous rumble.

The Doll closed her eyes.

When she opened them, she saw Osama bin Laden. George W. Bush. Missiles being launched. Men in robes firing grenade launchers. Great buildings exploding into balloons of fire. Women covered in blood. Hostages about to be beheaded. New York! Bali! Madrid! London! Baghdad! The Doll disintegrating into dancing squares of colour, herself pixelated, smiling a smile that was never hers.

A Fujitsu air conditioner ad came on and Wilder switched the tv off.

"It's like when I bought my Subaru Forester," said Wilder after a few moments' awkward silence, "and all we could see for weeks after were other Subaru Foresters—parked on the street, driving through the city, stopped at lights. But there are other cars, Gina, and there are other stories."

This was small comfort to the Doll. There was, she knew, much else on the tv, other headlines in the paper, other voices on the radio talking about other things. But all the Doll could see was her face, her name, all she could hear was one more opinion about her. And it was seizing her like a cold current and taking her somewhere she didn't want to go, just as the rip had carried Max out to sea.

"I'm not a car, Wilder, and this isn't another story," she said, lifting up a copy of that day's *Telegraph*. "Look here." And there, on the third page, was an article that declared "the story of the homegrown terrorist cell is shaping up to be the story of the year".

"And how's it end?" the Doll asked. "Do I get shot or

what? You tell me, Wilder. It can hardly end up as a mistake. That's not the story of the year—that's an embarrassment."

Wilder went quiet.

"It happens, Gina. They go crazy for a few days, then they move on like dogs. Besides," she said, picking up a *Sydney Morning Herald* and brandishing it like a sacred oracle, "not everyone's against you. There's something here saying how there's a climate of hysteria that could lead to innocent people being persecuted."

"Could?" said the Doll incredulously. "What's with the fucking 'could'?"

"It is here," said Wilder leafing through the pages as endless, as indecipherable, as irrelevant, as a phone directory, "somewhere." She gave up. "I'll find it later and cut it out for you."

"Wilder, no one cares about a shitty article lost in there. It's like throwing a corpse in the harbour," said the Doll. An image sprang into her mind of Fung's dead face staring out of a wheelie bin. She pointed at the *Sydney Morning Herald*. "You're the only person I know who reads it. Everyone else is like me—they just look at the *Telegraph* headlines and watch Richard Cody and listen to Joe Cosuk."

She never spoke to Wilder like this. Both felt a little stunned. With not a word more, Wilder led the Doll into her bathroom. Haircutting was one of a number of unexpected skills Wilder possessed, having done two years of an apprenticeship in a salon, before tossing it in to go to university, before in turn tossing that in to go work with a boyfriend in his landscaping business.

Wilder bleached the Doll's hair blonde, making the Doll

laugh as she worked. Any story was welcome now. As a hairdresser, Wilder said she was made for landscaping, telling tales
of perms gone bad and highlights turned technicolour. For all
the stories she told against herself, Wilder proved surprisingly
able, trimming the Doll's hair into a short bob, shaping it with
a slant running down the sides, so that it accentuated the Doll's
cheekbones and made her face look different, less heart shaped
than the images being run in the papers and on television.

When Wilder had finished, the Doll asked her if she could
have a bath. Wilder's home had an unrenovated bathroom,
which meant it had a real bath, deep and made of steel. The
Doll spun the hot water tap and the room filled with steam.
Then she cooled the bath just enough to make it possible to
sit in without scalding herself. When it was finally ready, the
Doll stepped into the bath and gave herself over to the blessing of water. And though the air was almost intolerably hot
and humid, she loved this feeling of letting her body return
to water, to which it seemed always to have belonged.

After a while, she felt better. If she craned her neck and
twisted, she could catch half a reflection of her head in the
mirror. She was pleasantly surprised at how different she now
looked. And not only that, she thought, sinking back in the
bath, no one knew her name anyway. What had happened
wasn't all that good, but perhaps Wilder had a point, for nor
was it all bad. After a time, she dozed a little, heard Wilder go
out to get Max and come back, and woke when the bath was
cooling and night was falling and the room darkening.

There was a knock at the door. It was Wilder, saying that
while the Doll had been asleep, *Undercurrent* had been on.
Richard Cody had named her as "the Black Widow". There

hadn't really been that much else that was new, though, said Wilder. There was to be an investigative special about it all the following night.

The Doll said nothing in reply. She turned the hot water tap with her big toe. She held a foot under its steaming flow, trying to lose herself in the pain, yet it was impossible to keep it there for longer than a few seconds. She let the bath warm back up, sank back and dozed off again in its pleasant waters.

But her dream was anything but pleasant.

Savage dogs were running at her. They had no flesh on their faces. The Doll saw that it was their nature to hurt. Again and again they ran past her, as if they could not see her. And then she saw herself reflected in the bathwater with a fleshless dog's face, and with that face she was kissing Tariq and flies were crawling from between his cold lips . . . there was a knock on the bathroom door and she awoke.

"Everything okay?" asked Wilder.

48

After her bad dream, the Doll summoned the energy to get out of the bath, dress in Wilder's batik dressing gown and make her way down the dark, toy-littered hall to where Wilder was standing at the door of Max's bedroom, gazing inwards.

"Sometimes I stand here for an hour or more," Wilder said softly, without turning to the Doll. "Just looking and listening." They both watched over Max lying curled up on his bed, his flesh the thinnest of coverings over a question mark of a body, the hush of the room occasionally broken by the snuffles and slight sounds, almost yelps, he made in his sleep. "It's my happiest time of day," Wilder said. "There's a peace in it."

The Doll said nothing. She put her arm in Wilder's. As they stood together in the half-light of the hall, watching a child sleeping, the Doll hoped for this moment—that would soon be forgotten and unknown and mean nothing—never to end.

"They have no words for it," said Wilder finally, still without turning to look at the Doll. "No one can name it and no one can take it from you."

"They can take everything from you, Wilder," the Doll said, sensing that for a second time she was going to consciously disagree with Wilder. She spoke in a hush, so that Max would not be woken. "They make these things up, they take something innocent about your life and say it proves you're guilty, they take a truth and they turn it into a lie. How can they do that? Like, there's this guy today at the ferry terminal, reading these lies about me in the paper, and he's shaking his head and swearing about me. I knew he believed them because up until yesterday I was like him, just hanging around, waiting for this or that, swallowing all the crap I read and heard, and then just puking all the crap back up."

And as parts of her day began coming back to her—the politician on the radio saying terrorists needed to be eliminated; the sight of Cody on the telly at Moretti's saying he knew who she was; the way on the plasma screens at the shopping centre they made her look like something off a porn movie—the Doll's voice began rising.

"But it's not true, Wilder. It's not true. And now, every hour, it's growing, like slobbering dogs they are, and now it's not even—"

The Doll was about to say Tariq's name, but then it all came flooding back—the phone, the alley, the Corolla and the tinkly Chopin and the vibrating flies and the boot lid bouncing and the stench rising, that stench that seemed to be welling back up in her nostrils now, and she couldn't bear to tell Wilder what she had seen. Once more, panic was gripping her.

"It's all changed," the Doll said. "Can't you see? It's me they're after, Wilder." And then she cried out, "They're going to kill me!" and the Doll could no longer hold back her sobbing.

"Don't be stupid," Wilder said, pulling the Doll's face into her shoulder to stifle her so she wouldn't wake her sleeping son, and bustling her out of the doorway and down the hall. "That sort of thinking is good for nothing."

"It's good for this—" the Doll said, pulling her head away from Wilder, "now I understand life. People aren't good or bad, Wilder, they're just weak." And with that, she dropped her gaze to the floor and repeated the word as if it were one she had never heard before. "Weak?" she said, "Weak . . . weak . . ."

Then the Doll's mind seemed to clarify and she looked back up at Wilder and, her voice now louder and clearer, said: "They go with power—you understand me? What else can they do? What the fuck else can anybody do?"

She scruffed hold of Wilder's shirt and pulled her in so tight and so close that Wilder could feel her shouting as damp wind on her face. Wilder tried once more to quieten her, running her hand through the Doll's freshly cut bob as if she were a child. The Doll jerked her head away.

"No, Wilder, no. You've got to listen to me," she continued, her voice edgy and brittle. "People like fear. We all want to be frightened and we all want somebody to tell us how to live and who to fuck and why we should do this and think that. And that's the Devil's job. That's why I'm important to them, Wilder, because if you can make up a terrorist you've given people the Devil. They love the Devil. They need the Devil. That's my job. You get me?"

But it was clear Wilder got none of it. For her there was goodness and only goodness, and the Devil didn't exist in her view of the world, and any talk of him or evil was just so much superstitious claptrap.

By now the Doll was hysterical. She had never thought such things before but having said them they seemed at once inescapably true and terrifying, and she felt as if some evil force were burning up her veins.

"I'm the Devil!" she was crying, and tendrils of hot snot ran out of her nostrils and rose back up with her sobbing breathing. "I'm the Devil, don't you get me?"

Wilder tried to calm her, saying it was all right, that everything would be all right, not listening to what the Doll was trying to tell her.

But nothing was all right anymore. Part of the Doll wanted to say to Wilder that it was all too late, that this was some sort of reckoning. She wanted to say that she did not disagree with such a reckoning or object to its justice or its injustice, its truth or untruth; no, the Doll realised that now all she wanted was to escape, but it was not clear how that might happen. And that was when she broke down completely and told Wilder that Tariq was dead.

49

Wilder was talking, but the Doll wasn't listening. The Doll no longer had any sense of what was the right or wrong thing to do. The inexorable chain of events that she had not initiated and that bore less and less relation to her life invited a certain fatalism. To do something or to do nothing, it made no difference: whatever was going to happen would happen.

Wilder had sat her down, saying,

"It can be fixed."

Wilder had brought her food: takeaway Pad Thai noodles she had found in her fridge and reheated, saying,

"You have to look at your options."

Which struck the Doll as not the same thing at all. The Doll had options, but none of them fixed anything. The Doll forced herself to eat, but after a few forkfuls she stopped. She was without hunger. Food seemed in some way an impediment, something that might slow her down should she suddenly have to run.

The first option, according to Wilder, was for the Doll to give herself up. But both agreed that the original problem was worse now: who was to say the police would believe the Doll or that they wouldn't frame her? The Doll pushed the noodles this way then that on the plate.

The second option was to do a runner. Everyone knew faking ID was easy, said the Doll, until you had to fake it, and without it she couldn't get out of the country. Wilder was unsure how you might do a runner when it was clear from television series and movies that the police could track credit and bank cards.

"Luckily I've never had them anyway," said the Doll.

But nor, as Wilder pointed out, did she have her cash.

The third option was to stay at Wilder's and wait until they found her. Both were sure it would only be a matter of time before the police came knocking on Wilder's door with questions. Or with guns. They would come, the Doll thought, as she was sure they had come to find Tariq, in black and with their high-powered rifles, ready to kill him. And who was to say they hadn't? Who knew whose gun had fired into his poor head?

"They shoot to kill!" the Doll suddenly cried out, dropping her fork and bursting into tears. And she would have sobbed for a long time, but some instinct told her she couldn't and mustn't.

Both women were quiet for a few minutes.

"My money," the Doll said then. "I'm not going to lose my money." On this, if nothing else, the Doll was determined. And as money had once been the solution to her life, now it would be the solution to her problems.

"With my money I can buy my way out of this," the Doll said, admitting in the next breath that she didn't know how she would do such a thing, but do it she would.

Wilder reasoned that if the Doll was too frightened to give herself up and even more frightened of waiting, if she was too frightened of fetching the money herself, then she should find somewhere else to hide tonight, and in the morning Wilder would go to the Doll's flat and fetch the money for her.

But where else to go? A hotel would be good, some busy fleapit where she was unlikely to be recognised. Wilder disappeared into her bedroom and reappeared.

"Here," she said, handing across a Visa card. "Take this. You're not going to get into a hotel just with cash. They'll want a card for security, and we don't want you putting across mine."

The Doll looked at the card. Punched in awkward block lettering across the plastic was the name Evelyn Muir.

"My mum," said Wilder. "She remarried not long before her death, that's why she's not Evelyn Wilder. But he died, then she died, and I got lumbered with the funerals and the credit card bill. I never got round to closing it down, and for some reason—maybe because she was buried as Evelyn Wilder—the bank never shut it down. The statements kept arriving, and I thought maybe one day it'll be good for something."

They got out the phone book and looked for a hotel. Although Wilder thought it might be safer, she knew her friend well enough not to suggest something out in the west, and she instead searched for something closer to the city. They made a few calls, got a few prices, and settled on a hotel near Double Bay that was surprisingly cheap. Wilder booked a room there for the next four nights, arguing that any longer might appear suspicious.

After a good half-hour wait, the Doll said goodbye and eased herself into the back seat of a taxi that smelt of aerosol deodorant and vomit. In front of an air vent a toy propeller spun pointlessly, for the obese taxi driver, encapsulated like some Jurassic embryo in the taxi's protective Perspex egg, seemed to absorb most of the air con's breeze as some cryogenic blessing, while exuding an ammonia-like odour as a flower does pollen.

In an attempt to expose as little of her thighs to the sticky vinyl upholstery marbled with Kaposi's sarcomas of oily grime, the Doll propped herself on the seat's edge. And at that moment as she sat forward, a thought, a vision of a person, a course of action, and a sense of relief all rushed into the Doll's mind and merged into one overriding purpose. Of course, she thought, changing her mind now would involve certain humiliations, yes, there would be no doubt of that, but she was up for it. It was still a solution.

"Forget Double Bay," the Doll said to the obese taxi driver. "I'm going to Mosman."

50

There would be a price, always there was a price, but as she rode over the Harbour Bridge, the Doll now realised that whatever it was she was only too willing to pay. She would go and see Moretti, the sooner the better; she would tell him of all that had befallen her, she would hustle and he would help her.

And having made a decision, life felt better—for the Doll believed that now there would be a path out of this mess. As the glomesh stilettos that were the North Sydney highrises fell away behind her, she thought how soon she would be back to covering her body with money and buying her own piece of the city. She would be happy and she would be free. She just had to do whatever it took, and if it took

Moretti and whatever revolting things he might ask for, well, so be it.

But when the Doll arrived at Moretti's mansion, it was not dark and quiet as she had envisaged. Nor was he alone. All the lights were on and there was a black BMW four-wheel drive and two Mercedes parked out front.

The Doll no longer felt quite so sure what exactly she would tell Moretti, or what she might ask him to do—how did someone explain all that had happened? Her situation seemed so extreme, so ridiculous, that for a moment she doubted herself. And wealthy though he might be, what, after all, could someone like Moretti do? Even if he understood, even if he believed her—what on earth could he do to help? And everything that had seemed plain and obvious only a few moments before now seemed complicated and idiotic.

The Doll would have turned and run at that moment, except that in her confusion she had already rung the doorbell, and a woman with bandy legs beneath a blue apron was there answering—some sort of servant, the Doll guessed from her dress.

Because she had to speak, the Doll said:

"Could you just tell Mr Moretti that Krystal is here."

The woman looked at her closely.

"What name?"

"Krystal," said the Doll.

The woman looked at her blankly, and the Doll felt humiliated when the woman repeated:

"Crystal?"

"Thank you," said the Doll, smiling at the lousy bitch.

The woman disappeared. From inside came the chilling laughter of the invited. After some time, the Doll heard the whir of an electric motor and Moretti came around the corner.

"Yes?" he said, not even bothering to say her name. Moretti's manner was the opposite of when she came on Monday mornings: it was cold and annoyed. Behind his red Porsche glasses his eyes no longer looked large and dopey, but small and sharp as lasers.

"I'm sorry, Mr Moretti," the Doll told him, because she had to tell him something.

And as she stood in front of his elegant cedar door, looking down at him in his wheelchair, her mind gridlocked. It was as if everything that had happened to her in the last few days appeared again all at once and her brain jammed and she could find no words to make any of her memories move.

Her own life felt to her only an ever more inaccurate reflection of what the media was saying about her. And maybe instead of fighting this, she began to think her real role was to find a way of agreeing with the television, the radio, the newspapers, not fighting and denying them, not coming here to Moretti's hoping to escape them. After all, it was important to agree and obey. One had to conform, that was what mattered, even with a new role she hated as much as that of terrorist.

And standing there, throwing herself on the mercy of a miserable fuck like Moretti, she realised this was madness, but then what wasn't? To agree with the world, to disagree—what was she to do? Something the Doll could not understand had happened, something so vast and so horrible that she had no words for it, but this thing had happened and somehow she was to blame. Standing in front of Moretti, she was simply aware of suddenly feeling strangely and terribly guilty. Perhaps what was wrong was not the world, she thought, but her in not agreeing with the world, and it was this of which she was guilty.

She needed to tell Moretti all these contradictory things, ask for his explanation of them as well as his protection. But her mind remained frozen, and still she had not one word for any of it.

"Your time is Monday morning," Moretti said. "If I want you any other time I'll tell you." He gave the cedar door a feeble push to shut it.

Realising she had to do something, the Doll put an arm out to stop the door shutting.

"I've lost my wallet," she suddenly exclaimed. She felt her mouth smiling and though her voice was trembling, she heard herself smoothly lying as if it were just another night in the club. "I think I may have left it here."

"I have seen nothing," Moretti said.

"You mind if I come in?" she smiled. "Quickly look?"

"I have guests," Moretti replied, his meaning clear.

The Doll said nothing, but nor did she turn to go.

"All right," Moretti said, finally relenting. "Let yourself out when you've finished." His wheelchair arced in a semi-circle as he turned to leave, then swivelled back around. "You'll need more than hair dye to save you," he said. "Consider our arrangement ended and this our last meeting." And with that he spun around and whirred back into the dining room.

The Doll remained standing in the doorway. She felt a slut; a lousy, stinking slut. She knew she should not have been there. She realised now that even if she had known how to tell Moretti about what had happened, he would not have helped, for clearly he knew a bit of it and his only concern was to cut her adrift.

Yet, not knowing what else to do, the Doll went inside. She passed the grand dining room, saw the dinner party taking place at the far end of the room, but no one seemed to see her. In the kitchen was a cook, the woman with bandy legs and a young woman dressed up as a waitress. The Doll poked around, pretending to search for her lost wallet. Finding nothing, she went into the library, where she could be alone.

A book of black and white photographs lying open on a side table caught her attention. She leant down and looked at a photo of a woman with a shaven head standing in front of a crowd. She turned the page. The photograph was one of a series showing the woman having her hair shaved. The title beneath the first photo read, "COLLABORATOR".

"Following the fall of Chartres, France, in August 1944, to the Allies", a caption below the title said, "a young woman who has had a baby to a German soldier has her hair shaven by townspeople in retribution."

The spectators, most of them women, were laughing and happy. Gleeful children seemed to be enjoying the day. Only the shaven-headed mother looked dejected, her eyes fixed on the baby she held in her arms.

The Doll made her way out. In the entry hall she paused for a moment by the ornate wooden cabinet and looked up at the Miró. What would she do? she wondered as she stared at the man who ate the sun. What could she do? And for the first time she noticed that misting over parts of the picture were small spiders' webs, and sitting between the print and the glass—just above the little man's forehead—was a white cocoon. Moretti, she realised, must never look at the picture of which he was so proud. There must be much else, she realised, that he only looked at very occasionally.

From the kitchen she could hear the caterers working; from the dining room came the sharp, dry sounds of a dinner party—glass and china and brittle laughter. She could see no one. No one could see her. She ran her fingers up over the large heads of the hand-forged Moroccan nails, reached up, took down the elephant, and lifted up its trunk.

51

Nick Loukakis looked down at the near-empty bottle of Penfolds Bin 128.

"Is it good?" he asked.

"I don't think I'd be drinking it if it wasn't," said Diana.

Next to the Penfolds Bin 128 was an empty bottle of Coriole Redstone. He realised he hadn't noticed that she drank every night now, at least a bottle, sometimes, like tonight, more. Perhaps it was because she never seemed drunk, never moved unsteadily, or seemed tiddly in any way. Only ever more angry. Her anger was absolute.

She never said they ought to split. He knew that final decision would be his alone. He felt like the navigator of a burning ship. At some point he would have to admit the fight was unequal, impossible. He would have to say,

"There's nothing left, it's over, this is what we must do, this is how we do it."

But not yet. He still hoped—but for what?

"You're so fucking petty," Diana said, "you know that, do you? Just how petty you are?"

It was true. Sometimes he was petty. It was also untrue. Sometimes he was unable to say anything in a way that to her didn't sound petty. They had lost a way of talking and being. What remained was flint striking steel. Everything rasped, everything hurt, everything caught fire. They lay in bed, him saying, "Please don't hate me, Diana, please don't hate me," over and over.

But she would hate him, she had to hate him, she did hate him. It was the measure of her grief and her pain; it was her right and her only hope of redemption, it was her pride and her dignity that he had always admired in her now determined and needing to smash to pieces this last beautiful thing, to make him understand it was over so that he would finally say,

"It's over, this is what we must do, this is how we do it."

Neither understood this. Both knew it perfectly. Both wanted it to end. Both knew they had to wait, and like wild animals in a trap not of their making, they savaged each other, weakened and maimed the other, waiting, waiting, waiting.

Their two sons had bickered and fought all day and nothing Nick Loukakis said seemed able to end it. Before dinner, he brought them both together, held each of them by the wrist and was about to say one more pointless thing, when he felt himself unable to go on. He realised in their pettiness, their hate, their constant backbiting and sniping over the smallest insults, that their sons, who loved each other, were but imitating Diana and him, and that this was now all that he gave his children.

He had hoped love would be enough. He wanted to tell his two sons this. That this was what he had hoped for. But it wasn't enough. It had never been enough.

"Please don't cry, Daddy," said Nick Loukakis's younger son. "It's not worth crying over."

52

As the Doll walked, her mind steadied. Unable to flag a taxi and unwilling to use her stolen phone to call one after she had left Moretti's, she had caught the last ferry back to town. She hung back after disembarking at Circular Quay, loitering on the jetty until it was empty, walking to its edge as if admiring the harbour views of a night. Reaching down, she took out her own phone and switched it on.

The phone told her she had twenty-three missed calls. Thirty-six text messages. That the memory was full. She didn't even bother scrolling through the call numbers and messages. She flipped the phone shut, hid it in the cup of her hand, and squatted by the edge of the jetty as though she were looking at something in the dark, littered water below. And then she let the phone slip out of her hand and into the harbour, to sink to where so many other secrets of Sydney lie hidden. She stood up and, for the second time that day, started heading by foot up into the airless city.

She was making for the Retro Hotel at the top end of Pitt Street. She knew nothing about the hotel, had only seen its shattered Perspex sign many times when riding in taxis, forever broken and never repaired. She wanted to stay there and not the hotel Wilder had booked, because for no good reason she felt safer in a dive in the CBD than in Double Bay. It wasn't the plan, but maybe, reasoned the Doll, it was better. She would ring Wilder sometime the next day and arrange to pick up her money.

So far, she consoled herself, there had only been some very grainy security camera footage, a few old and blurry happy snaps from a few years ago, and a crappy video of her dancing. None of the images looked much like the Doll in life even when they had been taken, and now with Wilder's haircut she felt it would be difficult for anyone to recognise her at all. But she had eyes and ears only for those who might recognise her, people who might want to turn her in, police who might want to shoot her. And so she avoided people's eyes, walked quickly and kept her head down.

Yet everywhere the Doll looked, there was the Doll. She was in snatches of conversation overheard in the street, as a statuesque woman leaving a suits' bar chirruped into the choking night air, "I haven't had the time to follow this pole dancing story properly at all." The Doll turned sideways as the woman brushed past her, and the smell of her perfume and the greasy stench of some effluvia from a nearby restaurant kitchen followed in her wake, a smell of hot fat and dirty dishwater and Chanel No 5. "I just hope they get her before she gets us."

The city, which she had formerly felt and known only as freedom, now seemed to be closing in all around her—the heat, the infernal traffic, the police sirens, the rumble and scream of building works that never seemed to stop—why was it that everything now appeared to her to be so oppressive and full of foreboding?

She looked up and saw a man wearily packing up his convenience store for the evening, taking in the wire-caged newspaper banners that yelled TERRORIST CELLS and TERRORIST LOVERS and IS SYDNEY READY FOR THE WORST? Seeing her looking at him, he rasped a hello. Then his gaze became a stare.

"There's something about your face," he said. "Can't place it. Is it . . . you're on television or something, right? You're famous. I'm so sorry, I just can't place it—is it *Big Brother?*"

"I wish," said the Doll, smiled, and walked on.

Nothing was as it had been. Martin Place, where once she had happily browsed fine designer shops, now appeared to her as empty and strange as the ruins of an ancient city that somewhere, sometime long ago, stopped making sense. For a moment she stood surrounded by colourful bunting and beautiful images that communicated nothing. Dolce & Gabbana. Louis Vuitton. What did any of it mean? On vertical banners pushing a designer label, models, no more than kids, were reproduced with their strange unfocused gaze, as if they had witnessed a massacre or horror they still could not comprehend. Versace. Gucci. Armani. The Doll had the fleeting sense she was looking at the remnants of some great lost civilisation that had become indecipherable, like the temples at Angkor Wat that Wilder had once visited and shown her photos of, extraordinary places, magnificent buildings, beautiful objects, wonderful art that only had purpose and meaning as long as everyone agreed it had purpose and meaning.

And then the sense was gone: it was once more a street at night, nothing other than a place to scurry through and leave, as she resumed her journey to the Retro Hotel.

53

Richard Cody sat in front of the monitor in the *Undercurrent* editing suite, a broom closet of a room with an oversized air con duct that blew an unpleasant smelling draught onto his aching head. It was so very late. Todd Birchall, the young editor, spooled back and forth. It was hopeless, thought Richard Cody. He lacked a skewer to run all the titbits of interviews together. He had less than twenty-four hours to get his special up on the lap dancing terrorist and he had nothing that made this a story.

Todd Birchall was regarded as a hot cutter. He was unfazed by the way connections had to be created, leaps made with cuts that perhaps there wasn't always a complete story to justify. "WHATEVER IT TAKES", as the motto inscribed on his baseball cap had it—the cap which, no matter the weather or situation, was always on Todd Birchall's head. But even Todd Birchall was at a loss what to do. He clacked his tongue stud against his front teeth.

"Maybe it's like maybe," he said, "just a fucking fuckup." As he thought on the problem, Richard Cody methodically tore an envelope to pieces. "I mean, she sleeps with a guy," Todd Birchall continued, "and then gets blamed for everything from the Twin Towers to Kylie's cancer. It's weird. I mean, why would someone like her want to be a mass murderer?"

Todd Birchall was starting to annoy Richard Cody. After

all, he did not say to himself, 'Given there is no real evidence this woman has ever done anything wrong, I will create an image of her as a monster.' No, because that would have been a disgraceful act of cynicism, and no true cynic can afford to be anything other than genuine in his opinions. Rather, Richard Cody began imagining an adult woman somehow so traumatised that she was incapable of feeling, a woman without empathy who could easily commit the most callous acts of cruelty. He felt quite overcome with fear at the thought of a monstrous woman out there, a human without emotion, capable of killing hundreds of people. But Todd Birchall's question remained: *why?*

And again, in his irritating way, Todd Birchall tapped his tongue stud on his front teeth, as though he expected Richard Cody to make something up there and then. Richard Cody was affronted. Todd Birchall, perhaps sensing an unease in the cutting room, went out to find some beer.

Richard Cody despised journalists who made things up. He hated the phrase "don't let the facts get in the way of a good story", for the art of journalism—and Richard Cody, who had won several Walkley awards and whose hobby as recently featured in a lead article in the *Women's Weekly* was watercolour landscape painting, firmly believed that in its highest incarnation journalism was most certainly an art— was to use the truths you could discover to tell the story you believed to matter.

And so, when he got on the phone and tracked down Ray Ettslinger at a Byron Bay conference on the parapsychological aspects of modern corporate management, Richard Cody was keen to hear Ray Ettslinger's answer to his question whether such a grotesque absence of emotion could fit with a profile of a terrorist bomber.

Ray Ettslinger paused because he was drunk, looked out through the open walls of the restaurant in which he sat, past some Aboriginal beggars to the beautiful Australian sea beyond and, before agreeing, put his hand over the mouthpiece of his sticky-taped Motorola, and to the other academics at the table, hissed:

"Media."

He rolled his googly eyes as though this were a wearying aspect of his daily life, rather than the only exciting prospect in his world at that moment.

Ray Ettslinger was a psychologist Richard Cody had last used for a story on poltergeists in the Sydney Opera House. Richard Cody loved using Ray Ettslinger: he was such wonderful talent. He had the biggest nose Richard Cody had ever seen, wild eyes, and a manner at once slightly pompous and completely authoritative. He took direction well, and never minded how Richard Cody cut him. Ettslinger *understood*.

In Byron Bay, Ray Ettslinger got up from the table and walked outside. He was, he told the Motorola, tired. He drearily complained about his back, his shoulder, his bowels and his students. But when Richard Cody mentioned the pole dancing terrorist, Ray Ettslinger was like a hard drive booting up. Richard Cody felt he could almost hear the low whirring of magnetic disks, of fans cooling Intel chips now processing the necessary information to arrive at the correct result.

Ray Ettslinger's Centre for Excellence in Executive Culture at UTS's western Sydney campus was not drawing the same student numbers as it had a few years earlier. He had just finished with his third wife and hadn't been offered a promotion since he turned down a chair at the University of Tasmania, because, he had joked to friends, he could never decide whether the position was promotion or transportation. His two ex-wives were back into him for more alimony, and his once profitable sideline in corporate management consultancy was no longer the lucrative joke it had for so long been. He needed money and he understood that to gain money he needed attention. He had written a well-received paper on "Cognitive Dissonance and the Suicide Bomber" for a conference in Stuttgart and was angling for a newly established chair in terrorist studies at the Australian Defence Force Academy. A pole dancing terrorist?

"Of course," said Ray Ettslinger. "It all fits."

And indeed it did.

Much as his fellow academics derided the commercial media, Ray Ettslinger knew it counted far more than any of them dared admit. And here was *Undercurrent* offering him a small but significant and, Ettslinger suspected, ongoing part in a national drama. It was irresistible.

"Predictable," said Ray Ettslinger, his tone now as bright as a new LCD monitor. "Who can really say what makes anyone want to blow themselves up other than some terrible emotional trauma?"

"How so, Ray?" asked Richard Cody. "She just seems, well . . . ordinary."

"Family?" asked Ray Ettslinger.

"Divorced. Also ordinary. Mother dead, car crash. No criminal records."

"Interview the father," commanded Ray Ettslinger. "And

then film me viewing the tape of the interview, commenting. Either he hates her, or is estranged from her—what better explanation for her terrorist sympathies?"

"A fuckup at the edges," said Richard Cody, beginning to tune in to Ray Ettslinger's thinking, which wasn't so difficult, given that he was merely developing an idea Richard Cody had suggested in the first place.

"Islamist ideology is irresistible for such a profile," continued Ray Ettslinger, who knew almost nothing about Islam. "It offers both a secure identity and the mechanism for revenge. Alternatively, her father loves her and dotes on her and she's spoilt—the Patty Hearst syndrome." Ray Ettslinger knew almost nothing about Patty Hearst either.

"An angry fuckup at the edges," said Richard Cody.

"Right," said Ettslinger. "Either way, she's a fuckup. Either way, I can make it work for us."

Richard Cody loved the "us". Ray was such a team player. And on and on Ray Ettslinger went, giving Richard Cody all he needed. And because nothing excites people more than sharing an aim, no matter what that aim may be, both were now far more animated. They agreed a time for the interview the following day.

"It's like Sudoku," said Ray Ettslinger before hanging up. "You just have to make the numbers fit."

Todd Birchall returned with a six-pack of Tooheys New. His cap was off.

"It's still so fucken hot out there," he sighed, offering Richard Cody a stubby.

Uncharacteristically, Richard Cody accepted, though he still wondered who else might have touched that bottle and what bacteria lurked on its seemingly clean surface. But he felt he now had cause to celebrate—a story, a program, a comeback. He would wash his hands later.

54

The red Perspex sign, partly shattered, revealed the neon tube that illuminated the wording:

THE

RE RO

HOTEL

The Doll followed a small monsoon of Asian tourists pouring into the hotel's lobby, the eye of their storm a woman with a long stick topped with a plastic sunflower. When the Doll finally reached the desk and handed over Wilder's credit card, the receptionist never even looked up at her face.

"Have a nice day," she said to the desk, handing back the card and with it the room key.

The Doll squeezed into an old lift jammed with more Asians. As it shuddered upwards, their heads rolled below her like industrial ball bearings.

In her tiny room the Doll undressed and took two steps across the fire retardant carpet—so brittle and dry it felt like shreds of melted plastic—to the bathroom. She stepped into the acrylic bath, its anti-skid dots black with grime, and with the miserly biscuit of hotel soap only partly succeeded in washing off the stench of the evening.

After, she lay down on the bed. She tried to ignore the

sharp odour of dry-cleaning chemicals; the cheap pilled nylon sheets that made her feel as if she were lying on hot glasspaper; the taut foam pillow on which her head rolled back and forth, up and down like a karaoke ball; she tried to calm herself by breathing deeply and slowly, but the air in the stuffy hotel room was sticky despite the air con and it was hard to breathe.

Above all else the Doll tried to pretend that what had happened hadn't happened, that here she was safe. She tried to imagine she still lived in the Australia where such things didn't happen. But as she lay in that wretched hotel room in the lucky country, the Doll was finding it ever harder to breathe.

She thought about Moretti's story of the Dutch soldiers who betrayed the soon-to-be-dead of Srebrenica. And it seemed to the Doll that the Dutch soldiers meekly handing over their weapons were the same people as the politicians and the security forces and the journalists, who, instead of protecting people, also betrayed them.

And then she was gasping for air. She stood up and went over to the window, but it could not be opened. As she stood there, trying to calm her breathing, she saw herself reflected in the window glass and experienced a terrible revelation. Wasn't she, after all, the same? Hadn't she that very morning ignored the beggar with the raw face? And only a few hours ago had she not rushed past an old woman being tormented by kids?

To her horror she saw that, as she had never cared or wondered or questioned, nor now would anyone care or wonder or question the stories they heard about her. As she had helped no one, how could she now expect anyone to help her? And as she had in a chorus condemned others, how could she be surprised that others in a chorus were now condemning her?

And she saw that all the people following the story of "the pole dancing terrorist" were simply behaving as she had. When they were frightened by her story, had not she felt similarly frightened? And as countless others would now fall asleep in their lounge rooms after watching her fate unravel on tv thinking little other than that it was about something vaguely bad and opposing it was something vaguely good—national values, national lifestyle, national security—hadn't she also dozed off at the end of a hundred other news stories thinking nothing?—nothing!

The Doll dropped two Temazepams, lay back on the glass-paper sheets and tried to imagine that she was not there and that it was all good. But it was not all good. As the drug took hold, she felt an immense weight build up behind her eyes as if sleep were imminent, but no sleep came.

Around her was gathering the most terrifying blackness through which she knew she must now travel alone, but it was not possible to move, it was ever more difficult to breathe, and in her heart a voice she had hoped to forget once more sounded. *You killed Fung!* it said. *You killed Fung! You killed Fung!* And in this way the night bore on, and even her truest friend, Temazepam, could no longer help.

55

Frank Moretti wanted to be part of life, to be part of Sydney, the two things being indistinguishable for him. With money, with lies, with grovelling, with threats, with bribes, with cheating, with charm, with determination and with spirit he would succeed; he had, and he would.

But he felt nauseous and the room suddenly seemed terribly overheated. He could feel sweat breaking out all over him. And accompanying these physical feelings was a sudden sense of shame and regret that only made him angrier, and his anger only made him sicker. Yet why did he now feel so fearful, so guilty?

Though he had tried all day, he could not stop looking at the newspaper. The photographs had not changed. It was him, Tariq al-Hakim, the programmer whom he had lately been using, twice to bring heroin out of Pakistan, once, more profitably, carrying coke from Kuala Lumpur; and with him, amazingly, that woman, the stripper Krystal. It was ludicrous, of course, or perhaps it wasn't. It was hard to say. What was clear to him, though, was that it was only a matter of time now before the authorities came to him, only a short time before they went through him, looking at his accounts, delving deeper, and then it would all be over. They would work it out soon enough, he knew they would, find out who he really was and what he really did.

After all, it was Tariq al-Hakim, with ideas far above his lowly station, who had set up his meeting with Lee Moon, for whom, presumably, he had also done some mule work. And it was Lee Moon's idea that Frank Moretti deal with the Sydney port part of his new operation, smuggling men into Australia in shipping containers, for Frank Moretti's contacts there, who had helped him in the past with his other imports, were of the first order: reliable and trustworthy.

"Women we do other way," Lee Moon had smiled. Frank Moretti knew well enough that meant bringing them in on educational visas to work in his chicken coops, which Lee Moon graciously invited Frank Moretti to make use of as his guest.

The deal was done, and Tariq al-Hakim had been meant to collect the cargo that morning, but all day had passed and most of the evening and Moretti had heard nothing. Worried, he once more tried to call him.

56

Nick Loukakis did not recognise the ring tone pulsing out from the car boot as Tupac Shakur's "Thugs Get Lonely Too". But even in the dim torchlight, clothes stretched taut by the body beginning to bloat and slow-moving maggots covering the temple in a twisting Turk's-head knot, he knew who the putrid corpse had once been. He looked at his watch. It was ten-thirty at night and everything felt too late.

Earlier in the evening, after talking to his sons, he had gone out for a drive. Every station on the car radio seemed full of the terrorist scare. There were other recurrent items— some deaths of old people blamed on the heatwave; a fresh outbreak of race rioting in the southwest suburbs between white supremacists and Lebanese gangs. But mostly it was about the terrorist threat: where they might strike—the airport, train stations, beaches, the Bridge or the centre of the city—and how they were going to do it. There was a strong sentiment playing out over several stations that it would be a dirty nuclear bomb that would cover the centre of Sydney in radioactive fallout. He switched to a music channel and pondered the tv news report he had seen a few hours before.

It was only then that he had seen the faces of the terrorists—until then he hadn't really taken much notice of the terrorist scare. But he knew straight away who they were. He was Tariq al-Hakim, a mule Nick Loukakis had tracked for a few weeks the year before, hoping he might lead them to Lee Moon's syndicate. Instead, all they came up with was a small-time dealer called Frank Moretti, who seemed to run a few different rackets, but none so stupidly that there was ever enough to nail him.

She, on the other hand, he knew as one of Wilder's friends, Gina Davies, a pole dancer. He had even once given her a lift back from Wilder's to her home.

At first he had been shocked—not that both a suspect and a friend of a friend might be terrorists, but that he hadn't twigged to it. He felt dumb as shit. How the hell hadn't he worked it out himself? He knew Tariq al-Hakim had been to both Pakistan and Malaysia several times, but he had always thought it was simply in order to bring back drugs. No doubt ASIO and the Feds and everyone else knew a whole lot more than a lowly drug squad detective sergeant could be expected to know, but he was amazed he hadn't picked up on any of it, and pissed off that no one had told him.

Nick Loukakis drove a long way away from Panania, but the night traffic was light and he made it to Darlinghurst in half an hour. He was retreating, as he always retreated, into his work.

He parked half a block away from the Doll's apartment building, then sat in his car for a while, engine idling, air con running, mind racing.

"Interface with the cosmos," said the car radio. "Nokia. Not a phone. A revolution."

Nick Loukakis switched the engine off, and got out of his Ford Territory. He wandered around the building in which the Doll lived. He was remembering when he'd first met her, how ordinary she had seemed to him, when walking past an alley he caught the odour of something very bad. His instinct in this, as it was whenever anything stank, was to seek to discover the cause of the stench.

But now, staring at Tariq al-Hakim's corpse, thinking back on what he knew about Gina Davies and all that he knew about Tariq al-Hakim, it didn't add up. It just didn't add up.

He would need to call homicide. But he wouldn't tell them everything. Not yet. First, he would drop in on Frank Moretti, about whom he knew one other odd fact that now seemed strangely significant: once a week Gina Davies used to go to his home and strip for him.

57

It was no mystery to Frank Moretti why he had taken up his small part as a subcontractor in people-smuggling. It wasn't "My humanitarian hobby", as he privately joked to himself, and sometimes even tried to believe, if only a little.

No; it was because his part was profitable. Easy and highly profitable: a few phone calls, some kickbacks, a hired people-mover and a man—Tariq al-Hakim—to let them out and take them away and deliver them.

With the exception of the women he paid for, Moretti rarely found human beings beautiful, but he was pleasantly surprised how trading in them could be so lucrative. Today another container had arrived, this time all the way from Shanghai, with its load of canned Albanian tomato paste— and twelve men. Why Albanian tomato paste would be coming out of Shanghai was a mystery to Moretti; it had been explained to him as old trading ties.

No wonder he felt unwell. What a night! First the stripper crazily calling, wanting God knows what, then after his dinner guests had thankfully gone and he was about to ring Tariq al-Hakim for the hundredth time, the doorbell rang.

A wave of fear and guilt broke over Moretti when he answered the door to a cop asking too many questions about the stripper. 'And my crime?' Moretti suddenly thought, 'what is it, and how is it different from what so many of my neighbours do for their money? After all,' he argued with himself, 'how is what I do poles apart from what we are all told to do every day?'

Then he remembered how Lee Moon had smiled over his tumbler of Johnnie Walker Blue Label the day they had met, and told him how free trade agreements lied, how in truth some things weren't exactly permitted, and some products were even officially disapproved of, but it was tacitly understood they too were part of the deal. Lee Moon was a pleasant-looking man who was always beaming, and reminded Frank Moretti of the Dalai Lama in an expensive dark suit.

"Yes, yes!" said Lee Moon, and his smile opened his face up further into what seemed delighted astonishment. "Organs of vanished backpackers, virginity of Mai Chai children—yes, yes; Frank, you know, yesterday I was offered collagen harvested from the skin of executed Chinese convicts to distribute here in Australia. Yes, yes! Is remarkable!"

And indeed it was. Lee Moon laughed. How funny it all seemed! Frank Moretti laughed.

"You know, Frank," continued Lee Moon, "what matters is not all these regulations—do this, can't do that—no," and here he held up a finger and leant forward. "No, it's the spirit of free trade, of this great globalised world, that is what matters. Yes, yes. The spirit of the age: buy and sell, Frank; everything exists to buy and sell. Even us! Yes, yes."

Frank Moretti laughed. Lee Moon laughed.

"Us!" said Lee Moon, raising his whisky.

"Us!" said Frank Moretti, raising his whisky.

And Frank Moretti had the momentary sensation of being strangely joined in this toast not just to Lee Moon, but to something vast and cruel that loomed over them both like a cold shadow of this world. He involuntarily shivered, but he knew this bad feeling would quickly pass, that more money would soon flow, and that before long he would forget this unsettling sensation. He drained his tumbler and with a smile shook Lee Moon's hand.

Looking back, thought Frank Moretti, what Lee Moon had said was true. That we exist to be bought and sold. That our natural laws, our destiny, our biology, amount to our capacity to cut a deal. That the world is a bazaar. And all this Moretti felt he had signed up to and lived in accordance with.

Yet worried as he was about his own situation when the cop came calling, Moretti found himself lying when the cop asked him about the stripper—not to protect himself, but to protect her, the crazy stripper—so strangely had he lied to try to save her. He said she hadn't been there for a month.

The cop had a Greek name and was smart enough to be friendly, and Moretti, rather than shut the door on him and call his lawyer, felt it wiser to appear helpful. It was, in any case, his way with authority, his Sydney way: to smile, help, offer hospitality and friendship.

And so when the Greek cop said yes to a late-night drink, they had one, then another, and the single malts led to a fine grappa and that in turn led to Moretti—when complimented on his art—growing a little proud and unable to resist taking the cop on a quick tour of the house and its more interesting treasures. And so—and not without a collector's desire to impress with their more exotic collections—he had the Greek cop open up the hallway cabinet to show him what was gathered there. He had already started in on the Beretta story when the cop looked down at him with a curious expression.

"It's missing," said the Greek cop.

Though shocked, Moretti recovered quickly, realising his obvious astonishment was an asset in proving his own innocence. He agreed with the Greek cop that it must have been an inside job—a tradesman, a waitress, one of several nurses who attended to him daily—but there were so many, he continued, it was hard to remember all their names. But when asked directly, he replied that it couldn't have been the stripper, for she had not been there for so long. It was such a stupid lie, and yet he persisted with it.

"And besides," said Moretti, "she has no idea what's in the cabinet, far less where the key's hidden."

He agreed with the Greek cop it was a mystery, such a strange mystery, and he knew the Greek cop didn't believe a word he said, and yet he hadn't betrayed her. It was inexplicable.

"Nobody knows what moves anybody," the Greek cop tried one last time as he was about to go. "You sure it couldn't be her?"

After the Greek cop left, Moretti realised that had he been taken into custody and grilled, perhaps he might have confessed what he had done, told them about all his many businesses—the forgeries of Aboriginal paintings and company memoranda, the phoney antiques, the smuggling of drugs and people—and even how he had done it; but it would have been the explanations as to *why* that would be impossible to give and, Moretti felt, impossibly annoying.

How could Moretti tell the cop that he had divined in the stripper the same passions that had led him to this house, these possessions, and this life of deception? For he too, after all, was what he had never told her: not rich, not from the eastern suburbs or the north shore, not from an established family of Italian vintners, but just another westie on the make, a westie who reinvented himself after his car smash with a new name for his new body and a desperate desire to rise. He had always hated wogs, and it seemed right to take on a wog name for the hideous mess of flesh he had been left to live in.

He should have told the cop all he knew about her and admitted it must have been she who had taken the gun. But how could he say she was him before his smash, and he couldn't betray her? He had agreed when Lee Moon said everything exists to buy and sell. But what if it wasn't true? What then?

He put on a CD of Dinu Lipatti's recordings of Chopin's Nocturnes in an attempt to calm himself, to remind himself once more of beauty and art. Once it began, he spun his wheelchair and was about to head over to the sideboard on which the phone sat, to call—but he had the oddest sensation. Everything felt unexpectedly heavy, and every movement became the most extraordinary feat.

Something was creeping over his body, at the same time as something else was emptying out of it. What was it tingling up and down his arm, numbing his fingers as he tried to find the controls of his wheelchair? Who was it pushing in his ribs? Who was it crushing his chest? Sitting on his lungs? Who was it tightening their fingers around his neck, pushing his tongue back, choking him?

"No! No! No!" he suddenly cried, terribly, terribly afraid. He began to panic, realising he must do something, anything. But all his concentrated effort to move only resulted in a rocking of his torso that grew ever more pronounced until he came so far forward that, losing his balance, he was unable to throw himself back.

He toppled out of his wheelchair onto a Renaissance chair with ivory inlay. But the fine pinpricks all over the chair, similar to those in much of his other antique furniture, were not some unusual finish but borer holes, so much dust waiting to be released from the mirage of taste in which it was imprisoned. One leg, rotten with woodworm, snapped as Moretti's small, heavy body pitched onto the chair seat. He slid sideways and fell to the floor, the side of his head smashing heavily and, the coroner would later determine, fatally, on the bottom shelf of a bookcase, and Moretti would never be conscious of rising in this world again.

All that could be heard in the house was the sound of felt-covered hammers attacking wires strained within a wooden box to an almost unbearable tension, as Chopin's piano notes continued playing over Moretti's dead body.

58

Richard Cody sat in his home study late that night, staring at the PC on which he had Googled his own name. His Vaucluse house had about it the sumptuous hush of truly large and rich homes. He could have been in a space station, with only the whispered assent of orderly machines for company, so remote it felt from life. On the screen there were several million entries. It should have been enough—his home, such calibrated celebrity, this comeback and its promise—but the more he rose, the more his spirits seemed to sink, and the greater his success the worse he felt.

He had introduced his famous and powerful friends to Australia's living rooms, preached about Australian wisdom and espoused Australian goodness and embodied Australian decency, led Australia keening at Australian disasters and Australia cheering at Australian sporting success, hosted telethons and Christmas carol specials, to say nothing of the several prominent Australian charities of which he was patron. But there was no peace at all. It was not enough, it had never been enough, and what was, what might be, he did not wish to know.

With his second wife Richard Cody had as perfect a marriage as it was possible to have with a woman he no longer shared anything with other than large debts, social ambitions and an adult son who worked in a hairdresser's—how did one talk about *that* at a dinner party?

There was, Richard Cody sensed, something about this world that would not allow him to do other than hurt. For a time he rued it, for a time he revelled in it; now, he simply accepted it as his skill for which he was rewarded. There was no peace, that was all. He wished he were able to talk with his son.

The image that came to him at such times was a childhood memory of a fallen seagull jerking in the sand. He had been at the beach, throwing stones at circling seagulls and with a lucky shot felled one. His heart rejoiced as the bird dropped out of the sky like a rock, then he watched with horror as the other birds dived on its still-writhing body and tore it to bloody rags.

"No peace, no peace at all," he muttered over and over to himself as he stood over the lower bathroom's sink and washed and washed his hands clean of the keyboard. Sometimes a man's life turns into a cancer, thought Richard Cody, but no one knows that he fears the cancer is him.

At such times he felt he had somehow transformed into that fallen seagull writhing before his eyes. There had been a woman he never slept with—she died in the mist of a Manhattan winter years ago—while he continued living in the bright light of Sydney. Each—her death, his life—seemed to him pointless. Ambitions, he had concluded, were largely pathetic fevers. He feared his greatest longing was for oblivion. How he wished to talk with his son.

He turned off the tap and, to avoid contamination from the towel, stood in the dark shaking his hands dry.

59

In the room next door a phone rang and would not stop ringing. The Doll, still unable to sleep, switched on a small Panasonic television that sat in a chipped woodgrain Laminex cupboard. A cable station was showing the perfectly preserved body of a three-thousand-year-old woman. The body had recently been found in a peat bog in Sweden. The fossil woman had been drowned, weighed down with stones tied to a noose around her neck. Her head had been shaved. A ritual death, a German expert said, for some crime that no one could now know.

Still the phone next door rang, and still no one answered.

As the Doll watched the documentary, she felt other women would have been mixed up with it—she could see all the women together, telling tales and getting high and mighty and het up—because they were scared too; scared that if they didn't accuse someone else, someone else might accuse them. There would have been some kind of crime, of course there would, just like she was called a terrorist now, and maybe back then she'd have been called a witch, but it was all untrue.

She could almost hear them—talking like they did in the club's changeroom, talking like they did on the talkback, talking about how wrong and how bad that woman had been even as she was drowning. And the worst thing was that the Doll knew she would have been one of those accusing women. She was, after all, a survivor and had done a lot of things to get by; she knew she was capable of far worse if forced.

She changed stations. A news channel was running a story on her by a smiling woman journalist with a vaguely American accent. For the first time she heard her name being used, following on, she guessed, from Richard Cody's story earlier in the evening. They also had several recent photos of her. And at that moment she felt sick: she didn't want to be the terrorist on cable; didn't want to be another bog woman drowning in some shitty swamp; didn't want to be the French woman she had seen in the book in Moretti's library with women laughing at her as they shaved her head.

But maybe, thought the Doll as she lay on her miserable hotel bed watching the tv, there was some need people had to hurt others, some horrible need, that hurting one woman in some way might make others feel safe and good and happy, like the smiling French women, like the smiling woman journalist.

And maybe she had to accept that she should be hurt, that maybe these things happen for the common good?

She turned the television off.

No, she thought, she couldn't accept that she should be hurt, she couldn't just give in and give up. She didn't feel hungry, but it mattered that she kept going. She ate a small pack of cashews and a Chokito bar from the bar fridge and washed it down with a Stoli mini mixed with tonic. And though at first her throat and stomach resisted, the nuts and chocolate tasted so very good, better than they should, and her body calmed with even such poor food as this, and the Doll realised how hungry and exhausted she truly was.

At some point long after, she must have drifted into a wretched, skipping sleep. She was vaguely aware of car horns and sirens wailing far below; of cries and shouting, and sometimes of people running.

Her dreams were claustrophobic, she was suffocating, images flickered back and forth in her mind ever more rapidly: the French woman unable to pull her head away from the open scissors; the bog woman screaming into filthy water; flies crawling from between Tariq's dead lips . . .

Some force from outside continued to rumble all the way into her room, and she found it harder than ever to breathe, and still a phone kept ringing and what was its message? What was it?

60

Though he slept well and hated being woken in the night, no news could have been more welcome to Richard Cody than the phone call that woke him shortly before midnight.

"I know it's late but I wanted you to be the first of our media friends to hear," said Siv Harmsen.

Richard Cody got up, and went out to the stairway landing.

"We've found Tariq al-Hakim," said Siv Harmsen. "Neat as a felafel in a roll, dead and stuffed into a car boot."

"My God," said Richard Cody, not because he was shocked, but because there was significance to this news and to the call that in his sleepy state he didn't fully understand,

and which he needed to draw out of Siv Harmsen. "Any leads?"

"There's a long way to go with the homicide investigation." A short silence followed. "You know how it is." Richard Cody waited. The air con sounded like the gentlest rain. "Completely off the record . . ." said Siv Harmsen finally. "Look, we share an understanding, don't we, Richard?"

"Completely," echoed Richard Cody.

"Well," said Siv Harmsen, "they're taking seriously the idea that it might have been another terrorist."

"That doesn't make sense, though," said Richard Cody. "Why would a terrorist kill a terrorist?"

"Well, it's kind of obvious, isn't it?" said Siv Harmsen. "He'd become too public, too well known, and therefore a liability. These people are ruthless, even with their own. What's that phrase I heard you use this morning on tv?—'the unknown terrorist'. It's them, the unknown ones, that can get away with the bombings. They're the ones to fear."

Rather than presenting a problem, the death of Tariq al-Hakim solved one of Richard Cody's key dilemmas. Jerry Mendes had gone cold on the Bonnie and Clyde title. As no one had yet come up with anything better, the special had only been promoted generally as "a chilling exposé about home-grown terrorism here in Australia". Jerry Mendes would, he knew, now agree to the special being focused on Gina Davies. And Richard Cody felt he had a new and perhaps vital element in his story. For what does a Black Widow do but slay her partner?

Richard Cody thanked his ASIO contact for having personally phoned, and was about to hang up, but Siv Harmsen was oddly talkative for such a late call.

"All this garbage about truth being suppressed with these new terrorism laws," Siv Harmsen went on, "you know *we* want the public to know certain things. And that's not me saying that, Richard. That's people much higher up than me."

"I'm glad," said Richard Cody. "We all need to pull together at times like this."

"Dead right," said Siv Harmsen. "You get it, you see, Richard. But a lot of people don't. And we need them to. My bosses like your boss, Richard," he added. "My bosses want us to help Mr Frith and you all we can."

As his wife grumbled at the disturbance so late at night, Richard Cody lay back on his pillow, feeling vaguely triumphant. Now his special had just about everything. He could even see the title that had come to him after Siv Harmsen's call. It would dramatically top and tail the ad breaks, backed by a deep voice announcing his comeback:

"*THE UNKNOWN TERRORIST* returns after this break."

It was enough. It had to be. How he wished he could hold his son. Nobody knows what moves anybody.

TUESDAY

61

WILDER WAS STILL DREAMING when she was lifted off the bed by the explosion. The sensation of once more flying, something she had not known in her dreams for a very long time, was so intense and pleasurable that the noise of the explosion, of her bedroom door slamming open, of men racing into her room, of men yelling, was for a fraction of a second absorbed into her dream before she was taken into their nightmare.

Not until other sensations took hold—her body starting to smart from the shoes and books she had landed on—did she slowly come to the awareness that somebody was yelling but the sounds seemed to be reaching her from far away. She knew not a next thing, but many things all happening together: her still-dark bedroom, her still-asleep mind, filling with ever more men clad in black, wearing military helmets and goggles and brandishing assault rifles, crashing through her home, and at that moment she felt their fear and their hair-trigger aggression as a complete letting go.

"Christ, she's pissing herself," she heard one man say.

Later that day she would tell the Doll,

"I was so scared, just so fucking scared. I thought they were the terrorists come to kidnap me, that's what I thought. They didn't look like soldiers. They didn't look like armed police or security guys. They looked like . . . like, unbelievable, really, Gina, I couldn't believe them, they were out of *Star Wars*, aliens, they were all in black, but their suits had special pockets and bumps and gadgets and what with their helmets and goggles they looked kind of like amphibious monsters, like killer toads crawled out of the sewers to kill us all, that's what I felt. I mean, they were so weird. They looked like death, Gina, like what happens when you die, and I just thought, I'm going to die."

And then the Doll could hear her crying some more, before gathering herself and going on.

"What I remember isn't the noise or even them, but the smell, that smell of animals terrified and excited all at once, just like kids get sometimes. And I was so fucking frightened I couldn't move, not even when they were ordering me to get up. I thought they were going to kill me, and it was some trick. They were pulling my home apart—drawers, cupboards, wardrobes, Max is screaming—looking for I don't know what.

"At first I couldn't understand what they wanted, then I realised they were police, that they had some sort of warrant, but even then it wasn't clear. Maybe it was drugs or maybe a mistake, and then I realised it was you, Gina, and only you, it was all about you. I was so shit scared, I wet myself again, there on the floor, and this man in black and goggles holding a rifle to my head, not moving, I told him, I said, 'If it's Gina, you don't know what you're talking about. She's beautiful. This is just mad. You don't know her.'

"And they just said: 'Have you ever thought maybe it's you who doesn't know Gina? Have you ever thought she might be trained to never tell or breathe a word to you?'"

The Doll said nothing, only moved the phone away from her ear a little. There were many sounds all around, Wilder's voice now just one. How many sounds equal the end of something and the beginning of doubt? There were cars, drills, sirens, building and road works, signalling that undertow of terrible movement that no one can understand nor predict, but which everyone must obey. The Doll could feel her feet losing their grip beneath her, could feel other forces sweeping up her body and taking it away.

"Gina?" said Wilder. "Gina, are you still there?"

62

A little over an hour after Wilder mistook the invasion of her home for the freedom of flying, Nick Loukakis, who in consequence of rowing with his wife was sleeping on an air mattress on their living room floor, gave up on the idea of sleep. His thoughts turned to his marriage and it suddenly struck him that they could no longer go on living together and that he must leave her. It seemed not simply important, but overwhelmingly necessary, that they talk. He got up and went upstairs to their bedroom in order to speak to his wife. But she was asleep, on her side, with a slight snoring burr to her breath.

Still there was the hopeless momentum of his need to change, to no longer live the way they lived, and though all this remained important and necessary in his mind, looking at her now he had no idea what he might say.

"Are you awake?" he began softly, hoping to wake her gently; hoping even more strongly the opposite, that she would not hear him and sleep on. She slept on.

He sat back up on the side of the bed, and, having nothing better to do, continued sitting there. He thought of a documentary he had seen about a great inland sea in Russia, the life-giving forces of which had always been taken for granted, until in a few short years it shrivelled up and disappeared. And somehow their love seemed to him like that inland sea that had simply vanished, that sea that seemed inexhaustible and immortal, and after a time he again leant over and once more whispered to her, because he wanted to tell her about that sea, and once more she didn't answer.

And so he sat on the bed until the dark night changed into a grey dawn, and he was no longer sure what it was that was so important and necessary, only that whatever it was, it was urgent. Through the course of the night the story about the vanishing sea had also transformed in his mind, until now it was only a tale that really meant very little. But still he hoped that together they might find some words for all the torment he now carried within him and, he suspected, she now also bore inside her.

But the dawn passed and the day came and when they saw each other in the kitchen an hour later, coffee cups in hand, it was as strangers who have no words other than the dullest and most obvious for each other. For, Nick Loukakis dimly realised, there were no words for any of it, neither the finding of love, nor its disappearance.

63

The Doll was still dreaming when the Panasonic television came on. A woman said:

"This is your in-house wake-up call. And don't forget, this week our continental breakfast is on special."

And then she vanished and the tv flicked onto Six's breakfast program, *New Day Dawning*.

"Well," a newsreader was saying, "the lap dancing terrorist story just keeps on growing."

The television cut to another angle, the newsreader turned to face it, and the Doll began searching for the remote control. She didn't want to hear any more. If she heard nothing, it might be possible to find a way through all this. But to listen was to become part of the madness. She would not watch, she told herself, she would not listen.

But the remote control was not next to her bed, and the new world in which she was no longer the Doll but someone and something else altogether continued rolling in, inescapable, tormenting, as undeniable and all-encompassing as the heat she could feel already building outside the sealed window's glass.

"In new developments, terrorist suspect Tariq al-Hakim has been found dead in inner Sydney. Police are treating his death as homicide. Meanwhile, fellow terrorist suspect Gina Davies, known as the Black Widow, remains at large. Police have issued the following image of Gina Davies, believing she may have altered her appearance."

An image flashed up of someone who looked like Gina with a blonde bob. It was a good likeness in the way an ID photo can be a good likeness but, in essence, unrecognisable. That, the Doll guessed, was something, but it didn't feel comforting.

"Meanwhile, in a police raid in the inner city suburb of Redfern early this morning," continued the newsreader, "a woman was taken into custody to assist police with their enquiries relating to terrorism rings in Australia. The woman has subsequently been released."

The Doll knew it must have been Wilder they had picked up, but she didn't want to know. She knew that Wilder would never now be able to get her money out of her flat and to her, but she didn't want to know that either. The Doll was up out of bed, looking for the remote control on the small writing table with its broken lamp. 'It could be someone else,' she told herself as her search grew more frantic, 'some real terrorist, some crazy fucking Leb like the one in the burkah. Or an Abo, they're always picking up Abos.' And then she felt bad, because maybe they no more deserved being hassled and harassed than Wilder, and maybe they were every bit as innocent, but who cared about Abos other than people like Wilder who didn't matter anyway?

The remote control wasn't on the writing table. She should ring Wilder, thought the Doll, then cursed herself for her stupidity. How could she ring her? What if they were listening in? The Doll's search became more determined.

"Attorney-General Andrew Kingdon has rejected criticism of the raid as an abuse of new anti-terrorism powers," the newsreader went on.

The remote wasn't in either of the two tub chairs, nor under the bed with the dust balls and a popped Viagra card.

"In a prepared statement, the attorney-general described the issues the nation was addressing as being of the utmost seriousness. He went on to say that the government did not have the time or resources to be playing games."

Then the Doll saw the remote, on top of the television, lost in the shadow of the television cabinet. It had many different coloured buttons, and in her panic she could remember the meaning of none of them. There were just coloured buttons, like little lollies.

Why listen to what wasn't true? If she saw and heard no more, perhaps her life of only a few days ago might return, her griefs and sadnesses might stay hers alone, and she would once more be able to pursue her hopes and her dreams.

The Doll hit several buttons, the television made a squelching noise as it turned off, and the newsreader disappeared.

The Doll went to her hotel room door and opened it, to escape if only for a moment, to breathe, to not feel trapped. A tunnel-like corridor, brown and not overly pleasant to smell, pocked with identical doors, came into view. The Doll felt something with her toes, and looking down saw a newspaper. The headlines read:

TERRORIST DEAD
ASIO RAIDS REDFERN TERROR HQ

But it wasn't that which caught her attention. It was the date. It was 6 March.

64

The Doll left the Retro Hotel in a rush. She headed down Pitt Street at a brisk pace toward the city centre. The sun had gone, and the sky had dulled off to the colour of a filthy pavement. Yet the lack of sun brought no relief. The cloud was a brown, prickling rug that seemed only to make the humidity and the heat even more unbearable. The smog spread a gritty fug over the windless city and left a burning taste in the Doll's mouth.

Everything was still, as if waiting.

She felt wretched with tiredness; her body at sixes and sevens with itself; one moment too hot, at another too cold; somehow slimy within and itchy and dry on the outside. Her head ached, and she felt a slight queasiness that was also a giddiness. As she walked the streets, her senses seemed at once dulled and overly sensitive, so that she was slow at registering that a traffic light had changed, yet nervously jerked her head around when behind her a mobile phone rang.

After a few blocks the Doll escaped the heat into the welcome chilled bowels of air conditioned shops.

A voice said: "Today only. On special."

A voice said: "Get to the red light now."

A voice said: but what did any voice say? There were so many voices now, so much being pushed, so little worth knowing, and the Doll, once so attuned to the white noise of the city, like a smart radio receiver able to find just what band related to her, what frequency she needed to hear, no longer heard any of it.

Such was her urgency that she walked into a Sportsgirl store, quickly picked out and changed into three-quarter khaki cargo pants and a white midriff singlet, and without getting back out of them handed over two of the four hundred-dollar notes she had left, got her eighty-six dollars change, and dropped her stinking Prada dress in a garbage bin not far from the shop.

As the Doll came closer to the Town Hall train station she found herself swimming against a growing tide of rush hour commuters, and she had to turn her body sideways to make her way through them. She bought a ticket from a machine for her trip and a can of Red Bull and a pack of Impulse mints for breakfast.

Then she descended several levels to the underground platforms. There were transit cops everywhere, armed with pistols. A sniffer dog snuffled at her legs. The Doll caught the dog handler's eyes and with a look that they both understood as fear stared at him.

"Don't worry, miss," said the dog handler, pulling the leash hard to bring the dog to heel. "There's a high level security alert out for mass transit. But we've got it covered."

Men in suits continued to read financial papers. *Telco to Make Play. All Ordinaries Sink on Terrorist Fears. Banks to Report.* Women twiddled with mobiles as they once did cigarettes, nervously. Kids watched the particular nothingness of it with an odd intensity. The Doll drank the Red Bull, ate two mints and threw the rest of the pack away.

Across the railway line was a large screen running the

latest news. Something about a bombing—was it Israel? Was it Iraq? Was it here?—vanished and like perfectly drilled soldiers the green dots leapt into another pattern that now read:

EXTRA RESOURCES BEING CHANNELLED INTO SEARCH FOR TERRORISTS

She looked in her handbag. All the Zolofts were gone. There was a rush of air, the noise of brakes, and as a train bound out of the city swept into the station, the video screen disappeared behind a silver ribbon that unravelled into brightly lit cabin windows. The train doors wheezed open, a few passengers alighted, a few more, including the Doll, boarded. The train was half empty. She found a seat by herself.

The train rushed through dark tunnels. It screeched and shuddered with the terrible force of tonnes of linked iron and steel. A man sitting two rows in front was reading a newspaper. From where the Doll sat she could see the front page. She could make out that the big photo splashed across much of the page was a still from the footage of her the night she had dressed up in a veil and stripped for the American sailors. A large caption above the photo read:

OUR BLACK WIDOW

Opposite the Doll sat a young Vietnamese man with earphones that dangled like a necklace. He held a digital camera out at arm's length from himself, gazed up into it, and was snapping a photo of himself sitting in a train carriage taking a photograph of himself when the Doll's stolen phone rang.

65

She pressed the talk button but said nothing. Then she heard Wilder's voice.

"Gina," Wilder said. "Have you heard?"

The Doll said she had.

And then Wilder told the Doll how she thought she had been flying and about the raid and how they wouldn't stop trying to tell Wilder that the Doll was a terrorist.

"Gina?" said Wilder. "Gina, are you still there?"

The Doll said she was, and then Wilder told her how they had taken her to some police office in town. "We're walking down this long corridor and one of the cops says to me: 'Listen, lady, your slut mate is in shit like you can't believe. It's not soliciting or joke offences. This is terrorism we are talking about.'

"I say: 'She's not a terrorist and she's not a slut.' He just shakes his head and leads me into this big room in which seven or eight suits are sitting, waiting. At one end was this fat old silver-haired bloke.

"'I'm the presiding authority,' or something like that, he says, and then he waffles on for ages, legal stuff, I didn't really follow it. They were videoing everything, it was so creepy, like, no one gave their name, each suit just said that, 'I'm here representing ASIO,' and then the next one, 'I'm here representing ASIO,' over and over, except for one who was a Fed. I tried to be tough and pretend I thought it was all crap, but inside I felt so sick and I was shaking so bad.

"'You can't detain me if you're not going to arrest me,' I say. 'What am I charged with?'

"'ASIO has a warrant,' says the old bloke, who was sleepy and yawning a lot. 'It authorises them to detain you for up to one hundred and sixty-eight hours without charge.'

"'Since when can they hold people without charge—' I started saying, and he just said since the Australian Security Intelligence Organisation Act was amended.

"'The what?' I say.

"'The ASIO Act,' he says and he yawns again, and they all keep on talking about this Act and each time it feels like a wall collapsing on me. 'As amended in 2004 and 2005 means they can,' the old man goes on. 'And one hundred and sixty-eight hours means seven days. ASIO has the power to detain without charge if it has reason to believe that you are likely to commit an offence, or if we think you have information about terrorist activity.'

"'What are you talking about?' I say. 'What reason? You have no reason—'

"'You are a friend of Gina Davies?' says a spook, a tall guy.

"'What about my son? What's my son got to do with this?' I say. It was like an insane dream, Gina, and you know you shouldn't be there, but you are. They said Max was fine and that he was being looked after.

"'But I have to tell you, Ms Wilder,' the tall spook says, 'your son is of security interest. Young people can easily be of security interest. Overseas, for example, attacks have often been carried out by young people.'

"'He's five years old, for Christ's sake,' I say. 'What can he know?'

"The tall spook looks down at me, as though there was something so bloody obvious I had forgotten, something so simple I couldn't see it.

" 'He knows Gina Davies,' he says.

"I didn't know where to look. What could I say, Gina? 'You don't know her,' I kept saying.

"He says: 'Have you ever thought maybe it's you who doesn't know Gina? You ever thought she might be trained to never tell or breathe a word to you?'

"I say: 'Oh yeah? You think an Islamic fundamentalist is going to work at a lap dancing club? You're crazier than I think.'

"He says: 'The best cover is sometimes no cover.' And they laugh. They thought that was real good.

"He says: 'Has Gina Davies made contact with you at any time in the last two days?'

"I say: 'No.'

"He says: 'You're lying. We know you're lying because your son has confirmed that she stayed with you the night before last. And that you two slept together.'

"Everything I had said up till then just sounded like a story after that. Even what was true didn't sound true any-more, somehow everything had become a lie.

"He says: 'Has Gina Davies phoned you in the last two days?'

"I say: 'I don't have to talk to you.' I say, 'I'm allowed to say nothing. You can get fucked.'

"Then I got scared, so scared, Gina. I thought they were going to hit me. But they didn't do anything like that. One looked like a politician, bit tubby, with a baby face. He just spoke real quiet, like. He says, 'You have no right to silence under the ASIO Act.'

"'What do you mean?' I say.

"'You can go to jail for up to five years for not answering our questions.'

"The fat old silver-haired man had fallen asleep for a moment, started snoring, then he jolts back awake. The Fed smirked. But not the politician spook. He leans in real close across the table and he says: 'I don't think you understand the seriousness of your situation, Ms Wilder. This is not a normal criminal investigation. This is a terrorism investigation. If new information is forthcoming we may seek to have your warrant renewed for another week. And who knows? Perhaps we may face the same situation the week after that. You can see what this means, Ms Wilder. We can just continue renewing the warrant. But if you continue to refuse to answer our questions, you can go to jail for five years. If you lie to us, same deal. Jail for five years.'

"Then he leans back and says: 'Did you receive a phone call from a mobile phone yesterday at approximately 2.24 pm?'

"I say: 'Can you be any more approximate?'

"They say: 'Answer the question.'

"I say: 'I don't know. I don't keep a record of all the calls I get.'

"They say: 'Telephone records show that you were rung yesterday at 2.24 pm on a mobile phone that had been stolen approximately half an hour earlier. The woman who owns the phone went back to retrieve it and has given police a description of a woman she saw walking away from where she had left it. The description matches Gina Davies.'

"And all the time I was worrying, Gina, about Max, about how he was. I mean, the poor little bloke has armed men smashing around his house in the middle of the night and he's screaming and screaming. And they take us both to some police station, and separate us, and I'm imagining Max is crying and then I'm crying too, I'm so upset, and I say that I'm not talking until they put us back together. But they won't.

"I look up at the old fat man but he's nodded off again. I can see he's even dribbling a little bit. I beg the spooks. 'Can I see my son, please?' I say.

"They say: 'Later.'

"I say: 'When? When do I get to see him? He's my son and he's terrified.' I told them I would go to the media and make a scene, tell them everything about invading my house, doing to Max what they did.

" 'Tell them what?' they say. 'Lesbian lover denies terrorist link?' They laugh, and then the quiet one who looked like a politician, he says:

" 'You talk to a journalist about this, any of this—tonight's raid, this, these questions—you go to jail for five years. Under the ASIO Act that's Australian law too, now. You breathe one word about your arrest, this interrogation, to a neighbour, your sister, your best friend, you go to jail for five years. Besides,' he says, 'under the ASIO Act the media isn't allowed to run any story about your arrest and detention or they go to jail for five years too.'

"He seemed a bit tired—it was like, I dunno, maybe six in the morning—and I think he was disappointed and bored with me because I guess I wasn't, you know, much of a terrorist.

" 'Unless, of course,' he says, 'we authorise the story. I hope I've helped make your position clear.'

"Then they went on and on, like some weird court it was, and when the interview was over they woke the old bloke, he said some more things and then they all left except a cop to guard me. Some time later the baby-faced politician-looking one came back. He said I could see Max now and that we were free to go. He was all friendly, the smart arse.'

"'Someone'll find out,' I say.

"'No,' he says. 'No one is ever going to find out. Those miners trapped down that gold mine in Tasmania a few years ago—you remember? Well, your situation is worse. Imagine nobody is ever, ever allowed to find out what happened to you while you were down that hole. And imagine all the things that can happen to people lost in dark holes.'

"And then a woman cop came into the room with Max, and Max runs to me and this creep smiles and, can you believe this?—he rubs Max's head with his hand.

"'Nice kid,' he says, and he looks up and he's still smiling. 'Imagine,' he says."

The Doll didn't feel safe sitting on a public train listening as Wilder continued talking. But she kept on listening anyway.

"But I didn't tell them, Gina, I didn't tell them anything, I swear to God, I'm sure they're watching me, hanging me out as bait. Don't come here, Gina, don't come back."

66

The train shrieked out of the dark and into the shock of daylight and sped past tin warehouses, railway sidings, stuccoed apartment blocks, under overpasses, past a suburban railway station at which three veiled Muslim women in dark clothes stood together and labourers in orange vests worked apart, and everywhere outside the Doll could see the terrible heat moving in visible waves, like some radioactive force. She took a Stemetil and her last two Valium 5.

She watched an African mother sitting at the carriage's end with a tired baby whose hair, the Doll noticed, was done in the prettiest plaits tied with red and yellow ribbons. The rails' comforting beat rocked the child to sleep as the train continued past green goods trains, shopping centres as bleak as penitentiaries, rusting corro roofs, concrete walls weary with graffiti, billboard after billboard brightly showing a huge face which in its geometric angles and gladwrapped smile appeared to have had the work done on it not with a scalpel but a power planer. Next to this bizarre face was a radio station's name and frequency, and the slogan "JOE COSUK IS SYDNEY".

Stretching away seemingly forever in the smoggy heat, the Doll could now see the west coming at her, an ever spreading delta of suburbs—Bankstown, Revesby, Panania, Macquarie Fields, Campbelltown.

The baby began to cry and her mother held her close. She was whispering in the baby's ear, and fanning her with a newspaper. 'Hold her,' the Doll thought. The newspaper had a photo of the Doll on its cover. 'Hold her and never let her go.'

It wasn't the Doll's way to go back in anything; all her life was a striving to go forwards. Family, home, memories: to the Doll they were all just a bucket of dust. She knew from the soaps she used to watch that such things could matter; the truth, she had discovered, was that they only mattered in the soaps. She had no home, no family, and there was no way back. Her childhood had been about little, how could it mean anything more now? But she wished she had more Valium 5, wished she had Zoloft, wished that she didn't feel so anxious, so uptight, so strung out, just because she was sitting on a train riding back into the burbs.

The baby had fallen back asleep, and the African mother stroked her plaits absent-mindedly while looking out of the window. This absent-minded look the Doll understood as that slightly complacent, slightly stupid, completely undeniable look of love.

The love the African mother had for her child was the same love the Doll had for so long repressed in herself and which now, despite her best efforts, suddenly rose up inside her as a huge anger. She wanted to rush up and seize that sleeping baby and throw it out the doors, dash it to death on the siding as the train rushed along. At that moment she hated that African woman, hated her blackness, hated her seeming lack of awareness that love is not enough, and she knew the only way the African woman would understand this was if her sleeping baby was cruelly and terribly taken from her forever.

And then the Doll realised the train had halted. She leapt up, panicked in case she missed her stop, and because she felt frightened of herself, fearful that her love might take over, horrified that out of love she had the momentary desire to kill somebody. She got off just as the doors began closing. Only as the train began to shunt away did the Doll realise that she was one stop too early.

Walking beyond the shade of the station, the direct sun enveloped her like a quick-drying treacle, slowing her every movement. Though there was still the traffic and commotion of a suburban main street, no one wanted to be outside. Anyone not working had retreated indoors and taken refuge near their air con vents and in cold beer and chilled wines. Some watched something on television and afterwards couldn't remember whether it was sport or reality tv or a documentary on Hitler. Some surfed the net looking at porn or eBay. Some hit their wives or screamed at their husbands or beat their kids. Most did nothing. It was difficult to sleep, yet almost impossible to move. It was easy to be irritated about everything that was of no consequence, yet care about nothing that mattered.

Outside a laundry that doubled as a Sri Lankan video shop, the Doll spotted the unusual sight of a stationary taxi in the suburbs. Grateful not to have to struggle walking a good half hour through the thick heat, she hailed it.

67

Wilder had just hung up from talking to the Doll when there was a knock at the door. It was Nick Loukakis. She hadn't seen or spoken to him since their affair had ended three months earlier.

He came in, and it was as if he were a door-to-door salesman. Neither knew where to look. Neither knew where to stand or how to hold themselves or what to say. There should have been many things to say, but neither knew how to say even one of those many things.

Nick Loukakis looked around her still trashed, only partly cleaned up living room.

"Your friends," said Wilder after a time. She said it with a double bitterness.

"Sorry?" said Nick Loukakis.

"I was the one raided in the middle of the night. That's why you're here, isn't it?"

Nick Loukakis looked around at the mess, the pots and pans spread out over the kitchen floor, the broken pictures lying scattered, the books spreadeagled. For a moment he looked as confused as the room.

"They want you to pump me and tell you what I know," continued Wilder.

Nick Loukakis looked up at her and she realised he hadn't known, but was only now putting it together.

"I'm just a dumb-arse detective sergeant in the drug squad," said Nick Loukakis. "If you think they tell us anything other than shit you're mistaken."

Their conversation dried up. She made coffee, and when she brought the plunger to the table she passed him a chair with a padded seat cover to sit on. He smiled. Wilder said nothing.

Wilder had four bentwood chairs with hard bases that she had bought some cheap padded seat covers for. Nick Loukakis had hated them. They were, he said at the time she bought them, "frumpy". This annoyed Wilder, but it was really no big deal to her whether they were on or off, and so she had taken them off and put them away. After it ended with Nick Loukakis, she got them out and tied them back on. But now she was angry: angry with what had happened to her in the night, with the mess her home was in, with the Doll for having allowed all this to happen.

"I like them," said Wilder, still rankling about the seat covers, about him, about the raid. "Besides, the chairs are too hard to sit on without them."

He drank some of his coffee.

He said, "You know, this is a nice place you've got here, Wilder. Stylish. Your style. But those padded seat covers—I dunno. They do let the place down a bit."

Wilder said nothing. Wilder knew nothing drove him madder than saying nothing. She changed the topic, knowing that made him angrier still.

"Why?" said Nick Loukakis after a while.

"Well, what are you going to do about it, Nick? What exactly are you going to do about it? Go back to Diana and get her wog seats for me? What, Nick? What?"

She was calm. After everything she was calm. She hated him when he was indecisive, when he gave in to her, when he wouldn't be the boss. So she goaded him some more about his wife, and the more she goaded him, the more she hated his wife and despised him.

In the depths of his soul, Nick Loukakis loathed what he saw as her jealousy when it manifested itself as such small-minded spite. But he also felt he had no right to show any anger. And besides, there were other things that mattered far more and he had to swallow it. Finally, in a voice that was somehow quiet but threatening, he told Wilder what he thought the Doll's real story was and why he needed to find her.

As he spoke, he tried to avoid looking at Wilder's breasts.

He tried to destroy the memory of gazing up at them when they had fucked, her belly heaving in and out, running his hand through her hair. He tried to forget how much they used to laugh, how much he liked just to listen to her stories.

"Where is she, Wilder?" he said.

"Your wife? Diana? Wifey, wife? You should know."

He reached across, grabbed both her wrists in a painful hold.

"Fuck you," he said. "Gina. Where the fuck is Gina?"

Wilder pulled her head back, stared at him and said nothing. He got up, and wrenched her off her chair. He held her wrists up so that one was either side of his face, and she was pulled into his body.

"Let go," said Wilder. "You're hurting me."

"I can help her, Wilder."

"I can't tell you," said Wilder, and then immediately regretted the words, for now he would know she knew.

"You've got to tell me, Wilder."

She tried to break his grip. She wanted to scream. But instead she smiled, because now he was doing what she wanted him to do to her.

"Wifey, wife," she said, smiling some more. "Wifey, wife."

'I'm worn out,' thought Nick Loukakis, 'and I no longer know what to do.' He let go of her wrists before he did anything even more stupid. He stood, picked up the coffee cups and took them into the kitchen, retreating into domestic routine to calm himself.

Wilder watched him from behind as he walked away. He had a rugby player's back. The taste of him, sweet and salty, came back to her mouth as she watched him washing the cups, then drying them and putting them away, an odd act of order in the midst of chaos.

Perhaps it was for the best, he told himself as he stood over the sink. What good could come of his knowing where she was? He realised he couldn't help the Doll, it was already too big, and he knew he would inevitably have to tell others, they would know he had visited Wilder, and then her fate would be theirs to decide, not his.

He came back to the table.

"I better go," he said. His voice was different now. "Sorry about this," he said, gesturing vaguely at the room, as though he were to blame. He went to give her a farewell kiss, quick and perfunctory.

But their arms went around each other and he could feel her breasts and she his back. They didn't drop to the floor; they didn't fall on each other in a frenzy amidst the upturned furniture, the strewn books and magazines and pictures littering the floor. They just stood there, holding each other awkwardly, as if their bodies were porcelain, as though the slightest movement might shatter whatever small thing was left into a million fragments.

To sleep in Wilder's arms, thought Nick Loukakis. That was all he wanted. To sleep!—to fall asleep holding and smelling her and her holding him and he at last at peace. Peace, how sweet it suddenly seemed to him, how he longed to rest. But it wasn't possible and he didn't know what to say.

For all her desire, Wilder had made up her mind that she would never sleep with him again. Something had left her. It was over. Unless he spoke, thought Wilder. Maybe then it would be different. If only he spoke, then one of the two ideas at war inside her head would vanish—that she didn't want him, that she wanted him more than ever. So Wilder told him about the Doll. She made believe that her telling him was fated to be. She tried not to think that she told him just so that he might say something to her, anything.

Nick Loukakis kept on holding her, longing to be at peace. He didn't know what to say. He wished she hadn't told him. He felt her hair in his fingers. He tried not to think of his sons. Of Diana. He didn't know what to do. He wished they had anything to share but this. He kept on holding her, the noise of the traffic, of Sydney, beginning to rise around them. He thought he would scream. He didn't know what to say and how he wished she hadn't told him.

68

"Just get in," said the taxi driver. His bead seat cover clacked as he waved an arm at the open door, seeming to resent the draught of hot air that accompanied the Doll into his cab. He was an overweight man whose red face was covered with crusty patches and his blue shirt with flakes of skin, like the scales of a fish.

"Rookwood," said the Doll. "I'll direct you."

Inside the taxi a radio announcer declared that they were "now going direct to the press conference being given by Police Commissioner Ben Holmstrom". The taxi driver turned on the meter and pulled out. On the radio a voice coughed, and then said:

"Well, I can confirm that we found a large sum of cash in the flat, along with a small amount of cocaine."

The Doll wanted to ask him to change the station, but didn't dare. She wanted to be invisible. She didn't want him to look at her, think about her, remember her. So she had to keep listening, as there arose a confusion of shouts from the media pack.

"Do you believe there is a connection between Islamic terrorism and drug running?"

"We are pursuing all avenues of enquiry and working with the appropriate government agencies," said the voice the Doll guessed belonged to the top cop.

"Is it true that this was the flat of the woman the media are calling the Unknown Terrorist?"

"The flat was rented in the name of Gina Davies."

"Is Gina Davies the same woman who works as a lap dancer at the Chairman's Lounge under the aliases Krystal and the Black Widow?"

"That is our understanding, yes."

"So there is a link, Police Commissioner? Can you confirm that the cell was financing its terrorist activities through drug running and the sex industry?"

"I can only repeat what I said a moment ago. But clearly these are disturbing developments."

The driver mumbled bitterly, as if all this were somehow personally directed against him, while at the press conference a different, distant voice rose above the clamour to ask:

"How much money did you find?"

In the all-pervasive heat even the air in the taxi was a clammy torment. The Doll tried to focus on the hoarse whisper of the car's air con vents battling a world that could no longer be cooled down. But when the cop said, "Close to fifty thousand dollars in one-hundred-dollar notes," she was unable to ignore the radio any longer.

"Stop!" she suddenly called. "Here—just pull into that hardware store there and wait for me."

The Doll stood for a moment on the street, trying to calm her breathing.

'My money! My money!' thought the Doll—and she knew it was all gone. Wilder had not got there in time and now could never retrieve it. It was all her savings, and she would never ever get it back. She could not prove she had earnt it legally and they would claim it had been obtained illegally. All those shitty, never-ending nights she had suffered for it; all those arseholes she had smiled at and cooed to; all that crap she had swallowed; all that money with which she had, bill by bill, slowly sought to put an end to her naked-ness, all of it had been for nothing!

She felt giddy, made herself walk into the hardware store though the floor was rising and falling away at the same time. For gone with the money was her dream of a home, and with the home, her dream of leaving dancing and start-ing a new life.

Then, as she searched up and down the aisles with a plas-tic shopping basket in her hand, she tried to find solace in her new situation. As she put a kitchen knife into her basket, as she took down a tin of Brasso and found a scrubbing brush, she tried to tell herself it didn't matter, that she could start again. She stopped and steadied herself by leaning against a Makita power tools display.

Perhaps, she thought, if she gave herself up, told them everything—including how the money had been made, how she had worked hard and honestly for it—then they would understand, clear the mess up and give her money back. She entertained this idea for some minutes; her desire for her money and the idea that the money was freedom was so strong that it for a short time overrode her fear. At the counter she added a bouquet of flowers to her basket, paid, then walked out and got back in the taxi. But as the taxi drove on, the Doll knew all that she was thinking was just so much dog shit.

"Grew up not far from here," the taxi driver said, as he spun the steering wheel, and the taxi swung off the highway and past a sign advertising the largest cemetery in the southern hemisphere.

"Seven hundred acres of it," the taxi driver said, scratching furiously at his raw chin. The Doll tried not to notice the pieces of his face falling away. "They called it Necropolis then. City of the dead. Like something out of a frigging Batman movie."

69

The Doll directed the taxi driver along the cemetery's narrow avenues, through its endless graveyards, old, new, this religion, that religion, no religion, beneath its palms, past its loud and large graves, its scattered, broken graves, its obscure and lost graves, through its occasional eucalypt groves, past sections of cemetery partly reclaimed by thrusting wattles and pines.

The news came on the radio, and they had a grab from the prime minister saying he had full confidence in the authorities' response to date in searching for the so-called

"Black Widow". He said that it was, however, necessary that every Australian remained vigilant.

"Vigilant!" snorted the taxi driver. "How's vigilant help?"

Shortly before the glistening black and grey marble mausoleums—elaborate warehouses of the dead into which the names of rich Italian families were inscribed in bold gilded letters—the Doll told the taxi driver to stop.

On the car radio the morning talkback had started.

"We're going to get the police minister on the phone," said Joe Cosuk. "He's got a lot of explaining to do to the Australian people."

"Go'im, Joey, thatta boy," said the taxi driver, as though the shock jock were a hunting dog.

"And if he won't talk to the Australian people," continued Joe Cosuk, "and tell us why terrorists can just run round seemingly at will, then I think the Australian people will judge him very harshly."

"How long you be, miss?" asked the taxi driver. "I can wait if you like."

"It's okay, my friend," said the Doll. "I'll walk to the train station and get the train home."

"Don't catch the train myself, lovey," the taxi driver said, scratching at his chin once more. "Lebs. They'll rob you and they'll rape you, they will. Fucken Lebs. Excuse the French. Where you going? We can agree a price, if you like, switch off the meter. Don't want to be on a train on a day like today with Lebs."

The Doll smiled briefly, paid him, closed the door, and turned. As she walked away she heard the taxi slink off. Above her there was no longer sun or horizon. A dirty gloom filled the baking sky and flattened those beneath it like a hot iron.

The rather miserable piece of land to which she was headed lay sandwiched between the determined uniformity of the Presbyterian Lawn on one side, with its regimented rows of plaques, and the Byzantine opulence of the Greek section on the other. This wretched patch of dust in the middle was called the Baby Lawn. Here the poor and those without religious denomination buried their newly born dead.

An old man and a small girl, no more than five years old, were tending a grave, weeding, arranging flowers, carefully positioning at the grave's centre a toy football on which was written "ROOSTERS". Though there was no real wind, clouds of dust occasionally kicked up and blew in little swirls around the girl's stick legs.

Running along the head of each row of graves in the Baby Lawn was a cracked concrete beam, not much more than ankle height, on which was fixed at regular intervals small bronze plaques of uniform size that served in place of headstones. Some graves were cared for and decorated with flowers, most not: abandoned, their small teddy bears and racing cars and porcelain dolls fading and rotting.

At the end of the newest row was a fresh grave with a small mound of gravelly soil not even a metre long, with some far smaller body lying beneath it. Nearby, beneath a grove of miserable gum trees, the neatly turfed lawn cut from the new grave had been laid in the forlorn hope of getting some grass growing there.

A white-haired woman dressed in black, carrying three

large plastic bags stuffed to the brim, came walking up the road. She halted, and with an odd, thirsty look stared at the old man and the girl for a moment as though she had unexpectedly come upon an oasis in the desert, and then walked on.

The Doll made her way up and down the rows of concrete beams until she came to a small white plastic horse, yellow fissured and brittle from the sun, resting beneath one more bronze plaque and some long-dead flowers.

Though she knew the words well enough, the Doll ran her fingers over the plaque's raised lettering.

LIAM DAVIES
LOVED SON OF GINA DAVIES
BORN 6 MARCH 2001
DIED 7 MARCH 2001

70

It was a lie. He had been dead inside her long before he was stillborn shortly before midnight. But he had been, she thought, he had been . . . but then the Doll became all choked up, for what he had been she couldn't say.

During her pregnancy the Doll had often imagined breastfeeding her newborn baby. Somehow it seemed important to the Doll that she would from the first feed her own child from her own body. After all, didn't the experts and the authorities agree that it was the best for a baby's health? But it was not only the baby's health that made the Doll dream of breastfeeding her child. In her dreams the child nuzzled into her milk-engorged breasts, found her lush nipples, and suckled a thread of gold out of her body that bound them together; magical golden threads of milk and love that nourished them both. She would love and be loved; she would have her due, no more, no less.

And that day, six years before, she had taken her baby to her swollen breast, brought his prune face and dead lips to her taut nipple and, looking at him, feeling him dead against her breast, she had shuddered with the impossible weight of grief.

They said, "Let him go." And then they said, "Let him go, you must let him go, we must take him now." And they would not let him stay and he was not allowed to live—and why? There is no *why*, the Doll thought. There is just *is*. The Doll did what she was told and offered no resistance as they gently unfolded her arms and lifted Liam out.

Only the big-breasted woman with blonde hair whom she had met in the labour ward before the birth was there afterwards. Only she held the Doll. The Doll let the woman hold her—she was past caring what anyone did with her—and in the end the Doll reached out and held on to the woman, a great boab tree in the middle of a cyclone, and the Doll felt that if she held on to her she might not be swept away. For nothing else was solid, nothing else was fixed. Nothing existed beyond her grief and then she would not let go until two nurses dragged her off so that the woman could feed her own son, born one hour before Liam. The woman called him Max. Her name was Sally, but everyone, she told the Doll, just called her by her surname: Wilder.

She thought of how Liam would have been six today, and how she had been nineteen when she had fallen pregnant.

Troy had been thirty-two and married. It was not possible, he told her, for his name to appear on the grave as Liam's father.

Of the time she had been with Troy it astonished her how little remained: an image of his face and the way he did his blond hair which, at the time, reminded her of certain movie stars she thought handsome, but now simply seemed vain and affected. Troy was an SAS soldier. At eighteen, when she first met him, that had seemed to the Doll something. Really something.

He bought her flowers. Presents. Took her to flash Chinese restaurants and knew how to use chopsticks. He would turn up without warning and leave unexpectedly. He talked mysteriously of places he had been, things he had seen, used phrases like "covert operations" and "the need to know principle, and you, baby, don't need to know" to explain the ever-growing number of things in his life about which there seemed to her no explanation.

He was a man who had success with women, but even in his thirties his taste for teenage girls seemed to be unchanging and unchangeable. Yet if there were something hopeless and unresolved about his womanising, it was also this that was somehow attractive to the women who fell for him.

She remembered aspects of his muscled body, and his odour, which was pungent and at first strange, for a time exciting, and finally repulsive. There were not even memories of fights and the slow, painful collapse of her love: rather, looking back, she could see it never really even started but had died as suddenly and inexplicably as their son.

And though it was all but over after that, they staggered

on a few months more. He would turn up drunk and scare her, mumble pleas and threats and grab her and shake her and then cry, and fall asleep and wet himself where he sat or lay. She had a restraining order put on him; he kicked her door in, she called the cops, he was locked up for a night.

The news of him having two kids to another woman in Fremantle had shocked but not surprised her in the way his death had, only four months after Liam's, in a training exercise up near Cairns: his body had seemed destined to outlast and outlive everyone. For a time, his death seemed to the Doll to vindicate his ceaseless womanising and bad behaviour, and she saw him as a man who must have known in some way his time was short and crammed what he could into those few years. But as grief ebbed, so did her sympathy. He was a mindless prick, and that was all.

And the Doll thought how hearts break in so many ways, and how hers was only one.

The Doll looked up at the sky. It had grown darker still. Black cloud clumps raced across its inverted maternal belly. She thought how if they had bothered to look at it, many people would have found the sky that midday glorious, at once moody and enchanting. But when the Doll dropped her eyes again and saw the sorry field of dust in which she had laid her stillborn son to rest, it seemed to her that the sky that day—like Moretti's beautiful possessions, like all things said to be beautiful—was simply cruel.

Near the end of her pregnancy, the Doll noticed that the kicks had stopped. For some days she hadn't worried, but then she went to the hospital. The doctor reassured her, but when they did an ultrasound they could find no heartbeat.

She was induced the following day. No one spoke in the hushed birth theatre.

After that day the Doll hated hush, quiet, silence. She had imagined such joy and such excitement at the birth, and, after, a home full of sounds: crying, laughing, cooing, singing, toys and stories and calls for help and calls of joy. But there was only pain and silence. After that day she preferred noise, any noise, to silence.

They told her the baby was macerated. He did not look like she had imagined. He did not look perfect. They told her she could hold him. They told her that some people chose to dress their child, to take photographs so that they would have memories.

She held him. His eyes were wide open. They were large and terrible, a dull blue. She brushed her hands over his eyes to close them and his eyelids fell off. He would not stop looking at her. He was hers. She was him. Dead. She did not dress him. She did not take photographs. He was dead, and she had her memories and she was him. She kissed his damp, stony face, his skin puckered like a prune. At that moment she was revolted by him. At that moment she loved him. He would not stop looking into her.

71

"You must have thought Mum would never come," the Doll said, squatting in the dust of the Baby Lawn. She spoke quietly, as if he were still in her arms and able to hear her very breathing. "Let's fix this up, then," she said as if talking about a child's untidy bedroom, squatting down and setting to work cleaning up the grave. The very dust was so hot she thought it might scorch her skin. Liam had not been good looking when he was born, yet within his prune-like face she had seen another, the face of a young, handsome man.

"My ugly Liam," she whispered as she cleaned the weeds out from around her son's small piece of crumbling concrete beam. "My ugly, beautiful boy."

With the new kitchen knife she had bought at the hardware store she cut away the tufts of dead grass encroaching on that half-metre of concrete beam that in her mind belonged to her Liam. She pulled out a lantana seedling that had risen almost level with the plaque.

She had photos of herself pregnant with Liam and kept them in a special album. No doubt the police had the photographs now. What would they see? What does anyone see? What did the suits in the Chairman's Lounge see when they peered so intently up between her legs? Eyes without eyelids that also couldn't stop looking?

After Liam's stillbirth, the Doll went to Melbourne. She told those around her that she was "going to find a better city". She found the same city, the same streets, the same dead stares, the same filth, the same indifference, the same grand decay, the same hive-like energy, bursting and building, killing and destroying, robbing flowers and fertilising flowers for no point other than to continue. She found all this and only the weather was different, and she knew every city henceforth would be the same for her, be it Berlin or Manhattan or Shanghai.

She returned to Sydney after a year, determined to change not towns anymore, but herself. 'I will begin again,' she thought, 'that's what life is, all it is, having to start over and over.' She remembered finding a job at a Qantas call centre, hating it, having every toilet break timed, and then seeing the ad asking for dancers at the Chairman's Lounge. She worked there for a weekend and never went back to the call centre.

Lap dancing didn't seem to involve either humiliation or pride. It offered money, and that was enough. And for a time—looking back she realised it had been a very short time—it made her feel somebody, feel proud, seem wanted. Instead of just taking it day after day from people over the phone, copping crap from the supervisors, she was up there looking down on others, and they admired her, they thought she was beautiful, they told her about their lives, all these men in their suits, all these older men who had for so long lorded it over her. She only had to put her hand between her thighs, push her arse into their faces, and they were lost; she could taunt them, have them hard and wanting her and only her and if they so much as touched her anywhere security would throw them out on their ears.

Really, thought the Doll, she didn't fool men, she just let men fool themselves. She was a goddess, unobtainable, better than them, beyond them, and they were nothing, not the Lebanese gangsters, not the television and music celebs, not the corporate executives, not the rich north shore boys out on a buck's night. It had been something, it so had, it had been like a party every night at which she was the centre of attention. Everyone came to the clubs, the dollars flowed, and without trying she was pulling over three grand a week, all of it black.

And the Doll felt she was finally going somewhere. She

wasn't exactly sure where, but for a time it felt good. Even the shock of her friends felt good. She was making real money, and she was proud, so proud. She looked better. With the exercise every night toning her right up and the clothes, the beautiful clothes and shoes and bags she could now buy, she looked like a movie star. Only sometime later did it become clear. She wasn't a movie star. She wasn't going anywhere. She was a lap dancer and she was falling.

Then the authorities banned lap dancing, and it was only tips from pole dancing or fifty bucks for a fifteen-minute private show, and somehow the clubs were no longer the thing, the place to go, but an embarrassment, and all the girls were sad, and all the men were mean, and you had to work twice as hard to make half as much. She was a lap dancer, no matter what she held on to nothing held, everything was collapsing and she was falling.

For a time the Doll worked elsewhere: a club in Perth where anything seemed to go; she lasted there three weeks until she was asked to do a full body soap slide. Apart from not wanting to do it anyway, it just seemed too ridiculous. For a few months she had flown to the Gold Coast to work weekends at a club there. Then she came back; tried to be proud once more. She was a dancer, an erotic dancer. It was an industry, not a game. She went back to the Chairman's Lounge: it was near where she lived, and that was enough of a reason.

'I am beautiful,' the Doll said to herself over and over, and men paid to admire her beauty and the way she displayed it. But in her heart the Doll felt otherwise. In her heart the Doll felt that they were paying for something else, and the more they paid, the more distant became that thing they sought. The Doll could now see that she had been no different from the men, that all the time the dollar notes had been rising over her body she had been falling further and further from what she really wanted—friendship, trust, serenity, love—that she had been falling and no one had said anything and everyone had known.

And as the Doll danced above the suits, their shirt tongues hanging out, she knew the men had to imagine she was thinking about fucking them, fucking anything, imagine that she existed in a state of sexual desire so absolute even they could enter it, a sexual desire that did not need another human being with a name, a past, a life, but just an assembly of flesh.

The Doll had to imagine other things. She imagined a life in which she had an apartment and an education and a job that people admired, a life in which she amounted to something, and her imagining became the plan, and the plan became the dream of dollar notes papering her body.

And once more, the Doll persuaded herself she was going somewhere, when all the time she was falling. She had always been falling but now she knew nothing ever changed. People lived, people died. There would always be women stripping for rich men, there would always be men paying to look at women, she would continue falling until death, and a month or two after her death only a few people very close to her, like Wilder, would remember her, and after a few years more even Wilder would have trouble recalling her face or her laugh, and out of her only lantana would grow.

The day of Liam's funeral had been a beautiful winter's day of the type that makes Sydneysiders smile and say:

"It's the best place on earth."

The air seemed full of joyful noise to the Doll. Everywhere were the sounds of children playing, of people laughing, pleasant music rising—and it was clear to the Doll that death was of no concern to such a world, where life was good and cheerful, and the appearance of suffering was an embarrassment, where she was falling and out of the dead only lantana grew.

72

Near where the Baby Lawn ended and the Greek cemetery began was a tap from which the Doll filled her bucket. As the water ran, the Doll saw two large Greek women and an older, small Greek man in an ancient cream linen suit set up in front of an ornate, beautifully kept Greek grave. They were sitting on director's chairs beneath an umbrella, chatting away as if it were a barbie.

One woman reached into a plastic bag, pulled out two salad rolls, passed one to the other woman, and they began eating. The man leant back, as though taking a break from some arduous task, reached into his pocket, and took out a metal cigarette case. He opened it and took out a cigarette, tapped it top and bottom on the case, then lightly ran it along the length of his moustache before putting it between his lips and lighting up. He leant even further back, looking very satisfied to be sitting in the city of the dead on such a splendidly hot day. And though they seemed somehow comic to the Doll, she envied them their ease. With them death had a place.

Then she made her way back to Liam's grave. The old

man and the small girl were gone. The Doll thought how the
Baby Lawn was a place where deaths were less easily
digested, life not so readily understood, and people frag-
mented rather than came together. No one set up director's
chairs. No one ate salad rolls. No one smoked. No one chatted. People came, remembered a few sad things, and then left.

The crack of a seed pod exploding open in the heat brought
the Doll back from her thoughts. Reaching into her plastic
bag, she pulled out the scrubbing brush and the detergent. But
when she began scrubbing the plaque, it came away from the
concrete and fell into the dust. A cemetery gardener drove past
on his mini-tractor, dull plastic kegs of poison jogging in their
brightly coloured lift-up tray.

"Good times, great value!" said the tractor radio. "Barbe-
ques Galore."

The Doll looked at the wet plaque now lying filthy on the
ground, the dust turned to damp dirt. She felt her heart grab,
but she would not let this get on top of her, could not let it
get on top of her: she would do as she always did, as she felt
she always must—she would start again, turn disadvantage to
advantage. She picked the plaque up, put it in the bucket and
scrubbed it until it was cleaned only in order, she knew well
enough, to be tarnished and dirtied once more.

The Doll had nothing with which to refix it to the concrete beam. She had some chewing gum in her bag, so she
got it out and, while polishing the plaque with some Brasso
and her handkerchief, chewed the gum, then pressed it down
on the concrete and pushed the plaque onto it, fixing it back
into a position as best she could.

She put the dead flowers away in the plastic bag and

arranged the already wilting fresh flowers in front of the cleaned and refixed plaque, then propped the plastic horse against the concrete beam.

A crow swore from a nearby tree.

She gathered her brush and detergent and litter into the plastic bag, and began walking back to the railway station in the stinking heat. She cut through an older part of the cemetery with its broken graves and fallen headstones, inscriptions lost to the erosion of wind and rain and sun. Berry bushes, pines, wattles, and lantana thrust up through graves, pushing aside railings, cracking concrete capping, slowly flattening headstones, gently, inexorably destroying with life the last attempts to pretend death wasn't forever.

The Doll thought of how Liam would never send her letters. Never text or email her. Never bring home a girl who would become a woman who would bring grandchildren to visit the Doll. Never hold her old unheld body and feel it soft in his strong young embrace. Never tell her stories, sing, make her smile with his laughter. Never kiss her thin unkissed lips, her wrinkled and papery cheeks. Never let her know she loved and was loved.

Beneath a stunted gum tree with low, sweeping boughs, the Doll saw a broken wooden cross lying on the ground. Tiny ants toiled in its rotting splinters. She looked up and saw Homebush Olympic stadium in the distance. When it was being built for the Olympics and she was a teenager, its wings had reminded her of angels. Now she could see there was so much that was more amazing than any angel, but that there was nothing left to believe. People put all their energy and brilliance into making things more extraordinary than themselves, only to have it make them feel that they were, in the end, less than nothing.

And somehow the ants in the cross and the people of Sydney with their Olympic stadium became the same thing in the Doll's mind, everyone doing what they did because they had to, and yet everything that was done seemed to serve no greater point, not ants toiling to make a nest out of decay, nor people labouring to make great cities and an Olympic stadium. And maybe that was why they wanted to be frightened of her, thought the Doll, so that they might think being like an ant was a good thing to be. But there seemed something wrong in this, or in her thinking, and then it all got too hard to hold in her head, and when her stolen phone rang for the second time, the Doll answered it instinctively, gratefully, and only after she had it to her ear did she wonder whether this was wise or not.

73

"Gina, listen. I had to call."

On hearing Wilder's voice the Doll felt relieved. 'A friend,' she thought, 'thank God, a friend!'

"After I rang earlier there's a knock on the door. I open it," Wilder continued, "shitting myself, but it's bloody Athens Loukakis.

"Look, you know how he's not a Fed or ASIO, he's a drug squad cop. He knew nothing about the raids. He told me he thinks ASIO and the Feds have got it all wrong. He thinks it's a terrible mix-up. He's not even sure Tariq was a terrorist."

The Doll did not know what to say. It seemed the cruellest of jokes.

"Who was he, then?" she asked.

"He was a man called Tariq," continued Wilder. "He was a computer programmer. He worked on the side as a mule bringing in heroin and coke."

The Doll could feel her upper lip smarting from the salty sweat beading there. It now seemed too stupid to be true—that who someone said they were, was, more or less, who they were. She wiped the sweat away with the back of her hand.

"He's dead," she said. "Does he know that?"

"Everyone knows it now, Gina," Wilder said. "The news hasn't stopped running it. Athens thinks a drug ring had him killed because he was getting too much publicity and they didn't want the police catching him and working out the real story."

The Doll had now reached the boundary of the cemetery, and made her way across a busy highway.

"What's all that noise?" said Wilder.

The Doll looked up and about, and almost told her where she was, but instead just said, "Cars."

"He thinks you're innocent, but he needs you to turn yourself in so he can prove it. He wants to meet you, and you can hand yourself in to him. Peacefully. No SWAT squads. He'll help you get your story listened to. No men in black with machine guns. He wants to avoid the possibility of anything bad happening."

The Doll walked past headstone shops. Behind their high Weldmesh fences were displayed glistening new marble headstones—black and red and charcoal—on which the names of the dead were inscribed in Cyrillic, Chinese and Thai.

"He tells me they think you're armed and he can't guarantee your safety. I told him not to be stupid, that you don't have a gun."

The Doll felt her hair with her hand.

"Then he told me you'd stolen one from that sleaze Moretti."

The wavy locks that Wilder had with such care straightened, which the Doll had avoided getting wet in the shower to keep flat, were, in the heat, resuming their natural kink.

"Christ, Gina," said Wilder. "What were you thinking . . ."

And the Doll listened to Wilder saying it would be best to turn herself in and agreed with her, agreed with her too that in Australia things always get sorted out in the end and the mistake would be rectified.

But the Doll thought no such thing. 'Have I become such a fool?' she was thinking while she talked. 'The mistake can never be rectified—I can only make sure I'm not caught.'

How not to get caught was something about which the Doll had no idea other than those gleaned from movies. And so she continued telling Wilder how it made sense to sort this out, to clear her name and put the mess behind her, while all the time thinking she would run—but to where? To leave Australia struck the Doll as impossible—she would need a fake passport and how on earth were such things to be got? What would she use for money to escape?

And the thought of money threw the Doll into fresh despair—here she was dreaming of escaping and she only had Wilder's mother's credit card and a little over two hundred dollars left in her wallet, enough money, if she was very careful, to survive another two or three days. And then what?

The Doll's mind pitched and swayed with the impossibility and hopelessness of her situation. To give herself up was madness, for they wanted her as a terrorist, no matter what Wilder or Nick Loukakis said, they wanted their victim. Nick Loukakis could be lying, he could be telling the truth. It didn't matter. The Doll sensed that no one would tell the truth about her once she was in their power. Too much had been said, too much done, too many powerful people were now mixed up in it. And anyway, who would listen to her, a pole dancer, a nobody, a westie, when they had taken the little truths of her life to make up a big lie?

With her hand the Doll flattened her hair against her scalp, a futile action, and, knowing it to be so, felt something close to panic as she continued to pat her hand as hard as she could against her head. She abruptly stopped, feeling more foolish than ever, fearing people were looking at her, wondering why on earth she was slapping her head.

"I'm frightened," Wilder said. She paused, as if waiting for the Doll to reach some conclusion that to Wilder seemed so obvious. "They'll kill you."

The Doll tried to stay in the shadows of buildings as she made her way toward the Lidcombe train station.

"I told him, Gina. I told him about the hotel. I told him about Mum's credit card. I told him everything. I told him because I believed in him, Gina, and if you won't give yourself up, it's better he finds you than they do." But the Doll was no longer listening, she was walking quickly, walking to

God knew where, while Wilder kept talking, talking. "It's not betrayal, Gina, it's friendship. He wants to help you. 'This is Australia, not Nazi Germany,' I told him—"

'They cut you up, eh, Wilder?' the Doll wanted to interrupt her friend. 'They make you into what you're not and then they condemn you for being who they say you are, then it's like, "Do what we say or we'll kill you", and then . . .' But her thoughts petered out, and she said nothing of the sort. In any case, the Doll knew such ideas made no sense to Wilder, while the cop's story, whether it was true or not, explained everything neatly, like the *Sydney Morning Herald*, like the ALP, like all her opinions: a mistake with the world that Wilder knew how to set right.

"Gina," Wilder said, "listen to me . . ."

But the Doll was remembering the bonsai garden Wilder treated so carelessly, where the only thing that ever seemed to grow was the mound of dope ash in the Bakelite ashtray and where the beautiful plants she had bought only to laugh about withered in the terrible heat and then died.

"Are they listening, my friend?"

Before Wilder had even replied, the Doll knew the terrible truth.

"Of course," said Wilder. "Why do you think that nicked phone hasn't been disabled?"

"Tell Max happy birthday," the Doll said, and hung up.

74

The Doll now found her opinion of the world once more in flux. Whatever had seemed true yesterday no longer seemed true today. Everything was constantly altering. It was not the first time: as a child everything she'd held dear and true was revealed to her to be rotten and false, without foundation. And so she started again, on another basis, with the belief that she could make her own family and that family would embody all that was good, and through and with her family she would find love. But then the screw on which life depends snapped once more; with Liam, it died before it was born.

Once more she rebuilt herself, her life, her world, believing less and hoping only for small things. She did not ask for large things, and she did not dare hope for happiness, or ease, or luck. She would make her money, no matter how hard the making. She would buy an apartment, no matter how many years in the paying. And she would make a home, no matter how little and insignificant. She would put herself through university, train herself, and have a job that was secure and from which she might derive some small pride. And always she would hold her soul close and precious, allow no one to take it from her and trash it. These seemed neither large nor foolish things, but something solid, a rock, on which to build a life.

For a long time, all that time since Liam's death, this had been the Doll's sole vanity—to believe she had reckoned with the harshness and unpredictability of the world, building her life on foundations that seemed unshakeable. If not harmony, wasn't there at least a deal she had made with this world—how could it not endure?

But still these things had happened to her, and it appeared to her that her rock had been shattered into a million pieces of gravel, that her life had been ruthlessly broken, and her soul was somehow being taken from her, and all she could feel, in spite of her innocence, was the most consuming shame.

Wilder, thought the Doll, Wilder, my best friend. Wilder, who believed in goodness. Far better, thought the Doll, to believe in only the bad things: people let you down, people lie, people are cowards. Such beliefs never let you down.

And then the Doll felt hot tears in her eyes. She angrily rubbed them away with her knuckles. Whatever did she expect? That in the end she wouldn't be betrayed? After all, hadn't she betrayed Fung? She now saw that she had been deluded, that all were deluded, both the strong and the weak, for all hurt and exploit one another. All that differs is the degree of success—Moretti less successful, her best friend, Wilder, it had turned out, more so.

She dropped the phone in a garbage bin, and after it threw the plastic bag with its dead flowers and scrubbing brush and detergent and Brasso. When it hit the cans and takeaway containers, the phone made a noise like crap hitting crap, a soft, forgettable nothing of a sound.

75

Richard Cody's head hurt more than ever. He stood out in the Six studios backlot, in the short shadow thrown by the large building, because he had needed to think, and to think he needed to get out of the cutting room and the office. But the bitumen only radiated more heat and there drifted up from a group of smokers standing a short distance away an acrid aroma that only added to his sense of something about to explode into flames. He hoped it wasn't his reputation. He was a cautious man, he had built his success out of careful positioning and careful words and careful friendships, and he began to fear he had staked much too much on the gamble of this story.

Getting a half-hour special up in two days was no mean feat even with the best of stories, but it was already past noon, and with less than seven hours to go before they went to air, he still didn't have anything like the best of stories, and what he had didn't work.

Worse, he had been told by Jerry Mendes that Mr Frith's lunch the previous day with the prime minister's secretary had gone very well, so very well that Mr Frith had declared "our feeling" was that the special now ought to run for an hour. But the material had not proved as juicy as Richard Cody had hoped and, worse, promised, and the longer format was only going to highlight its weaknesses.

And at that moment when Richard Cody felt utterly weary and dejected, when the whole project seemed impossible, when he felt his career was once more about to go down the dunny, his phone rang.

It was Siv Harmsen.

He told Richard Cody that "an anonymous package" would be left at Six's front desk in five minutes' time. It had footage, said Siv Harmsen, that "had fallen off the back of a truck" showing a pro-Islamist rally in Cairo in 1989. Siv Harmsen apologised for the quality, and then gave him the number of "Bill", who would be willing to be filmed as an anonymous security source. He would identify one of the figures in the footage as an Islamic fundamentalist who happened to be Tariq al-Hakim's uncle.

"And get this," Siv Harmsen continued, "there's ten seconds of Uncle Tea Towel protesting outside a New York court in support of the 1993 Twin Towers bomber." The package would also contain photocopies of travel records showing that Tariq al-Hakim had travelled to Pakistan four times in the last two years, and twice to Malaysia.

"So he was in a terrorist cell?" asked Richard Cody.

"Well, mate," said Siv Harmsen, "that's where they're so clever. You see, you don't have to be in a cell to be part of a cell. Once you start thinking that way the rest is inevitable."

Richard Cody liked this way of thinking, whereby the fact of something missing could be used to prove the idea of it actually existing. It would help enormously.

"And look—here we have bombs, a Muslim whose close family has demonstrated dangerous Islamist tendencies; a Muslim, moreover, who travels regularly, mysteriously, to al-Qa'ida hot spots—well, it's a lay down misere."

Then he gave Richard Cody two other names: one of a former US Special Forces colonel, and one of a retired senior intelligence analyst who just happened to be in Sydney that afternoon in a hotel close to Six's studios. Both would say these very things to a camera, promised Siv Harmsen, but far more persuasively. Now he had to run, or he would be late for a lunch appointment. The phone went dead.

Richard Cody blinked once, twice, and his eyes filled with water. Though this could have been confused with tears of joy or relief, it was his blue-tinted contact lenses, irritated by the hot, abrasive smog.

Todd Birchall, on viewing the new footage half an hour later, was delighted.

Richard Cody's eyes were once more clear and focused. "Now take me," he said, "from a fuck to a flame thrower."

76

When he got back to the station in the city, Nick Loukakis rang Tony Buchanan, who was riding high as operational manager at the Counter Terrorism Unit. He and Tony had started out together, pounding the beat out among the slopes in Cabramatta, and when Tony's second wife kicked him out, it had been Nick Loukakis who had taken him in.

None of this meant much to Tony Buchanan when Nick Loukakis explained why he believed Gina Davies was innocent. Tony Buchanan thought how some stories are good to hear, and some aren't. This wasn't good, not good at all.

"You know how these things are always in the details, Athens," Tony Buchanan said when he finished, "and you don't know those details."

Nick Loukakis had run enough interviews to know when he should be talking and when he should be listening.

"Do you, Athens?"

Nick Loukakis's feet felt so wet with sweat in his shoes it was as if he had stepped in a bath. He wiped the back of his neck.

"How can I know them?" Nick Loukakis said.

"That's right, Athens," Tony Buchanan said, "you can't. Even I don't. But the security boys know what they're doing. There's the Feds and ASIO and—"

"What if it's not the truth?"

"Yeah, well, fuck me, there is that. Is that the same truth

257

you worried about, Athens, when you fixed Harry Tait up with the planted coke to get the initial conviction?"

"He was a killer."

"Sure. But the coke wasn't the truth. And these people are killers. Look, Athens, I gotta go. I've got a meeting in Parramatta in half an hour." He was about to hang up, but he felt bad. "You know, we have to get back out on the water soon. On that beautiful harbour of ours. You'd love the boat I've got now. Thirty-five-footer. Magnificent."

Nick Loukakis rang Jenny Rhodes in the Feds, but she was out. He left a message. He rang George Sziporski, who was working as liaison between the New South Wales force and ASIO. George Sziporski seemed to be taking it on board, until he said there was an interview going live on Joe Cosuk with the minister. George Sziporski said he would ring back.

Nick Loukakis searched through his desk until he found the small portable radio he had bought when he used to jog at lunchtime, before his wife confronted him about Sally Wilder and he still cared how he looked.

By the time he had the earphones in, the radio on, the station found, the interview was nearly finished, but he still heard enough to know what it meant.

"It's like a wild pig hunt," the minister was saying. "It's frightening and we don't know where the pig is. But we're trained, we're ready, and the pig won't escape."

The shock jock laughed. The shock jock said,

"It's good to hear a politician speak in a language all we Australians can understand. Thank you, Minister."

"Well, thank you, Joe," the minister replied, relief palpable in his now deeper, easier voice, as if he had been the hunted and not the hunter. "The Australian people need to know we are going to get this suicide bomber before she gets Australians."

"Fucking fuck them," said Nick Loukakis loudly because he was wearing earphones, and when a young woman cop walking by raised her eyes, he flashed her a smile and tried not to feel foolish.

The radio babbled with ads until the news came on telling of how, in the wake of the failed Homebush bombing and revelations of terrorist cells containing native-born Australians, the government's previously sagging approval ratings had risen to record highs. Frustrated by his own inability to change anything and not knowing what else to do, Nick Loukakis continued listening.

His phone rang. With some relief he pulled out his earphones and answered. It was Jenny Rhodes, but he had barely started on his story when she told him to forget about it.

"Dopey Sydney cops should stick to being dopey Sydney cops," she said, reprising a private joke they once shared, "and leave security to the people who know what they're doing."

George Sziporski didn't ring back. Why would he?

77

The lights of the train carriage went off for a minute then flickered back on just after the train had been sucked back into the tunnel and its darkness, heading into the city. Then the train stopped and the air con with it, and the Doll sat in the increasingly sweltering carriage, waiting.

After several minutes armed cops moved through the

train with sniffer dogs and mirrors on poles and along with them came word that there had been a bomb threat. To hide her face, the Doll picked up a newspaper that was lying on the seat next to her. Its front page had a new photo of her topless, breasts pixelated, with the caption:

DANCER OF DEATH

From her haircut it looked like it had been taken a year or so ago, and the setting suggested some private show she had difficulty recalling.

As the cops went by, as the dog sniffed around her ankles, the Doll tried to keep her hand steady, her breathing slow, and concentrate on the newspaper. She opened it up, aiming to find something to distract her. One page had the headline—

OUR TOP 10 TARGETS

and under it the Sydney Opera House with a bullseye printed over it.

Further in, there was a cartoon she didn't really follow, showing women in burkahs pole dancing, with the caption—

THE MULLAH'S LOUNGE

Simultaneously, a memory and a feeling of dread came over the Doll. She remembered what Tariq had said to her only two nights earlier about raster graphics—how it was what they—the powerful—would like to do with real people if they could. But Tariq only changed images, dot by dot, until

Elvis was an ostrich. They were doing something far bolder: turning her from a woman into cartoons, headlines, opinions, fears, fate. They were morphing her pixel by pixel, the Doll realised with terror, into what she wasn't, the Black Widow, the dancer of death, the unknown terrorist.

She looked up from the newspaper. At the end of the carriage a mother was telling her small son stories in loud Vietnamese, oblivious to the cops and dogs. Every so often they would both burst out giggling, and the son would repeat something the mother had said, and she would nod agreement, pretend to frown, or to be angry, and then she would continue as if it were all very serious. The little boy looked up at his mother with the broad, open face of complete trust and love.

And the Doll had the overriding sense that, though she was full of many faults, she, like the Vietnamese woman and her son, was love. But for reasons that were not clear to her they would not let her love. Whatever it was—life, the world, fate—it had not let her love the father she had wanted to love. It had not let her love the son she had wanted to love. It had not let her love Tariq whom, perhaps, she would have liked to have loved. Then they lied to the world that she was hate, and deserving only of hatred. Hate was to be hunted with hate and, when found, destroyed.

She returned her gaze to the newspaper. The dog moved on and its handler with it, and then the cops and the dog passed on into the next carriage. Within the newspaper was a celebrity magazine. Here, thought the Doll, was some relief. She flicked through articles on Hollywood stars' battles with cellulite and eating disorders, somebody's bulimic daughter, Princess Mary's depression, and then there, spread over the centre pages, was the headline:

POLE DANCER'S SORDID PAST

There were photos of whorish-looking pole dancers, and one of the Doll where something strange had been done to her eyes to make her look cold and nasty.

"Jodie McGuinness," the article began, "one-time close friend of pole dancer cum Australia's top terrorist suspect, Gina Davies, said, 'She used to make jokes about threesomes.' "

The Doll knew she should stop reading, find something else to read or do or think, anything else. But she didn't. She read on.

"Those who worked with Gina Davies at other pole dancing venues said that 'some rich clients would pay very well for group sex and Gina loved making money.' "

78

After the Counter Terrorism Unit summit meeting, Tony Buchanan went for lunch with Siv Harmsen, who was there as ASIO's delegate on the committee. Siv Harmsen was to Tony Buchanan a mystery. At thirty-eight he had an ungainly gut and had grown fleshy, but this seemed only to accentuate his baby face. Once a champion cricketer, for a short time even being rated a chance for the national team, he had started out in the force, a strange cop, but since becoming a spook he had grown a lot stranger. He had risen rapidly in the security services as they swelled post-September 11

and his youthful looks and bad suits belied the high standing he now enjoyed. These days he was said to be close to
the attorney-general and sometimes even have the ear of the
prime minister.

They went to a bad pub in Darlinghurst because Siv
Harmsen claimed the steaks were good there. The steaks were
awful, but Siv Harmsen's enthusiasm was unaffected. They
talked generally at first: property prices, wives, cop gossip. But
all the time Tony Buchanan was thinking about what Nick
Loukakis had told him. He had run interference for his Greek
mate before. Mostly Nick Loukakis was right. Occasionally
he was wrong and when that happened, he, Tony Buchanan,
had paid the price. But this time, Tony Buchanan felt he
might just be right. When he had finished telling Siv Harmsen the story Nick Loukakis had told him, Siv Harmsen burst
out laughing.

"We've got the biggest national security threat in our history," Siv Harmsen said, "we are in the second highest stage
of security alert, there's a lunatic stripper about to blow God
knows how many innocent people up, and you want *me* to
believe some copper who's been busted twice and nearly got
thrown out after the Royal Commission?"

"I'm just saying it doesn't add up," said Tony Buchanan.

"Tony, have you followed this thing at all? In the papers,
the talkback, the telly? I mean, people are seriously frightened. Do you think we could get something so important so
wrong?"

"It's possible, Siv, that's all I'm saying. Possible."

"You've gotta be fucking joking," Siv Harmsen said, looking Tony Buchanan in the eye, "if you think this is a mistake.

Everyone from the prime minister to fucking Richard Cody agrees on this one."

Tony Buchanan averted his angry gaze. Below the pocket of Siv Harmsen's peach-coloured polyester shirt, he noticed little flecks of pepper sauce spreading an oily areola. He looked back up at Siv Harmsen.

"I trust Athens on this," said Tony Buchanan.

"That dick for brains," said Siv Harmsen, "has got an SBS mind in an MTV world."

"What if he's right?"

"I don't think so," said Siv Harmsen. "Gina Davies has got motive, she's got contacts, and we can trace a connection through the people she's been with and who they've been with directly back to terrorist groups in the Middle East. The experts, the psychologists, have been telling us for a while how a terrorist today doesn't look the way a terrorist did yesterday."

Tony Buchanan cut a larger portion of his steak into several smaller portions, biding his time.

"Sure, she's not Muslim," said Siv Harmsen. "Sure, she's Australian. But she's a loser, Tony, and she wants to settle scores and prove something, and she fell in with the wrong crowd, who have shown her how to get back at the world. Do you seriously think the nation's top security bodies could have this so wrong and one half-bent, dopey Greek copper be right?"

The knife was blunt and the gristle was formidable, but Tony Buchanan kept cutting the meat into ever tinier pieces, feeling such activity was preferable to swallowing.

"I'm telling you, Zorba's a gyros strip short of a souvlaki.

Tell him to lay off banging his bouzouki and get back to his real job."

"What if it's true, though?"

"You want what's right, Tony? You want what's true? Kill a dozen or so Poms and you're Ivan Milat and in prison. Kill a hundred thousand Iraqis and you're George W. Bush and in the White House. One's powerful, one's not. Do you know who gives a rat's? No one. Besides," said Siv Harmsen, his tone altering from being aggressive to something gentler, albeit slightly mocking, "she can turn herself in. *She* can prove to us she's innocent."

"How?" asked Tony Buchanan, piling all the little pieces of gristle into a mound of watery fat at the side of his plate. "How can she, Siv? What if she's too scared? What if she thinks, God forbid, that she might just be about to get fitted up? What if she does a runner somewhere and somebody shoots her?"

At the mention of the Doll being shot, Siv Harmsen looked up with mild amusement.

"The little cunt getting shot might just be the best solution all round," said Siv Harmsen, smiling. He tapped the edge of Tony Buchanan's plate with his grease-smeared steak knife. "Not hungry?"

79

Sitting on the train, the Doll realised she no longer had anywhere to go. Her home had been raided, Wilder's was being watched, and her hotel room, she guessed, would well and truly have been staked out by the security forces now. And after the cops had been by with their sniffer dog and pole mirrors, the Doll realised that she simply wanted to be free. Her freedom, about which she had never thought, now seemed to her the most precious thing in her life.

The Doll decided she would spend whatever time she had left just wandering the streets of her old haunts. If she was recognised and caught or shot out there, so what? Until that moment she would be free. She wanted to have a good day, a perfect day—who knew? maybe even a few days, a week or two?—determined not to acknowledge what was happening around her. She would have a coffee. See a movie, maybe. Go window shopping. It was crazy, of course—*random*, as Wilder might have said—but then, what wasn't?

And so when she walked up out of the city train station, she went straight into a café, determined to enjoy a moment of normal life. But as she approached the counter, she looked up and saw on the wall behind a plasma screen. A uniformed cop was on, saying that police had reason to believe Gina Davies was armed and dangerous.

Outside, there was a screeching noise of tyres braking too quickly, then the abrupt sound of colliding metal and shattering glass. Inside, the waiter behind the counter had come between the Doll and the tv and caught her eye, and it was suddenly too late and too difficult to leave without drawing attention to herself. The Doll knew she was shaking. Her nerves were shot. The waiter had to ask her twice what she wanted. Maybe, she told herself, they would just think she was one more junkie needing a fix. Christ knows, she probably looked like it. She sat down at a table. She tried to avoid the tv and people's eyes by staring at a small stand of free postcards that sat next to her table.

"Turn it up," barked a middle-aged man at the counter, "this is important."

She wanted to be free, to once more do the simple things free people do. One postcard oddly moved her and she took it down and, with a pen from her bag, began writing on it, in order not to see, in order not to listen, in order to be free. But it wasn't possible. The waiter had turned the tv up and how could she not listen? The world insisted you listen. And it was, after all, thought the Doll, about her. She stopped writing. What if they finally admitted it was a mistake? Or suggested there was now some doubt about the Doll's involvement? What if there was some vital piece of information that might prove her innocence?

When she heard the cop say how the New South Wales police force was "interfacing with over sixteen different state and federal agencies in the hunt for Gina Davies" she had to look back up from her unfinished postcard. The day before they had merely wanted her to assist with their enquiries. Now they were hunting her like a dog, a mad dog. Watching the cop on the tv, the Doll was convinced that the world no longer existed for any reason other than to destroy her. She was just waiting to be found, for police to come crashing in, for shots to sound; preparing herself to run, to freeze, to hide, to do something, to do nothing. And part of her wanted that confrontation, that moment of destiny to come, so that it might be over.

Perhaps in consequence, her body felt astonishingly alert. Her eyes darted everywhere, her ears tuned in and out of conversations around the room. She could feel the smallest breeze caused by someone moving past her, could sense anger, affection or weariness in each person sitting near her. She was in a bizarre way aware of everything. And above all, what her hyped-up body could sense was fear—that this same fear that had hold of her was in everyone. It seemed so tangible, she felt she could smell fear and taste fear, all this fear they were breathing in, drinking up and eating, all this fear they lived by and with.

And then she wondered: what if people could not live without such fear? What if people needed fear to know who they were, to reassure themselves that they were living their lives the right way? If they needed a hit of fear even more than a hit of coffee or beer or blow? For without fear, what meaning was there to be had in anything?

On the tv a large, florid man had replaced the cop. His name and the words "American Ambassador" appeared across his suit jacket. He welcomed the effort of Australian authorities in their counter terrorism work; indeed, he went on, in his experience Australia was almost unrivalled in its homeland security measures.

"It is not policy," he said, "to disclose what American agencies do or do not do with the agencies of friendly countries when dealing with the terrorism question."

These words, *terrorism question*, thought the Doll, what do they mean? She mulled over them as the waiter arrived with her order. But try as she might, they made no sense to her. She repeated them over and over, till they sounded in her mind like just another trance beat to which she had once danced in the Chairman's Lounge. Everyone else seemed to understand what the words meant, and it was clear to the Doll that it must only be because she was particularly stupid that she couldn't.

Sitting in that café, looking at her undrunk macchiato, flicking her uneaten focaccia with fingers still grubby from grave cleaning, trying and failing not to see, not to hear, not to be afraid, waiting for a cry, an accusation, a shot, she had the odd idea that the *terrorism question* had become a fad, like body piercing or flares; a fashion that had come and would go like this season's colours. Maybe, thought the Doll, if it was just like fashion, it was simply about a few people building careers, making money, getting power, and it wasn't really about making the world safer or better at all. Maybe it was like Botox, something to hide the truth.

The Doll wiped her mouth with the tips of her fingers and felt the grit of the city of the dead rubbing, wearing away at her skin. It was a stupid idea, really, but it made her smile. The stupid idea, she thought, of a stupid woman. But if it were true, she sensed that perhaps these few people needed terrorists, for without the terrorists what would they do and where would they be? And part of her felt oddly, stupidly, proud, as if she had been specially chosen for this clearly necessary role.

The tv said: "And now we have the man who has done more to put this incredible story together than any other, Richard Cody. Good to see you again, Richard."

"Good to be here, Larry."

Richard Cody looked far younger and more vibrant than he had that night in the club. It was as if the terrorist story were for him an elixir of youth.

"Richard, the question I suppose on everyone's mind is why? Why would an Aussie girl allow herself to get mixed up in all this madness?"

"What the experts are telling us is how terrorism constantly mutates," said Richard Cody, "like a super virus—a bird flu of the soul, if you like. So, first, it was a Middle Eastern phenomenon; next it spread to countries like Chechnya. Then in Britain we saw English-born Muslims turning into suicide bombers. In Gina Davies we are seeing the latest morphing, with an Australian woman—not, as far as we know, of Islamic belief or ethnic background—making common cause with the terrorists. This is an entirely new phenomenon, and it is why Gina Davies is viewed by the authorities as so dangerous."

"It's shocking to think an Australian—one of us—could do this, Richard."

"Indeed, Larry. And when people see our *Unknown Terrorist* special tonight, they are going to be well and truly shocked. I know I was. It's sad, it's disturbing, and it's on tonight at six-thirty."

80

As they were leaving the pub, Tony Buchanan offered a final defence of Nick Loukakis. They were standing in the shade of the pub awning, pausing before having to once more move in the heat.

Out on the pavement a short, stocky man, clad only in board shorts, came hurtling along on a large skateboard pulled by a dog in a harness. He was travelling at such speed that a woman stepped back into a pavement table to get out of his way. Tony Buchanan looked up and shook his head. Siv Harmsen yelled out, "Fuckwit!" then turned back round.

"Listen, Tony, even if you're right," he said, "you couldn't change any of it. This story, you know, it serves a bigger purpose, the big picture, right?"

Tony Buchanan watched as Siv Harmsen used his fingers to extract a shred of steak from next to his eyetooth, and then swallowed the rag of recalcitrant meat.

"Let's suppose we're wrong," said Siv Harmsen, closing in now. "Just for a minute, let's suppose that. You with me?"

"Guess so," said Tony Buchanan.

"And you know what? It's still important that the public know these bastards are out there. That this is going to happen here. And that they need people like us to stop it. It's important that the public know they have people like us looking over them. That's very important. I'm sure you can understand that. How bad would it look if we were wrong? What a victory for bin Laden's bastards that would be! People out there don't understand all the threats, all the issues, how we have a war between good and evil happening here. How can they? People are fools, and we need to give them lessons as to what is important and what isn't, don't you think?"

"I think people need to know the truth, Siv."

"Look, mate, I went to Bali. I saw what the arseholes did. That's truth. But Australia didn't see that truth. Not the bits of charred goo that was someone yesterday. The terrorists want to turn all our cities into Baghdad. It's bloody frightening, Tony, and people need to be frightened. And that's part of our job, too."

"I thought you just said people were already frightened," said Tony Buchanan.

"Not enough," said Siv Harmsen. "Never enough." He sprayed some breath freshener into his mouth, put the spray back in a trouser pocket, then extended his hand to shake farewell and smiled. "People are fools. It's the Rohypnol rape decade, Tony. People can't remember anything. They just have a vague idea something bad's gone down. Stiff titties. Unless they're terrified, they won't agree with what we do and why we have to do it."

A strange and terrible thought formed in Tony Buchanan's mind.

"Those three bombs, Siv," he said. "Who did make them?"

"What are you talking about?"

"The truth," Tony Buchanan said, surprised to hear himself repeating what now sounded a trivial point. He realised his voice sounded thin and unconvincing.

"Anything is better than another Sari Club," Siv Harmsen said evenly. He gave a strange smile, an expression of weariness and knowledge that unsettled Tony Buchanan. "Australia feels like me, Tony. Just think about it."

And so Tony Buchanan shook hands and went back to work. He did think about it. The air con was off, the office a furnace. He had a new wife, an over-extended mortgage and alimony payments. He had a new thirty-five-foot yacht. He had taken out a second line of credit for it, secured against his Elizabeth Bay home, debt chasing debt. He was still a chance, distantly, it was true, but still a chance for an assistant commissioner's position sometime in the next five years. He would do nothing, he reasoned to himself, for what else could he do?

And then he had the answer.

He would go sailing on his next free afternoon. The thought of sailing always calmed him, and he imagined himself out on the water, thinking how beautiful Sydney was and how so few people really got to see its full charms, and how lucky he was to be able to enjoy it.

Yet something made Tony Buchanan ring Siv Harmsen one last time. He had been thinking of Tariq al-Hakim, how his murder was said to be the work of the woman, how Nick Loukakis had thought it an underworld job, but now he could see another darker, far more sinister explanation.

"Who killed Tariq al-Hakim?" he asked.

There was a strange laugh at the other end of the line, a *how-fucking-dumb-are-you?* laugh, and then Siv Harmsen said, "I would say people with an interest in terror did that. Wouldn't you, Tony?"

"There's always a paper chain, Siv."

Siv Harmsen said nothing. Tony Buchanan recognised the old interrogator's trick, of Siv waiting for him to implicate himself in a nervous rush of words. But this wasn't an interrogation.

"Always documents."

"I was an altar boy, Tony, you know, a child of God. Did I ever tell you? And the needs of the state, Tony, are like they used to say about God: everywhere apparent and nowhere visible."

"Always a record, something, Siv, that connects the highest to those who have to get their hands dirty."

"Once upon a time," said Siv Harmsen finally, "maybe. I wouldn't know. But now, mate, there's just people like us. We don't even have to share our knowledge verbally. We just have to share an understanding."

Tony Buchanan felt himself filling with terror.

"You get me?" asked Siv Harmsen. Then he hissed one word that suddenly sounded so sinister. "*Mate.*"

And Tony Buchanan finally connected with Siv Harmsen

at some deeply buried place where he understood that to share power was to share guilt.

"This heat," said Tony Buchanan, pulling at his collar.

"Yeah," said Siv Harmsen. There was another long silence. Then Siv Harmsen spoke again. "There's drinks at the minister's office next Thursday. Why don't you come?"

"It's getting unbearable."

"Yeah," said Siv Harmsen, his voice as flat as Bankstown. "Unfuckingbearable. Six pm. I'll send a car for you." He hung up.

Yes, of course, thought Tony Buchanan, that was the solution: he would go sailing, not sometime soon, but now, today, this very evening. In such stinking heat the harbour would be particularly glorious. It was extraordinary how many millions of people lived in Sydney and yet never used the harbour. If only they knew how foolish they were! He would let the spinnaker out, feel the sail belly, the yacht yaw like a great beast waking, and as the yacht pulled forward toward Shark Island its acceleration would push him slightly back and he would feel the salt breeze on his face. Life was beautiful in this most beautiful of places where it was possible to forget everything.

He smiled to himself, leant back in his chair, dreaming of sailing, dreaming of passing Sydney by.

'No doubt about it,' thought Tony Buchanan, 'people are fools.'

81

The café's air con seemed to be freezing the sweat that coated the Doll into frost. A newspaper scattered over her table said that they had sold out of gasmasks in the Blue Mountains. The television was singing "I Still Call Australia Home", but Australia no longer felt like any sort of home to the Doll. Australia felt like a war. It wasn't the war against terrorism that everyone kept talking about, but some other war that nobody was talking about, and the Doll had ended up on the losing side.

A radio from the café kitchen said: "Nissan Maxima. Wow!"

It was a war against everyone, and it didn't matter whether you were Muslim or Christian, a Leb or a lap dancer—there was only this war and whatever you were, whatever you thought: nothing like her; something like Wilder—you were going to be sucked into it no matter what.

The paper said: "Learn strategies to build up your wealth *and* self-esteem! Call us now!"

But the war was vague, thought the Doll, difficult to nail down, camouflaged in words and messages that wearied you and seeped into you like the ceaseless heat.

"What kind of scumbags?" the radio asked. "Islamic scumbags."

The tv said: "Four hundred mill Pantene Pro-V. $4.95. Today only. We're the fresh food people."

The radio said: "And it's not politically correct to say it, but I'm saying it."

"Yeah, I'm with you, Joe. My uncle was in the war, and he said the only language they understood when he was in Syria was a good boot up the arse."

"Maybe we should listen more to our old people who fought for our freedom."

"You get me, though, Joe?"

"We all get you, Trev, and, what's more, I think we're all

with you. We're the land of the fair go, but these trouble-makers who come from elsewhere need to know that's not the same thing as weakness. And if the government won't do it, sometimes it's up to the people to show what our standards are, to make it clear what discipline and punishment mean. And if that's beyond us as Australians I don't think we should be living here either. I'm Joe Cosuk and this is *Australia Talking* on 2FG. Now, my friends at Toyota have come up with a beauty . . ."

Out on the street, a woman with her head out of a car yelled abuse at the car in front of her.

The Doll felt everything blurring, and taking her away from some understanding she had momentarily known. She was unable to recall what it was she had been thinking just a few seconds before. The noise of radios and tvs, the sight of endless magazines and catalogues and papers that spilled over the café tables were like Temazepam, setting her adrift from reality and heading her back down a deep tunnel.

"Fucken elites," a thin, bearded man was yelling outside, so loudly that it cut through the radio and the tv and chatter inside the café. Startled out of her thoughts, the Doll turned and looked out, and by accident caught his eye. He stared at her. "Fuck you!" he yelled even louder. "FUCK YOU!"

The bearded man gobbed, and smeared on the glass at the Doll's head level, not an arm's length away, was a green scallop of mucus. As the man disappeared along the street the phlegm slithered slowly down the glass like a snail, and then stopped level with the Doll's mouth.

Her thoughts scattered like snow.

82

The Doll walked outside and, simply to escape, opened the door of a parked taxi. When the driver asked where she was going, she said, "Darlinghurst," because it was what she mostly said to cab drivers. But she had no intention of getting out there. No, she would just drive around for a while and compose herself, confident in taxi drivers' utter lack of interest in any customer. But he too had his car radio tuned in to another talkback show.

"Well, that's what I reckon, Ron," a caller was saying. "She's as guilty as sin. You know, if you sleep with terrorists, if you look like a terrorist, and, look—I'm no racist—I have Aborigine friends . . ."

She would drive around and then return to the Retro Hotel. Although she knew it was highly likely the police would have tracked her there, the Doll now merely wanted to agree with her destiny, not fight it. She wanted an end to her own fear, and submission seemed the best way of ensuring this. It was fine to be free, but free to do what? To go mad? To endlessly hear your own name being talked about with horror and fear? To know that whatever you did, wherever you went, you were doomed? And besides, where else could she go? She was weary, so heavy and weary with it all.

"Some of my best mates are Aborigines," the shock jock's honeyed voice oozed in. "Jimmy Little. Mark Ella. It's not racist, Terry, to speak honestly—"

"—well, she's dark, isn't she?"

"Here will be fine," the Doll said to the taxi driver, trying to control the quaver in her voice. "Please, just here."

Walking, she thought, even in this intense heat, would help

calm her. But it didn't help. To the contrary, almost everything was panicking her now. When she heard a rolling whoosh coming up from behind, she overreacted, jumping backwards and knocking a café table at which two women sat.

A short, heavily muscled man, wearing only Quiksilver boardies and leather belts tied around his oiled torso, rolled by on a large skateboard, dragged along at a clip by a pit bull terrier to which the board was harnessed.

"Fucking Ben Hur," said one of the women with a scowl. She had an upended apricot Danish stuck to her skirt. Two men talking intensely at the pub's entrance looked up and one swore before returning to his conversation. The Doll put her head down and walked on. She made her way through some back streets, and was cutting through the Cross, trying to think of nothing, when her path was blocked by a small crowd gathered outside Happy Hockers.

Two young men were kicking a body that lay curled on the ground. One of the young men wore Industrie three-quarter pants and a Morrissey t-shirt, while the other had a neat Mambo singlet and Billabong boardshorts. Both had sunglasses and baseball caps on, both, thought the Doll, were hotties, with the well-cut arms and calves of gym junkies.

The body on the ground moved with their blows like a heavy mattress. It made no sound other than the dull groan each kick forced from it. The body—its rags, its crumbling bomber jacket, the plastic shopping bags stuffed with trash that lay spilled around it—was clearly that of some beggar or another.

Though most people walked quickly around the scene, anxious not to become involved, a small crowd had gathered.

"Leave him alone!" yelled an old woman.

The men stopped momentarily and turned their aggression onto the onlookers.

"What the fuck are you going to do about it?" said the shorter man, his handsome face wet with exertion, his splendid biceps moist as if freshly waxed and oiled.

Realising nobody was going to do anything, he took a step toward them. He took off his Diesel baseball cap, his Revo sunglasses, wiped the sweat off his forehead like a man unnecessarily challenged in the middle of a necessary labour, then thrust his gleaming head forward and scanning the dozen or so spectators, looking each one in turn in the eye, sneered:

"Well, what the fuck are you gunna do?"

The crowd was going to do nothing. They stepped back, and began dispersing.

The Doll looked down. The scabs, the thin, ratty hair, the bomber jacket: it was him, the beggar she had given money only a few days earlier. His face was covered in blood and filth. His blue eyes were open and caught hers. They asked for nothing. *That is how it is*, they seemed to say.

The Doll avoided acknowledging his gaze, those terrible blue eyes. Like everyone else, she abruptly turned away and resumed walking.

Under her arms, on the wrist beneath her watch, on the back of her knees, under her chin—everywhere, the Doll could feel herself sweating. Sweat trickled down her cleavage and sweat furrowed her back as she scurried townwards. She could feel it slimy between her buttocks. She could feel it in the way her damp bra gripped her body unpleasantly, and her singlet caught on her wet body and held more heat against her.

And behind her they kept on for a few minutes more, kicking him as if he were to blame for everything in that dirty, dead decade they were all condemned to live through, a sack of shit that had once been a man, in a place that had once been a community, in a country that had once been a society.

83

The Doll turned into William Street and walked past a hairdressing salon. She halted, turned and walked back. Through its front window she could see the salon was empty. A young woman stood at a small counter looking at her nails.

I'll begin again, thought the Doll. I will—but then she realised that no new beginning was possible now. There was no starting over, there was no choice, no freedom, only the time left waiting for fate to seize her. There was no home, no family and no friends. There was no belonging. Everything, everyone had to cut out and cut off. There was no hope, nor was there despair, only certain events that felt to her ever more predestined. Everything had to be shaved off. Everything.

The Doll summoned her courage and went in. The salon was a long, narrow room, little more than an enclosed alleyway. The hairdresser seemed uninterested in the Doll's request.

"It's a bit weird, I know," said the Doll, feeling the need to say something.

"I've had plenty weirder," the hairdresser told the Doll. "It's about all I have," she continued, a little ruefully, pointing to a chair for the Doll to sit in. "Weird people. Weird requests. One woman wanted extensions to her pubes. Can you believe it?" She couldn't.

The Doll watched in the mirror as her damp hair fell in short blonde hanks to the floor, and a hideous white scalp and a stranger's face were slowly revealed. She felt she looked like a skinhead. An ugly, dykey skinhead. She felt what she wanted to feel. She felt nothing.

84

When the electric doors of the Retro Hotel slid open and the Doll walked in, grateful for the chill damp of the air con, she felt a dim sense of disappointment that there were no police waiting with guns and black uniforms. Nor was there anyone in her eerily empty hotel room.

She had, she realised, no gift for evasion. There was no longer anywhere or anyone to run to. She felt an exhaustion so complete it required a great effort to walk the last few steps across the room. She drew the heavy hotel drapes, and when she switched off the lights the room was darker than any night. She lay on the bed, her head heavy, her limbs without energy, thinking she would simply wait there on her bed for them. Whoever they might be—men with guns, police, soldiers; whatever they might do—arrest her, beat her, lock her away forever, kill her, none of it any longer mattered to the Doll, only that it end and end soon.

But no one came.

She closed her eyes for a long time, waiting, and still there were no police. The Doll felt both relieved and irritated. Where were they? What would she do if they did not turn up? They were a kind of solution, and she had no other.

The Doll now forgot that just three days before, she had

been happy, her griefs and worries seeming no better or no worse than what other people had to bear, and she had conducted all her affairs with one single rule in mind—to make and save money—and this rule had seemed to her infallible in pointing her ever ahead in the right direction.

In that complete darkness the Doll wanted to think that somewhere life was good, that truth was not chaos, that the world was not random, that a good person could build themselves a good life . . . but then these just seemed thoughts with no basis, rooted in nothing. So instead the Doll tried to think of what had been good in her life, and she thought of her friends and she thought of how when she was a child her mother used to take her fishing in a little dinghy, and how her father would lose his temper with her for tangling her line, or being scared of a fish being landed, and he'd yell at her and then give up and take the boat back in. And so it was that there was no good memory that somehow didn't seem to lead into a bad memory: her parents fighting, her mother leaving and the death of someone from *Home and Away*, Wilder's friendship and Wilder's betrayal, Tariq's kisses and Tariq's corpse, all her money and all of it gone and the fishing lines and Wilder's hair all tangled and she could undo none of it, none of it . . .

85

The Doll jolted awake. She looked across at the clock radio. It was 6.30 pm.

Green button taut beneath her finger, the Doll held out the remote control. She tried to ready her body for what was to come, as if it were about to absorb a punch or a fall, but her stomach was watery and she felt somehow seasick. She was, she realised, terrified. Until two nights before, she had never featured in the media, and the shock of it had quickly honed her responses such that she now scanned every screen, every paper, every broadcast only for mention of herself, and there was more than enough about "the pole dancing time-bomb" in the news to see only herself everywhere, screening out all other matters.

She knew for most watching and listening she was a won-derful story—mysterious, sleazy and sinister—all in the form of an instant celebrity. She was, as Wilder had predicted, going to get voted off soon. Everyone knew it; the interest in the tale was simply when and how it unravelled. Perhaps she, a long-time *Survivor* fan, instinctively thought that the rules and logic of the show she now found herself in would be revealed if she too just watched carefully and patiently. Maybe then an omnipotent presenter would appear and an immunity challenge present itself whereby she would have the chance to save herself for another week.

But, as yet, nothing had become clear to the Doll. No pre-senter had outlined the rules of an absurd challenge and handed over a clunky bead necklace in an act of evening sal-vation. For the Doll was alone in a world without divine saviours, a world without rules, a world in which she could see nothing and everyone could see her. She realised that her life was no longer what she made of it, but what others said it was. For the first time she clearly understood her fate. There was no choice, she had to know, and so she pressed the green button.

The special had already started and at first it was familiar enough to the Doll: a bomb appeared and armed police took up positions; once again there was a bearded man; again Tariq and the Doll hugged; and once more the children's bodies were laid out in Beslan, where someone dressed in black brandished a machine gun. Twin towers fell. Bali burnt. Madrid bombing. London bombing. Uniformed police officers. Suited politicians. Robed terrorists. The Doll naked. Missiles. Explosions. Blood. The Doll dissolving, smiling a smile that was never hers. An ad break. New cars. Welfare compliance warnings. The special returned with Richard Cody standing on the steps outside the Sydney Opera House, his best side facing the camera.

"The Sydney Opera House," he said, extending an arm to the scalloped sails behind, "one of our greatest national icons—and one of our most prominent targets for terrorists. But why would an Australian want to destroy it? To answer that question we set out to get to know our unknown terrorist."

There appeared on the tv a face she recognised: a sickly old man, sitting up in a bed, skin like the cellophane window of a business envelope, tubes running in and out of his nose.

"After Gina Davies' mother abandoned her daughter, Gina Davies was raised single-handedly by her struggling father," said Richard Cody in voiceover. "This man devoted his life to his daughter. Yet tonight we can reveal how Gina Davies has not visited her dying father, Harry Davies, for many years."

A caring Richard Cody was now to be seen sitting at Harry Davies' hospital bedside, speaking in a gentle, sad tone.

"How many years exactly is it, Harry, since Gina visited?"

"She left at seventeen," said the old man, with a deep roll in his voice. "Saw her a few times over the next year or so. But since she was eighteen, nothing."

The Doll could see that what little he had to say might seem to people moving. No doubt, she thought, he would have told the tv crew other things, bitter things, but she knew that they would never be shown.

"And you have a terminal illness, Harry?"

"Yeah. Emphysema."

"This must be very hard for you?"

"Daughter first a stripper then a terrorist? Well, you know, she was up to no good from the beginning."

"What do you mean by 'no good', Harry?"

"Well, it's a terrible thing to say as her father, but she was always, well, a cold fish—I don't think Gina knows how to love."

As her father went into a coughing fit, the Doll realised he was repeating more or less what he had said to her at thirteen when she asked him to stop touching her between her legs and to stop kissing her with his tongue.

"Have you got a message for your daughter?"

"Yeah, don't hurt others like you hurt those who love you."

And that too the Doll recalled him saying, along with his most repeated endearment:

"You little slut . . . you little slut . . ."

Harry Davies had drunk more than ever after the Doll left, his smoking grew heavier, and though the charges laid by the Doll's schoolfriend were dropped for want of evidence and a desire by her foster family to protect their daughter, he never felt better again. His coughing grew worse, until he was diagnosed as having terminal emphysema.

He sold his pest control business, blaming government regulation for the small price it fetched, and blew his savings in just six months on the pokies. He stayed at home, using what breath remained blaming a mining company for whom he had worked for three months as a twenty-year-old for his declining health. Before long he was hooked up to oxygen bottles, which he only disconnected for a smoke and to blame doctors, nurses, aides, for anything, or to speak in terms befitting a saint of his long dead wife, whom when alive, both before and after she left him, he had blamed for everything.

To his own surprise, and that of all who knew him, Harry Davies did not die but continued living, albeit in ever more dismal ways. His life was miserable, his house increasingly squalid, and when he thought of his daughter, he only thought of her badly, and he would say between coughing fits:

"The little slut . . . the little slut . . ."

The Unknown Terrorist special returned with photos of Troy in his SAS uniform, Richard Cody describing him as "Gina Davies' partner of two years", and talking about his tragic death in a training exercise. A retired US Special Forces colonel speculated how this might explain why the Doll first developed her hatred of the state. Richard Cody asked the ex-colonel if the Doll could have acquired knowledge of military tactics from Troy.

"It's possible," he replied. "Frankly, you would have to say highly probable."

And then the Doll shuddered. For Richard Cody was

now standing in the dust of the Baby Lawn, in front of Liam's grave. Little of what he said registered with her, other than a few phrases such as "emotionally frozen" and "abandoned grave". The Doll realised he must have been there only an hour or two after her that very day, because the grave was freshly weeded. Yet how strange it looked, for missing were her flowers and the prancing horse, and lying in the dust once more was the bronze plaque bearing her son's name.

The Doll's head dropped.

When after some time she found the strength to raise it and look back at the tv, Richard Cody was in a soft voice tracing a line of evil connection that started with Islamist groups in Egypt in the early 1990s. A photo flashed up of what he said was an anti-USA protest in Egypt in October 1991, organised by a group sympathetic to al-Qa'ida. There was footage of a protest in 1994 outside a New York court in support of the 1993 Twin Towers' bomber.

The profile of a shadowed face appeared, with the caption "Former Senior Intelligence Analyst". In an electronically distorted voice, he identified one of the men in the photo and the footage as a mullah who, he said, was the uncle of the late Tariq al-Hakim. He made much of the mullah's influence on the young Tariq when his family visited Egypt in 1996, speaking over what he said was home video footage of the trip. Tariq looked to the Doll just a bored kid. Richard Cody went on to list Tariq's later travels outside Australia and, before they went to another ad break, ran slow-motion footage of the mullah embracing Tariq as a kid, back-to-back with the security camera footage of Tariq as an adult hugging her.

'But he was only a boy,' thought the Doll. 'Just a boy.'

There were more experts, more opinion, the story of Tariq's unexplained death, a shot of the Corolla in the alley, more ads, until Richard Cody was once more back outside the Opera House. He dropped his head slightly, brought his hands together so that the outstretched fingers touched, and slowly walked toward the screen, like some kindly, wise teacher pondering weighty matters as he talked.

"We asked eminent psychologist Associate Professor Ray Ettslinger what Gina's life story suggested about Gina Davies' personality and motivations."

"Gina's case," replied Ray Ettslinger, standing in front of a bookcase, "certainly fits the classic profile of someone profoundly emotionally damaged and unable to empathise with other human beings. The ability to be a table-top dancer, to see their body merely as a commodity, and sex simply as a commercial transaction, somebody unable even to grieve for her own child, indicates someone unable to feel as normal humans do . . ."

And on the psychologist went, knitting all the disparate stories into one large untruth: a sad and bitter woman with vengeance on her mind, corrupted by a closet fundamentalist.

"Is it true that this profile fits with someone who could execute a major attack on civilians," Richard Cody asked when Ray Ettslinger finished, "and have no feeling for the loss of innocent life?"

"Sadly," said Ray Ettslinger, "yes."

"It is, of course, Professor Ettslinger, a large leap from a profile to a terrorist—is it not?"

"Of course. We need to recognise this is not a madwoman. These are the rational acts of a rational human being. In understanding one woman's history we can better understand why these terrible atrocities occur."

"But in your professional opinion such a woman could become a terrorist?"

"If that is the form she wished to channel such sociopathological behaviour." Ray Ettslinger paused. The Doll thought she caught his lips counting two beats like a good professional. "And it does appear that is the direction she wishes to go."

"Is Gina Davies our very own black widow?" Richard Cody asked.

Before he could answer, the Doll changed stations.

A man with a mike was walking back and forth in front of a studio audience, with the happy authority and plasticised hair of a tv evangelist.

"And tonight," he said, "we'll be using the Worm, a line running across the bottom of your screens which rises when you feel frightened, and falls when you feel reassured."

Two SMS numbers appeared at the top of the screen, one titled "NOT FEARFUL", the other, "FEARFUL", and the screen cut to people crying outside the forever burning Sari Club in Bali.

"Let's start," he said.

It was as if some invisible force were ripping open the heavens and splitting the earth and leaving everyone somehow outside of themselves, unknown to each other, frightened of shadows on cave walls. And shaping the lightning bolts breaking the world apart were the new gods—the pollies and journos, the spinners and shock jocks and op page parasites—playing with the fate of mortals, pointing at shadows of fear and hate on the wall to keep everyone in the cave.

The chorus of radio and television, the slow build of plasma image and newspaper and magazine photograph, the rising leafstorm of banners and newsflashes not only made any error impossible to rectify, they made errors the truth, the truth became of no consequence, and the world a hell for those whom it randomly chose to persecute.

The Doll pressed the remote.

She pressed it and pressed it and kept on pressing it.

But the next channel was the same, and the channel after, and after that, everywhere, all the Doll could sense was the same darkness amplified a millionfold, unavoidable, a mudslide of binary signals brought on by the ceaseless rain of fear. All the Doll knew was that they had taken not only her money, but stolen her very soul, and all the Doll could see were more bombs armed police Tariq's apartment block bearded man Tariq the Doll children's bodies man woman black machine gun the Doll naked New York Bali Madrid Beslan London Baghdad Sydney the Doll dancing uniforms suits missiles robes blood dead children's bodies herself disintegrating, smiling a smile that was never hers.

86

The Doll continued sitting on her bed in her miserable hotel room for a long time. The Panasonic portable continued on, and she continued staring at it, but none of what was on registered with her any longer. She listened to the rising wind occasionally bumping the window like a drunk pinballing down the street. Everything felt to the Doll to be waiting for her—her moment, her action, her response, her statement, her guilt, her punishment, her hair-shaving, her ritual death.

For the first time she sensed her wretched fate was as accidental as winning a lottery and, like winning a lottery, as undeniable. The only thing that puzzled her now was why she had never seen signs of her impending fate, when all around her every day there were people suffering similarly. Why had she not realised this was the real nature of the world, that everything else was an illusion? Why had she not understood that everyone was allotted a part to play in such tragedies, whether they were Richard Cody or the pollies or the cops or her?

People chose not to care and not to see and not to think. And the Doll could now see that she, while thinking she was a good person, had actually been the same.

After all, every new attempt at a new life—the baby, the move to Melbourne, the move back, the hundred-dollar notes—she now saw was just a different way of agreeing with what the world was, one more attempt at getting on with that very power that was now turned on her. On her, who had always agreed that those who were judged as evil were indeed evil! On her, who had never questioned the right of those who made the judgements to be the judges!

And it seemed to the Doll that she finally understood what had happened, for the world was this way because she was this way; and the world's judgement of her was only as stupid and cruel as her judgement of others had been. Wasn't it she who had said they should be hunted down like dogs? And once more a voice rose within her, telling her she had killed Fung by failing to warn her of Mr Moon's visit to the Chairman's

Lounge. Only, this time the Doll didn't deny it. She had, she knew, betrayed and killed Fung as surely as the hitman.

She remembered how the beggar had caught her eye when she abandoned him, and how he had seemed to be saying with his eyes, *I am so sorry, but that is how it is, you see. People are cruel to one another. I can't change them.* And she realised that it was his pity—his pity for her, for all people and their hopeless, inescapable cruelty, his rotten pity for all their stupid, necessary deceptions, his foul, stinking, vile fucking pity—that it was this she had hated above all.

The air con continued to rattle and wheeze. The world pressed in on the Doll from everywhere. The room felt tight, fit to burst with humidity and a heat which did not move but seemed to slowly set like glue over her body. She wished it could be a night like it had once been—another night pulling money at the club. She remembered Jodie telling her how Richard Cody had taken to visiting the Chairman's Lounge early Tuesday evenings. Perhaps he would be there tonight. And then, in the stupor of the room, a new thought took form in the Doll's exhausted mind.

She got up from the bed, found her handbag, took out the roll of foil, shook the coke onto the woodgrain Laminex side table, and shaped it into a line between the black micro-craters formed by cigarette burns.

The Doll knew what they would say afterwards—hadn't they said it before? It made no difference. It would help, that was all. There was truth, but it would never be told. She found her Prada Saffiano leather wallet, took out the last hundred-dollar note she had left and rolled it into a straw. There was truth, but perhaps the world needed lies. The Doll leant in to the table and flattened a nostril. Perhaps it was ever so, she thought. She put her nose down, and snorted back.

Everything ran away from her and everything came together; everything broken was joined, and family and home and past and future and her father and her son, Tariq in bed and Tariq in the boot, all were finally one. She was spinning around the brass pole and life was spinning beyond her—life itself, miraculous life—and everything was as it should be, the approaching night, Sydney, her thoughts and her feelings, the past few days, the sounds of cars, radios, laughter and the cough of Ferdy and the sight of him standing there at the edge of the table, wanting to speak to her, the inevitable summons:

"Krystal," he was saying in a low voice, "dance, just dance."

But the Doll no longer wanted to dance.

87

The elevator doors opened and the Doll strode out into the hotel's ground floor. She was heading through a large open entrance in one side of the foyer into the café next door when she sensed the police moving into the hotel foyer behind her. But she was already moving again, in control, walking out of the café, smiling at one of the grim-faced cops as he bustled past her. So dopey, the cops now seemed to her, almost childlike, like Maxie playing, and—if only for a moment—they weren't frightening in the least.

And with this coked-up confidence and purpose that both dazzled and perplexed her, the Doll headed down the street, while inside the hotel and inside her heart everything was turmoil and confusion.

For the Doll was remembering how she had once believed it was possible to remake her world again and again. But now walking up Pitt Street, sensing the police cars massing behind her, festooning the hotel with their flickering lights, it was clear to her that all this was just a dream, and that life had always been there waiting for its revenge on those who think they can shape it. As the traffic tensed then halted because of the raid, she saw that any attempt to shape life, to make of herself something new, all of that was just so much crap. There was no end to this world, and no end and no reason to its sufferings, its joys, its senselessness.

At the first cross-street that had flowing traffic, the Doll dropped the postcard in a letterbox, then put her hand out for a taxi. As she waited, she became aware of a noise rising to compete with the industrial moan of the city, a distant rumbling she recognised as the roar of a hailstorm some kilometres away. In the gap above her a darkening steel blue cloud filled the city with a strange, new light. She could feel a slight breeze, the first wind in weeks, and sensed this new air cooling her shaven head.

A taxi halted and the Doll got in. She was mildly annoyed to see an Asian driver, for in addition to not trusting Asians, they always now reminded her of Fung. Instead of the normal radio talkback of most taxis, piano music was playing. The almost hesitant, shy piano notes seemed familiar; the way they rose to some strange assertion of their own beauty reminded her of something—what was it? The mysterious tinkling sounds and the awkward moments of revelatory silence between notes, together reaching some dark, terrible truth—but what was it? What?

"Excuse me," the Doll asked. "What are you playing?"

"Chopin," the taxi driver replied. "His Nocturne in F Minor. Very beautiful."

'How could I have forgotten?' wondered the Doll. And as she continued listening, the piece began affecting her in a new and entirely unexpected way. How was it possible that for so long she had believed that in comfort and ease was to be found life? Hearing Chopin as if for the first time, such an idea struck her as being as dumb as searching a real estate guide for love.

As they pulled to a stop at a red light, the Doll looked out of the window into the shadowed ravines of Sydney's CBD. An old man sat on a bench, ranting at the passing cars and pedestrians. He dropped his head between his knees, vomited on the pavement, quickly looking back up in order to keep on yelling at the stationary traffic, strands of loosely plaiting puke slowly falling from his mouth, long vomit tendrils stretching and breaking, then forming all over again. He would occasionally stop yelling to gulp silently, like a landed fish fighting death.

And as the taxi pulled away and the man disappeared from her view, it suddenly seemed to the Doll that there was ranting everywhere, that it fell out of the opinion pages, the radio airwaves, the tv current affairs programs. It was the vomit of journos and pollies and shock jocks thinking life could be theirs, and it was as vile and stupid and pitiful as the man on the street corner yelling at the world as it went by.

But here in the taxi, thankfully, was something else in these strange piano notes; something that spoke of truth, something that seemed to grab her soul and explain what it was that had happened to her, what it was that she felt, and the music clarified in her mind what she now must do, something as terrible as it was unavoidable.

"In Saigon I train as pianist," the taxi driver was saying. "I love Chopin most."

The Doll leant forward.

"We're going to the Cross, my friend," she said. "The Chairman's Lounge."

88

"I want play Chopin to people," the taxi driver continued, nodding his assent. "I want play love. But here Australia—what can do? Drive, is all."

But all the Doll was hearing was the music, as it told her about life in a way she had never known and had no wish to know, but having realised it, her world was shaken to its very foundations and nothing could be as it was ever again.

"Drive and make money and back up next morning and drive again. Make more and drive more to make more—why?"

And still Chopin continued playing and the music was terrifying to her now, it was insane, it would not stop reaching into her, it would not stop telling her it knew everything about her. And then the Doll hated the music, feared how it was cutting into her and through her, how it was taking away all the things she had set up to defend herself.

"Australia," murmured the taxi driver, as if answering his own question.

The temperature was plummeting. The roar of the approaching hailstorm grew louder and louder, and the Doll could no longer hear the city, the traffic, only a growing drumming coming up over the piano. The taxi driver's only response was to turn up the volume.

Hail began to fall, not just ordinary hail, but hailstones the size of golf balls. They pounded the taxi's roof so loudly it sounded as if it were being hit by hammers. The traffic slowed to a crawl, headlights and streetlights came on, then there was a slow screech and the sounds of metal crumpling, glass smashing, a car alarm wailing, yet all these sounds formed only the dullest background to the drumming fists of hail on the taxi roof. The taxi driver turned up the Chopin once more, though now it was to no audible effect for the music was drowned out. The Doll was grateful to no longer be able to hear that terrible music. And then there was an odd deafening stretching sound, and the windscreen went white as hailstones smashed the glass.

"I so sorry," the Vietnamese driver yelled in order to be heard. He pointed to the side of road. "Must stop."

Not far ahead, prominently sited on a crest at the intersection of several roads, the Doll could see the massive Coca-Cola sign looming ominously, the hailstorm having brought the dirty sky so low the red American sign was supporting black clouds along its ridge. Of a day it looked as beaten up and washed out as the junkies who passed beneath it. But of a night it transformed into a latter-day Lighthouse of Alexandria, a small sea of roiling red and white neon waves announcing the way to the Wall and its rent boys on one side and the entrance to the Cross on the other. The Doll yelled back that she would walk the last few blocks.

"No, no," shouted the taxi driver, who seemed genuinely worried for her. "No charge."

The Doll could only guess what he was saying from his lips and his action in flicking off the meter, because neither he nor Chopin nor anything else could be heard above the roar of millions of hailstones smashing the city. The Doll held out her last hundred-dollar note, still slightly powdery.

"Too much," the taxi driver mouthed, shaking his slender-fingered hands in front of her. "Too much." He pointed to the meter. It showed the fare as $8.20. The Doll took his fingers and folded them around the money, flashed a smile, and stepped out of the car.

For a moment she looked back toward the city down the long strait of William Street. The hail had temporarily halted. At the street's far end, she saw the sun sinking into Sydney as if it were being swallowed, a huge and blinding presence framed between two tower blocks that rose like black entry portals to the city's heart.

A murderer's light spilled out from the sunset. It flooded William Street with its ruddy glow and ran beneath the blue-black hail clouds and up the boulevard like hot blood. The hail was already melting on the street, and the steam that rose passed through this strange light to create a red mist that the Doll could feel filling her lungs.

The Doll shivered, turned back to the Cross and began walking quickly, a strange, skating walk, for in order not to lose her footing she had to slide her feet in under the hailstones that, in places, rose up to her ankles. Her scarlet body chased her lengthening shadow up the hill, heading into the faded ochre bars and swirling white lettering of the Coca-Cola sign.

Behind her a police chopper was arcing up the street, shuddering the ravine of William Street with the relentless blows of its rotor blades. There were sirens sounding ever closer. The hail began falling again, quickly growing heavier. Pole banners broke loose and were shredding. People were running for cover. Cars were sliding and smashing. The Cross looked as if it were covered in snow, but no one any longer looked. There were screams, distant. No one regarded them.

The Doll took shelter in a doorway. She saw that she was standing in a brothel entrance on the doorway of which was a small notice advertising for workers.

Ladies required killed at pleasure.

The Doll burst out laughing; she thought how she must tell Wilder about it—but then she remembered what she intended doing and how she might never see Wilder again. 'No,' thought the Doll, 'nothing is funny. Everything is about hate. The world only exists to hate and destroy. Every joke, every smile, everything happy exists only to cover up this truth.'

And then, as if in confirmation of what she had just been thinking, directly opposite her, beneath the awning of Centrefolds Sex Show, two beggars oblivious to the storm were quarrelling, pulling a piece of bedding back and forth.

From doorways and shop alcoves a small crowd of the ragged watched, some laughing, some egging their favourite on, everyone happy to observe such a pitiful spectacle solely to be amused. 'Yes,' she thought, 'even beggars make war on other beggars—that's life.'

She broke cover and began running.

She ran past Club X, her breath even, her stride strong, accelerating around the few people still out on the street, deftly skirting obstacles. She ran past the Spice Bar. Fuck hotels. The World Famous Love Machine. The Pleasure Chest Cruise Area. Maddonas. The chemist with "Nite Lady Sandals" on special out front. She could not hear her own cries above the huge roar of the storm smashing into the city.

As the hailstones thrashed her bare arms, her shaven head, the Doll felt life and her separating. She felt a growing distance from everything around her, even her own body. She observed her pain as she was now observing so much, from some strange, detached other place. And part of her welcomed the pain, the hurt, the way in which her agony finally could be faced and felt as something real, and every blow, every frozen ball hitting hard as a rock, seemed to her necessary and good and cleansing.

She saw hailstones forming a gravel garden around a Big Mac wrapper, and next to it a dark-complexioned woman lay on her side on the pavement, back to the wall. The woman had the most beautiful black hair. It trailed away from her head and lay strewn over the pavement, flecked with white hail. At the corner of one of her burning dark eyes a fly waited.

Run, Doll, run, she told herself.

There had to be a judgement. She understood that. There had to be a sacrifice. She understood that too. She had always understood it in some way. The bog woman. The French woman.

She felt something warm running down her cheek. Then the salty taste of blood came into her mouth, and she realised a hailstone had cut her head. Yes, it was clear what had to happen. Blood had to be spilt.

There was no point in asking why. It was a need, that's all. Everyone felt it. Everyone agreed. No one these days wanted to admit to it, but that was simply part of the deceit of the age. It was nothing. She was ready. Her shaven head felt cold; her shaven head felt good. It no longer contained many conflicting thoughts, only a single purpose.

Run, Doll, run.

She wanted to live . . . how she wanted to live! But the things that held her to life seemed to her to be falling behind as she ran further down the street and deeper into the Cross, and with each controlled pant, something else seemed now gone and forever irretrievable . . . her father . . . her son . . . her home . . . her money . . . her friend . . . and then the Doll lurched to a stop, put her hands on her hips, and took some deep breaths.

She did not know what she was going to do, only that she was always going to do it, like the ending of a movie she had seen before but could not remember. She did not realise until then that she had the Beretta, that it was the pistol's metal warming in her palm as around her the world iced over. But she understood she was always going to end up here, going back to where it all began, her finger on the trigger, and that everything else had been as unavoidable as it was now inevitable.

The only thing she was unprepared for was how calm and peaceful she felt. For the first time since she had woken alone in Tariq's bed, she was not filled with a panic that left her unable to make even the smallest of decisions. She lifted her head up and smiled.

"A good night, my friend?" she said.

And with that walked up the red carpet between the brass poles and the fancy rope towards the great white-clad figure who kept guard outside the official entrance of the Chairman's Lounge.

90

"We are lucky gods," Richard Cody was telling some Six executives with whom he was drinking inside the Chairman's Lounge. He was working hard at changing his own rather bleak mood. "Why, just look at our world! A more wondrous variety of food and wine in one suburban supermarket than Nero could have found in his whole empire—and all that just for another evening meal!"

As wonderful a week as Richard Cody was having, he was still troubled by something that he reasoned should not have troubled him at all. The day before, he had overheard one of his producers, a young woman who Richard Cody felt had a lot to learn, talking about him with a research assistant, another not unattractive young woman.

"Not an idea in his head," she had said.

And yet it had been a remarkable week, and today had

been particularly glorious. Why, only that evening, after watching the special at the studio, he had just been about to come to the club when Mr Frith himself had called.

Mr Frith said he personally wanted to pass on to Richard Cody the news that "those who matter at the highest level" had already rung to congratulate him on the special. Six, Mr Frith had been told, was helping not only the government but the nation and freedom itself. It was something, Mr Frith felt, that would not go unnoticed when the contracts for the next government advertising campaign on a welfare clampdown or a new tax regime was apportioned among the media conglomerates; nor when the laws concerning media ownership were reviewed. And nor, Mr Frith added, would he personally forget Richard Cody's part in it all.

But it was hard to take pleasure in that memory when all he could hear in his mind were the two women talking.

"Know why they call him Shitcart?" said the research assistant—"Screw him into a septic tank one end and watch the shit stream out the other!"

And they had both laughed and laughed.

"We live far longer than anyone before us," Richard Cody continued, quoting almost verbatim from an article he had read online only the night before: "We have wondrous machines doing our bidding, we look better and we can look at better things"—here he raised his eyebrows, and the other men laughed as they surveyed the high breasts and wide smiles of the women who wandered the room semi-naked.

But all Richard Cody could hear in his mind was the sound of the two women's tittering and their voices saying:

"Shitcart! Oh my God! That's hilarious! Shitcart!"

And while Richard Cody continued in the lounge with his philosophy of a wondrous west, outside the Chairman's Lounge Billy the Tongan's dark eyes came to life. Even with her shaved head he had no trouble recognising her.

"People been round, Krystal," Billy the Tongan said, his snub nose spreading even wider as he spoke. "Asking questions."

The hail was easing, but it was still hard to hear anything over its cacophony.

"People always asking, Billy," the Doll said loudly, still catching her breath, knowing she needed to humour him, to have him onside and not suspicious. "Only they don't stop till you give them the answer they want."

Billy the Tongan smiled. He raised a great white arm, gesturing with his open hand to the door. As the Doll walked past, he didn't look at her but away, up and down the street. It was something he had learnt when he had been a bodyguard.

Keeping the Beretta hidden behind her handbag, the Doll marvelled at how it felt little more than a toy, something Max might play with. Only its compact weight in her hand reminded her otherwise.

91

She walked on down the neon-arrowed steps, around the corner and past the cash register where Maria was on duty. Maria—who told anyone who would listen how she "was, like, blown away" when she found out Krystal was "really a terrorist, you know, a real celeb"—broke into an excited grin and waved. The Doll gave a small smile and continued on, halting for a moment at the entrance to the main lounge.

The deafening noise of the hail was gone and here in the dark and doof music it was any time, any season, any place. Looking through the swirl of light she picked out some of the usual crowd, a few casuals and, sitting at the bar's far end with Ferdy and a few other men, just as Jodie had said, there was Richard Cody. The men were all laughing, as men always laugh.

It was then, as Richard Cody was finally beginning to forget the overheard taunt and fill with the particular joy of his life and world, as he began taking some pleasure in his success that week, that he sensed something going on in the bar other than his own conversation. He twisted around on his bar stool and looked up at the exit. All he could see was black.

And then, for the last time, the Doll emerged out of the darkness. With her bald head and glistening face, blood smeared, she looked more beautiful than Richard Cody remembered. Far more beautiful and more delicate—almost a child's body—than the crude, pixelated images that had in a few short days filled tv screens, posters and newspapers.

He stared at her for what seemed to the Doll a very long time. He opened a hand, extending his fingers—those awful, fleshy fingers—outwards. But his face made no expression, was—though the Doll could not know it—rendered by Botox incapable of expression. And it was this perfect, terrifying blankness that now convinced the Doll that he had never believed a word of what he had said on television, because if he had, he would have been afraid.

A suit next to Cody seemed to sense something and pulled his stool back toward the bar. Ferdy had disappeared, and the Doll knew he would already be phoning the police.

She didn't mind: he had to. He needed protection, friends, publicity. He needed them, they him. The Doll knew she had only a short time before the cops arrived, but it was more than enough for the little she had left to do.

Someone had turned the music off. Everyone was watching. The Doll began walking toward Richard Cody. Covered by her handbag, she felt her fingers flick off the ambidextrous safety catch.

"Well, look who's here!" said Richard Cody in a loud voice to the lounge, spreading his arms wide.

No one else said anything. Richard Cody laughed. A few laughed with him and then stopped.

"Jesus," someone stammered.

For a moment the Doll had no idea why she was standing there in front of Richard Cody, nor why it wasn't just another night when she would smile, uncover herself and make money and go home and cover herself back up with hundred-dollar bills. Nothing made any sense, not the club, not her life, not the last three days, least of all the stranger sitting in front of her, smiling, a man whom she had exposed her body to just a few days before.

"Well, well," Richard Cody said. "If it isn't the unknown terrorist."

And then the Doll remembered why she was there.

92

Nick Loukakis had been driving down William Street, heading back to work from his home, trying to make some sense of Gina Davies' world, trying to think what she might think, trying not to think about what had just happened at his home, when the traffic snarled in a hailstorm.

He had told Diana it was all over, and she had simply stood up, walked out of the house and driven off. Though he had wanted them to do it together, he alone told his sons he was leaving. He said that he still loved them and not to worry, that love was for keeps.

"Yeah," said his eldest son, then returned to gaming on his Sony PlayStation. "Whatever."

And his son was right—this love didn't help Nick Loukakis because he had no words really, no words that would do, no words that might explain a life or justify what was going to happen. It should have been better, different, but his love had betrayed him and destroyed him and would, he feared, for ever after poison all their lives. He tried to find something they could all hold on to, to bring them all through. But there was nothing. He could think only of a sea of plenty transformed into a poisoned desert.

As Nick Loukakis waited for the storm to end and the traffic to start moving, he noticed a young woman with a shaved head for a moment haloed in red light up near the Cross Coke sign. Then he forgot her. His thoughts returned to Gina Davies and, for perhaps half a minute, he kept running through his mind all that he knew about her, and all that didn't make sense about her story.

And then in his mind's eye he saw once more the woman with the shaved head, and the odd way she had been walking through the hail, not taking refuge, not hiding, but seeking something, heading toward some destination, some destiny.

These things came to him dully, as thoughts tended to come to him in traffic jams. And then he jolted upright in his car seat. It was her, he realised. *Her*.

Swearing at himself, he drove the police car up onto the pavement, opened the door and, with some difficulty, got out and began running. He was forty-three years old, twelve kilos overweight, and none of it came easy.

The hail had turned the Cross white, the white was drumming madness, and his burning chest and his wounded heart, his past and his future, were coming together in that wild, deafening whiteness into which he was now lumbering.

He made his way as quickly as he could up Darlinghurst Road, twice having to stop to catch his breath and once nearly tripping over a junkie lying on the pavement. Out the front of a chemist an Aboriginal trannie in a red vinyl mini and black croptop was wiping tears from her cheek when, upon seeing Nick Loukakis bearing down on her, she abruptly turned and started running away awkwardly in her stilettos.

And so he continued deeper into the embrace of the Cross, of the city and the destiny that was eating them all, until at last a red carpet appeared to welcome him and in his pathway reared a large human figure, much larger than almost any bouncer he had ever seen, and his clothes were of the perfect whiteness of the hailstones that littered the city.

93

The Doll was very close now. She dropped her finger to the trigger, took up the tension. She wouldn't miss. She wouldn't mess up. She had fifteen rounds saved from Srebrenica. Fuck Srebrenica! Fuck terrorists! Fuck this world!

She felt in control. The Doll realised that she hadn't really known she was alive until she had felt bad enough to want to kill. How was it possible to say that being a murderer or a terrorist is something in this world now, but being the Doll was dying over and over? That she had been shut out of this world, so she had made another world? That when love is not enough, what else can someone do?

Maybe guns allow a way back, thought the Doll. Maybe this is what people do when they get written out of this world, when they get turned upside down and remade into something people can only hate, into something people become afraid of, into something no longer themselves. Maybe that's all anybody's got left. It's not right and it's not enough, she thought, but then what is right and what is enough?

She could hear Wilder telling her how you can have anything you want, only you have to pay the price. No one was going to pay the price for the Doll, no politician or journalist was going to speak for her. And all she had to speak with, to pay up with, was Moretti's Beretta. It would help make it clear, if only for a split second before the trigger eased back and the chamber emptied, that she was herself and not an invention, a prejudice, a label.

It was strange to her that he—who had said the worst things about her, who had called her a killer and an inhuman monster—did not know what she was going to do next. The Doll knew that she would never do so human a thing again in her life. It was all good. She raised the Beretta into view.

"Krystal?" said Richard Cody. Yes, he thought, that was her name.

BLAM! went the gun. Richard Cody's chest tore open, his right arm kicked up and out, and he fell backwards. Someone screamed.

The Doll's eyelids were wet with sweat. She was very weary and wished to sleep. But she had things to do. In that quiet that follows catastrophe the only sound was something scratching frantically beneath her.

She looked down.

It was Richard Cody on his back on the floor, his feet flailing as he wildly attempted to push his body away. But his body wasn't moving. All she could see were escaping rays of bright red sun. They shone in splatters and specks on people's clothes. With her free hand she flicked the sweat out of her smarting eyes, then brought it back to the pistol. Then she could no longer hear her own heart banging, nor Richard Cody's feet scratching away. All the Doll could hear in her mind was Chopin. She knew he understood. She could explain none of it.

The Doll took two steps closer to where Richard Cody lay squirming on the ground. He reminded her of an upturned cockroach attempting to writhe away, with his limbs jerking, his repulsive fingers twitching. Though his tinted eyes danced with terror, his strange face remained oddly frozen, like an insect's. As the piano rose to its final notes, other sounds began coming back—screaming, shouting—and she could feel the pressure of the Beretta's trigger again growing as she brought the gun close to his head and once more eased her finger back.

94

Nick Loukakis was running down the steps, following the purple neon tubes, when he heard the first shot. His throat burnt, his side ached with a stitch and his calves felt as if they were made of lead. He could hardly hear over his own rasping breathing as he raced past the small entry table where a near-naked woman cowered into the wall.

From the docile way the bouncer had behaved, Nick Loukakis had been sure nothing had happened. Even after the shot sounded, he wanted to believe that there was still time for him to save Gina. As he lurched and wheezed, he was praying, hoping he could set one thing right, that he could make one person safe from the horror, that he might make some reckoning, find some balance for the Vietnam vet he had killed all those years before.

As he made it to the corner that led into the main lounge, he realised there was no music, no talk. He thought he could hear the human sound of breathing. He was listening, hoping, praying, trying not to think that the wolf might already be inside. How could he have known the wolf was him?

95

BLAM! went the Beretta again, the pistol's handgrip pushing back into her palm like a jolted coffee cup, no more, no worse. BLAM! BLAM! BLAM!

The Doll never heard Nick Loukakis then yell to drop her weapon, neither saw him raise his pistol nor heard his pistol by accident discharge as Billy the Tongan threw him to the floor.

The Doll felt only the murky waters of a three-thousand-year-old swamp abruptly rising up over her body, saw simply the relief on the other women's faces as she took their guilt, as she felt the hot metal that had slashed a thousand innocent women's necks slam like a hammer into her head.

She was once more with Tariq. Liam, now a young boy, slept peacefully nearby. Their hands did not find each other hungrily, clumsily; those awkward erotic gropings of a first coupling. Everything took a long time and time, which had always seemed a panicky confusion to the Doll, now stopped. There was time for everything, and when they were ready they came together and when they were finished it felt like they had only just begun.

But in her final moment she realised all this too was just an illusion; there was no redemption, no resurrection. There was only this life from which she could feel herself ever more quickly leaving. The bullet was smashing apart bone, nerve fibre, memory, love, before it came out the other side of her head, leaving a hole the size of a ten-cent piece behind her left ear. She was twenty-six, claiming to be twenty-two, and she would never make twenty-seven.

"Fuck you!" cried the Doll. "Fuck you all!"

But she was already dead.

THE IDEA THAT LOVE IS NOT ENOUGH is a particularly
painful one. Had the Doll, as she walked into the Chairman's
Lounge that fateful evening, understood what she was now
going to do as arising out of love and its impossibility?

Not at all. She simply saw a string of images—her father
smiling, her son's lidless eyes, a swarm of flies—that added up
to a tale of forever leaving and never arriving, the story of
her life.

As a story it did not have the scent of place, nor the hope
of home. Nor did it offer the reassurance stories sometimes
can have and perhaps ought to have. It is the ruffian on the
stairs, and the ruffian may very well be you. Who can say
what any of us might do if denied the possibility of love?

For a split second, the Doll thought back on how only

three days before she had been lying on Bondi Beach in an odd harmony with life. But the beach and the sea were the last things left in the city that reminded people that the measure of all things was not man made; the beach and the sea were not the city, were no longer of this world.

The world had deliberately shed itself of all that reminded people of their impermanence, their fragility, their capacity and need for transcendence. The city was no longer the most marvellous of human creations, but the most oppressive. Nothing was left to balance the horror of life. Power and money were what were to be admired as life atrophied: except at the beach, beauty was to be despised and the contemplation of the world decreed as a sickness, depression, maladies.

Power and money were to be all that remained, and politics was what ensured their primacy. Politics places man at the centre of life, and in permanent opposition to the universe. Love, to the contrary, fills man with the universe.

As the Doll stepped forward into the light she could hear Chopin begin playing. In listening to what Chopin could not explain, she heard an explanation of her own life.

Love is never enough, but it is all we have.

At the Chairman's Lounge the following night it's business as usual. Salls and Jodie and Maria are called out and climb up the same metal steps onto the same purple felt-lined tables. As they take hold of the same brass poles, they give the same smiles, glad that once the same music starts they will have a few minutes before they will have to say something, anything.

Outside, a crescent moon sits like a fairytale ending over a fairytale town. In her Redfern backyard, Wilder lights another joint, and turns the postcard of a bonsai plant over and back. It arrived that day, addressed to her. She stares at the back of the postcard, at a blank column. There is no message, nor name of sender.

She feels anxious. She longs not to think. To forget, and not think. Finally she stops staring and sets the postcard of the bonsai plant alight. When it scorches her fingers, she drops it to the ground and watches it curl in slow flame. After a time, everything is ash.

Down at the wharves a Chinese man awaits death in blackness. He is locked inside a shipping container he and eleven other men had been hidden away in a month earlier in Shanghai. Then they dreamt of many things. Now he hopes only for water. He tries not to think about the stench, the heat, the sight, thankfully lost in the darkness now his torch batteries are spent, of the other men dead. Because if he thinks about any of it he will lose his mind. One last time he bangs on the side of the container's cruel steel walls with a can of Albanian tomato paste.

The odd dull tapping carries up past the rising rows of stacked containers to the harbour beyond where motoring back on its once more silky waters is Tony Buchanan in his thirty-five-footer, trying to think of little else other than how chill, how sweet will be his first beer when he gets home. This is what he does, he thinks, attempting to feel pleased with his lot, this is who he is.

But in his heart he feels there is something intolerable in continuing to live for an unspecified number of years more and the dominant, undeniable feeling in his soul is boredom. For a moment he fancies he hears a repetitive thud but he is too tired, for a moment he thinks it is his heart, or something falling apart in the Gardiner diesel below decks, but then the noises simply join back with all the other noises of the city, cries that once understood need no answering.

Siv Harmsen continues working into the night, boosting his overtime readying fresh warrants for further arrests. Among them is one naming Sally Wilder, citing her for breaching the ASIO Act by twice telling others—one a known terrorist—of her arrest and interrogation the previous day. The case is clear-cut. He expects that the act will be applied in its full severity and is quietly confident she will be locked up for five years.

He has a sticker above his monitor that reads: *Family Values Value Life*. He intends taking his family to Fiji for his fifteenth wedding anniversary. He has never fought with his wife; he loves his kids: his is an exemplary life. There is talk that he will be offered a post within the prime minister's office. He cannot deny to himself the sense of intense pleasure the news of Gina Davies' death brought to him.

But that exquisite joy has evaporated. Though the heatwave is now over, the air in his office is heavy with something he finds unpleasant and incomprehensible. He will in the morning raise the matter of a bravery award for Nick Loukakis with the minister. This idea reassures him. Like every self-made man, he knows he deserves his success and happiness.

The minister tells Zoe LeMay on *Undercurrent* how he wishes to add his tribute to the many that have been pouring in all day honouring a courageous journalist and great Australian, Richard Cody. He announces the government's intention to establish in his honour a multi-million-dollar journalism scholarship scheme. He tells the nation that "Gina

Davies' murderous actions prove what we've been saying all along. We can only be grateful that the possibility of a far greater tragedy was averted by the courage of Detective Sergeant Nick Loukakis."

Nick Loukakis picks up a snakehead streetwalker in his Ford Territory, perhaps hoping in this final degradation to arrive at some truth. All day he has called Wilder, all day there has been no answer. He has watched from his car, he knows she is home, and he understands only that he loves her and that they will never talk again. He has resolved to live without love, one more resolution that he knows life will doom him to break. As the streetwalker unzips his trousers, he asks where God is and why he allows such a world. He no longer knows what he is going to do or whether he can continue and, unable to get hard, he pays her and lets her out.

As the snakehead gets out of his car she looks up, and her body shudders. Driving past in the opposite direction is a shiny black BMW four-wheel drive with two men she knows sometimes work for Mr Moon. The two men go to the wharves, and from there steam out to sea in an old prawn trawler loaded with twelve corpses that need to be dumped, while police paddy wagons work the Cross, and the fallen and the wretched, the hopeful and the hopeless, those who need compassion and those who need to give compassion pass the evening in that run-down strip mall that bears too big a name for suffering so everyday.

Everything takes its accustomed course even when life is at its most terrible, and people know, they always know, but life goes on and the excuses for doing nothing other than going on with it are made. Near the fountain, ten policemen circle one bearded man in a crumbling bomber jacket who brandishes a blunt Wiltshire kitchen knife. Tragedy happens while an order is placed for an Oporto flamed chicken burger, as twelve corpses dully slide into the sea, as ten policemen wait, as one woman beneath a blue neon light with bruised white legs and iced veins asks, "Hey, you want some fun? If you don't want *that* fun, do you want to score?"

And the men after something else again pass her by, on their way to the Chairman's Lounge where the women wait, all of them creatures shaped by another light, the red light of blood— the blood that will never be completely steam-cleaned out of the still-damp carpet and tub chairs below; the blood that's colouring the sky and flowing in rivers and filling the seas.

They know only without understanding that they now must belong to some place, to some idea, to something; they understand without knowing that not far away, on an ever rising sea, the scattered corpses of those that don't belong float for the shortest time like storm-tossed kelp leaves, before disappearing forever.

Ferdy, his hair brighter than ever, looks up into the lights and for a moment can see nothing, neither the semi-naked women, awkward and waiting above him, nor the clothed men, relaxed and comfortable in the death-shadowed darkness below. Then he fixes his face into a smile for all to see and claps his hands together.

"Dance," Ferdy says.

Though he speaks in little more than a whisper, everyone hears his order.

"It's time we all got back to dancing."

ACKNOWLEDGEMENTS

I wish to thank Baronessa Beatrice Monti della Corte, Bobbi (Bobbi's Pole Studio), Larry Eaton, Arabella Edge, Brian Edmonds, Donald Graham (NSW Police), Wayne Hayes, Terry Hicks, Jo Jarrah, Sally Jooste, Sam Jooste, Aphrodite Kondos, Kate Law, Peta Murphy, Sally Novak, Paul 'Canada' Richardson (NSW Police), Deborah Rogers, Meredith Rose, Sarina Rowell and Geoff Smith; and make particular mention of my publisher of ten years, Nikki Christer, to whom I, along with many other Australian writers, owe much.

I took this novel from everywhere—ads, headlines, gossip, bar talk, along with the grabs of politicians and the sermons of shock jocks— no-one, after all, was doing contemporary fiction better. While the bones of the plot I owe to Heinrich Böll's *The Lost Honour of Katharina Blum* (1974), the sub-plot of stripping for a rich man though recognisable from Paul Cox's *Man of Flowers* (1983) comes not from that film, but life, a story a woman once told me.

Though art is mostly theft, larceny is no guarantee of worth. Whatever resonance this tale possesses, if any, must be rightfully attributed to those men and women who have created our own times. As Shakespeare—who rarely invented his own plots and so well quarried such sources as Raphael Holinshed's *Chronicles*—wrote in *Henry IV, Part I*:

"Wisdom cries out in the streets, and no man regards it"
—a most beautiful line lifted from Proverbs.